Praise for *Dep*

"In this cinematic thriller, crippling insomnia infects the tourists and residents of a small town following the appearance of a mysteriously silent orphan . . . A well-paced action thriller with a wide-eyed premise . . . to shake readers awake."
—*Kirkus Reviews*

"Be prepared for sleepless nights, because once you start this multi-layered psychological thriller, you'll find it impossible to put down . . . and when you've finished, you won't be able to stop thinking about it!"
—Linda Hepworth, ***NB Magazine*** (5 stars)

"Freirich delivers thrills and suspense in some of the sharpest writing of any American author working today. The language is so precise, the details and disparate collection of vacation islanders so acutely observed, that when the seemingly impossible happens—no one on the island can sleep—you never doubt for an instant that the living nightmare that follows is terrifyingly real. Insomniacs be warned: this page-turner guarantees a very late night."
—David Angsten, author of ***The Night-Sea Trilogy***

"A twisty psychological thriller that reminds us that the greatest monsters are to be found within."
—Tom Epperson, author of ***Roberto to the Dark Tower Came*** and ***The Kind One***

"A rattling read! Claustrophobic, unsettling, visceral."
—Alice Clark-Platts, author of ***The Flower Girls***

"A beautifully crafted trap. At first, the reader imagines that it will be one of those classic horror-thriller books, as all the ingredients are there—a vacation island, likable but life-scarred characters, strange events leading to random violence and satisfying gore. And yes, you can absolutely read *Deprivation* as a great beach novel, along with the latest Stephen King, Peter Straub or Dean Koontz. But it conveys a much deeper and disturbing reflection on humanity, not far from Albert Camus's *The Plague*, José Saramago's *Blindness* or Josh Malerman's *Birdbox*. Beyond the mystery lies the question on mass hysteria, modern technology and the slowly dissolving of empathy in our society. Extremely well written, with precise and convincing descriptions, realistic characters and deep-reaching plot, *Deprivation* is a must-read."
—Seb Doubinsky, award-winning author of
The City-States Cycle series

"Set in a sleep-starved beach town, *Deprivation* is a stark psycho-thriller told in prose that's at once elegant, lucid, and more than a little hypnotic. With deft pacing, hip atmospherics, and above all, his brilliant style, Roy Freirich evokes the sensory distortions that come in transit between wakefulness and dreams. Truly, *Deprivation* is a rare piece of work, a thriller that succeeds as both art and entertainment."
—Kurt Baumeister, author of *Pax Americana*

"A smart literary thriller, *Deprivation* kept me guessing to the end."
—Keith Rosson, award-winning author of
Smoke City and *The Mercy of the Tide.*

ALSO BY ROY FREIRICH

WINGED CREATURES

DEPRIVATION

A NOVEL

ROY FREIRICH

Meerkat Press
Atlanta

Library of Congress Control Number: 2019955315

Cover design by L. Mai Designs
Author photo by Marie Buck Photography

Printed in the United States of America

Published in the United States of America by
Meerkat Press, LLC, Atlanta, Georgia
www.meerkatpress.com

contents

#day_two

#

Innocently, they come in August to Carratuck Island and the end of sleep. From ferries out of Long Island's North Fork, or from the south ports of Rhode Island and Massachusetts, the sojourners disembark in chattering, impatient lines at the old Bay Haven dock to trudge—with roll-ons and duffels and backpacks, a toddler crying, a dog barking—to their weekly rentals, share houses, motels. On to the broad shining ocean, along gray planks of boardwalk and over the dunes from the sandy lanes, a pilgrimage, a peregrination, they cross the narrow island. In flip-flops, struggling with coolers and umbrellas and mesh bags bearing floppy hats and tubes of sweet-smelling sunblock, they come—the tourists and weekenders, the clusters of couples and friends and families reunited yearly for these last fleeting days of summer.

From the beachfront Cape Cod or cedar-sided architectural second homes, the ad and publishing executives come, the bond traders and middle-aged trust-fund children, with a folding chaise and towel and a Kindle or tablet, for even just an hour to inhabit a perfect moment of sea, air and light, to cling to, as in a lingering farewell, a moment somehow so lazy, insouciant, redolent of youth.

A Frisbee seems weightless, coasting slowly and improbably straight through the sodden air, until giving in to gravity to skid into a wet footstep near the tide line. Kids grapple over it, pushing, giggling lazily, all knees and elbows, jams yanked, and taunts muttered like endearments, almost sweetly: "aaassswiiipe," "biyatch," "bite me."

Women frown down at their shoulder straps, melted ice sloshes in coolers as their lids creak open, and there's the snap and hiss of a pop-top, the smells of baloney sandwiches gone warm, yellow cheese cubes in baggies, peeled oranges.

Teenagers thumb cells, texting each other from yards away. Laughter erupts, dies. Tinny music leaks from earbuds, chunky thrash guitars, sibilance of cymbals, angry indecipherable vocals.

A young mother lies on a spread towel; she stares up at nothing, her eyes wide, unblinking, the tender skin beneath darkly bruised. Her fingers absently clutch and release the hot terrycloth, holding on, letting go, holding on.

Nearby, her little boy sits cross-legged in the sand. His hair is tufted to a point on one side by dried salt, his trunks are crooked and the skin on one hip is pink and etched by the damp waistband; his eyes are bluer than the ocean, fixed on the bright little flashing square in his hand—his GameBox—and the funny, tiny figure there leaping and dodging glowing balls, fleeing, or to the rescue. Points! Sparkles! A bouncy song of bleeps!

A gull floats nearby, hovering in the scantest breeze, wingtips trembling.

On his screen, the little hero leaps a platform, a cloud.

A wave hesitates, and spills lazily ashore.

#day_four

1

Carratuck Island's local surfers like to call themselves the Dawn Patrol; when they find the Boy standing mute and staring seaward, day has barely begun on their pale stretch of beach, or across the lanes of share houses, or at the Bay Haven Marina where Sam lies aching in the bunk of his forward cabin, watching the deck hatch brighten above him.

The sheets cling, damp with humidity, a hint of mildew under the tang of bleach. It's already too hot, too airless. Weighing the throb in his head against last night's excesses, he's lucky to feel no worse.

Was it three or four plastic cupfuls of Chateauneuf-du-Pape? After the half-joint of indica, the hour of easy chatter and laughs and another of enthusiastic sex, he had lain back and waited, and waited, for the usual dependable sounds—the idle slosh of current on keel, the creak of dock lines in cleats—to lull him into unconsciousness and a few blessed hours of forgetting.

He would turn over to face the close mahogany wall along his bunk, just to trade the pressure on one hip and shoulder for the other, but he might wake Kathy there beside him, her sleep deep and trusting, beautiful to see. His own eludes him too often of late, but from triple shifts at med school to the wakeful nights of these past months, he's learned to hope; a kind of purposeful drifting can sometimes almost work, and end the endlessness, if only for a while.

Unbidden, randomly, the faces of the summer's patients come back to him, the tourists gathered at Carratuck's day clinic in jams and tees and faux-batik beach wraps, with an ear infection, or the heaves from a bad steamer clam, or alcohol poisoning. Most present with a sheepish sense of their maladies as minor or self-inflicted: the Hannah or Heather with itching mosquito bites, Frank from Rhode Island with an angry sunburn, tipsy college kid Max with a foot cut on a horseshoe crab's broken shell. More than the usual absent regard, though, lately a few seem to offer a commiserating look, as if for a kindred weary soul. Or maybe worse: almost a kind of recognition, in glances met and slid away. And what about that other girl? The plain-faced teenager, Cindy or Cynthia, in for a headache, whose pupils when he checked seemed to darken and dilate, as if some faintest shadow had passed between them? Stoned, likely, and who wouldn't want to be at her age, trapped in an Airbnb with her parents bored or bickering?

Faint chiming begins. His cell? He climbs quickly, silently, out of bed. Kathy barely stirs behind him, one ankle nudging her other's tattooed bracelet of thorns, as he pads naked through the cabin and its clutter of last night's detritus.

Where is it? He spots and plucks the little cell from where he has forgotten it on the companionway shelf, and answers with a finger swipe. From its tiny speaker, as it sometimes has over the last few days, a wave of static surges and disappears. A word becomes audible, like something surfacing, a question: "Sam?" It's Paula, his clinic nurse, voice harsh, too loud and too soon on this day to bring good news.

"I admit it." He does a half-turn, aiming his lowered voice out the cabin door so Kathy can sleep in, her luxury since quitting her waitress job at the local Coffee Spot.

"Sorry to rush you this morning."—the line is clear now, her voice sharp—"but we got a little boy here, surfers found on the beach, alone. He won't talk, or can't."

An image floating up: silhouettes against the gleam of the ocean, leading a smaller one away. The lost child, found. Not news in a summer resort town like Pines Beach, but a boy with a disability, or purposely silent, suggests more amiss. "Huh. His parents—?"

"Nothing, Sam. Who he belongs to, where he's staying, nothing. He bolted a Cup o' Noodles and a bag of chips, but shied at a washcloth."

He makes his eyes wide, rubs the bridge of his nose. "On my way."

"Say hi to Kathy."

He clicks off, and behind him she appears—a glimpse of nude hip by the stateroom door, her wry sleepy eyes and teasing smile. "Whatcha got? Bee sting? Sunburn?"

He hesitates, torn, but grabs her sweatshirt from the dinette and flings it across to her. "Hi to Kathy."

Sam rushes his routine, skipping the shave and finding a tee and cargo shorts. Unimpressive, but clean enough for work.

Kathy's already set for her morning—iced coffee in one hand, eReader with *Destination: Tuscany* cued up in the other, the little galley TV tuned to *The View*—when Sam bends to brush her lips with his own, and a small hint of lingering.

"I realized, we've got it all wrong," she says. "I'm supposed to pine away on shore for you, while you take to the deep blue sea."

They trade their crooked smiles and he heads up the cockpit steps to work the tarnished latch and open up on gray-white daylight, blinking as his eyes adjust. The world sharpens into verticals and horizontals—stays and masts and blue canvas-covered furled mainsails, down the long multi-fingered float of Bay Haven Marina—fifty-odd slips filled this time of year by weekenders from Greenport, Nantucket, Hyannis.

He steps into the day, from the cockpit onto the deck to leap a bit jarringly down to the float. He climbs onto his rusting five speed Rudge and pedals up the ramp for the dock, sun warm on his back.

Through the open gate, he glides onto the quay where tourists are slowed as usual in idle groups before Carratuck's kitschy clip joints, ogling the same stacked tee shirts and coffee mugs, the laminated faux-nautical charts, the cheap bikinis and Chinese Ray-Ban knockoffs. There's enough belly fat for twice as many people here, on what looks like a whole bowling team, outer borough or Jersey commuters with Bluetooth headsets and big showy laughs, taking their summer ease from middle-class city jobs—police, transit, fire.

A clutch of teenagers whispers urgent business, probably trading pot for Ritalin or mom's Flexeril, or just gossip: who's back this year, who's hooking up, who's a total bitch or, forever unforgivable, just lame. A few clients back in Boston were teens suffering the slings and arrows of high school, anointed or exiled on a dime, self-medicating with anything handy, or hiding in their cluttered bedrooms, tweaking their online profiles, counting their friends and followers, lost in the data cloud.

Among these, the girls of summer stand giggling, fifteen- or sixteen-year-olds with salty, tangled hair, mahogany tans, fleeing childhood in the uniform of the day—cutoffs and unbuttoned, baggy sheer shirt over a two-piece, flip-flops, rawhide bracelets, pale lip gloss. He recognizes one he treated weeks ago—Cody, or Cortney? Was it food poisoning? Smirking and aggrieved, redolent of menthol cigarettes, her mother had dragged in the mortified girl, whose eyes now find his again in a fleeting glance. Her hand tips vaguely upward, before she's nudged by a girlfriend and they all bend closer to a cell phone one holds, exclaiming, "Oh my God, could I just die, please?" and "Oh my God, I have so gone longer!" Whatever it means, they crowd in, twitching with the eager joys of bragging rights or schadenfreude.

Up ahead, there's already a line at the Coffee Spot window, with its peeling redwood sills and red-eyed, hungover barista trying to keep up. It's the only restaurant with a service window on the boardwalk, and no doubt the owner lobbied one alderman or another with the usual inducements for the honor—a cut of the till, a campaign contribution—more than free coffee, it's a safe bet.

As Sam passes, a tourist in pricey Gore-Tex "walking gear"—everything but the goofy ski-poles, it seems—chides the barista in stagey, confiding tones: "Hey, I know it isn't Starbucks, but that latte yesterday wasn't decaf. My fiancée was up all night. Just a heads-up, between us, right?" Sam's heard a thousand iterations of it—the uneasy tolerance between sulky islanders trapped in service jobs and finicky, demanding tourists who have planned and saved for a few days of having their way, right now and just so.

No time for the usual iced grande today, Sam presses on.

"Doctor Sam, hey," a voice floats out, mild and lilting, and Sam lifts a hand in a casual wave to Carlo slouched in his beach chair, under his striped umbrella, beside his cooler-cart of bottled water and ices.

Now he coasts by a pair of local fishermen, Dwayne and Hank, both too leathery-looking before their time, sunblasted as boys on their dad's charter boat, chumming off the stern without a shirt or hat in the halcyon days before anyone connected sun and melanoma.

"Yo, doc," Hank offers.

"Gentlemen." Sam indulges them with customary, dry subtext; these two will never qualify as such and take full pride in it. Dwayne will tell anyone how he coldcocked a Soho performance artist at the bar at Claude's for whining about all the Guns n' Roses on the jukebox. Today he has a bucket in one hand and his surf rig in the other, a ball cap low on his forehead, eyes shadowy, downcast.

A flash turns Sam to see sun glinting off the chrome of Chief's patrol Jeep, slowly cruising the town's last straightaway of boardwalk. Should he stop and tell him about the foundling at the clinic? Better a quick nod and keep on; chances are the parents have already shown up to claim the child, and he and Chief are glad to keep things need-to-know, both wary of false alarms and wasted time.

After a last hundred yards of sandy lane, past stands of dusty bayberry and mildewed bungalows, Sam pulls up outside the clinic with its peeling sign, *PINES BEACH URGENT CARE*. He leans his bike against the rough-hewn cedar siding, and through the plate-glass storefront window (the place was another kitschy gift shop before the township eminent-domained it), he can already see med tech Andrew laughing into the phone behind the check-in counter, and nurse Paula nowhere in sight—probably in an exam room debriefing the foundling's embarrassed, contrite parents.

Inside, the waiting room's empty. Magazines are scattered, the place could use a dusting, and the TV silently displays a commercial for nothing short of happiness, apparently: a mom and dad and child in their kitchen high-fiving, laughing. The image freezes and scattered, solid-colored squares flicker, and then the picture recovers and becomes a talk show. After just a few months on the island, Sam already knows: a gull has built its nest in the island's cable TV head-end again, probably, or someone needs to check the TV inputs for corrosion, not the first time. Andrew, as usual, ducks his head and whispers last words into the phone with a sideways nod.

Sam pauses to wash up, and then steps around the doorway of Exam One to see Paula and the Boy there. In baby-blue shapeless scrubs and her glasses-on-a-chain, she's a trim, Black, no-nonsense sixty-one from Medford, ever on alert, always appraising.

The Boy's skin is smudged with grime, his hair dark and matted with sweat, but his eyes stop Sam with a look Sam knows—haunted, from someplace well past grief.

"Well, we've made friends, I guess." Paula peers over her glasses at Sam. "But he doesn't want to tell us who he is or write it down. Do you?" She smiles winningly back at the Boy, whose gaze has never left Sam's, and now holds a glint of something deeper, unsettling, almost accusing.

Sam's shoulders tense, an odd reflex he shakes off, trying a smile of his own. "That so? Can't get you to write anything down?"

The Boy's silence is filled, it seems, with other sounds: the phone gently ringing out at the admittance counter, the murmur of voices there, the distant sighing of the ocean a few sandy lanes away, broad and deep but barely audible.

Sam eyes the comma of grime crossing the Boy's cheek, the smudge on the side of his neck, and turns to yank on the exam room sink tap and adjust the temperature. "Maybe we'll just clean you up a little, for now. How's that sound—?"

"Sam . . ." Paula's warning voice spins him back: the Boy cringes there, wide-eyed and gasping at the gush of water bursting from the faucet. Sam flashes a hand out to slam it off. He smiles, too fast, too big. "Or not—later works, too!"

He and Paula trade a glance that at once suggests and agrees on the likely but vague initial diagnosis: trauma, and what it first requires—slow, careful going.

As if in agreement, the Boy has reached into his shorts pocket and pulled out his black little rectangle of a handheld electronic game. He grips it like something ready to fly off, and the gaze he turns to Sam now beseeches.

It's a relief, for the moment, at least. Any semblance of normalcy is welcome for any sense of calm it might restore. Sam nods, and pitches his voice soothingly. "Hmmm. One of those, sure." Sam looks closer at the inert thing. "Looks like the batteries are—" He checks himself. "Let's see if we can find you some new ones."

2

Heat seems to descend all at once this morning, baking the damp planks of the boardwalk in a torpid haze. Chief slows his patrol Jeep by the seaward rail near a group of teenagers eyeing him sideways, a few of them girls in a giggling huddle. He gives them his wry wave as he rolls by. *Square, loser,* is no doubt what they all think, but ten years from now, they'll be getting jobs and knocked up and less hip by the minute.

Near the end of the broadest section of boardwalk, Chief steers for an access ramp to the beach and trades a nod out his open window with Sam Carlson just biking by, on his way to the Pines Beach clinic, somehow on time today, go figure.

Down on the sand, Chief slows again along the kelp-strewn high-tide line, near folks spread out in groups of gaudy towels or folding beach chairs, with their noses in those sleek eReaders, or their ears plugged with iPod or -pad or -phone buds, wires dangling. Why show up at all, just to tune everything out?

Not that anybody misses it, but there used to be plenty more drama: benders turning into bar fights, bachelorette parties ending ugly with blotchy shouting faces streaked with mascara, frat guys breaking limbs on dares. Of course, the place invites it. With no cars but beach taxis, it's always been a DUI-free-zone, where a .12 blood-alcohol level is anyone's hangover to have. The Pier View, the Pelican, Claude's Clam Shack—for years, none of them cut anybody off until they couldn't stand, and customers did get plenty clumsy sooner than later, with cheap well drinks at Happy Hour prices all night long, or tall-highball themed concoctions of sugary crème de menthe and rum, "The Haymaker," or the standby "Sex on the Beach," featuring peach schnapps and vodka.

Last few years, lawsuits have made bar owners wary; doormen check IDs, and pourers prefer their customers ambulatory. Kids who used to get wild seem busy with their own gadgetry now, and at their worst, content to just appear menacing—it's a fashion statement these days.

Just ahead, four college guys try to look like players who mean business, but their sleeveless college tees showing off pumped "guns," their surf jams, rapper shades and gleaming spiky hair are just more MTV beach party. They share the same goofy white-boy, pimp-roll gait, pausing to laugh with a hand hovering over their crotches, bending stiffly forward and back at the waist. Bozos, out from the local schools, SUNY at Brookhaven, or Hofstra, probably.

Chief looks away as he rolls by and heads down an emptier stretch of beach, where somebody's bonfire last night has left telltale gray cinders and a charred log, ready for any sun-dazed tourist to blunder into and maybe get burned. He pulls up and climbs out, not so fast since sciatica has been nagging him and sending a funny-bone-like tingling down one leg. He squats to check the log: dead cold. But a yard away a flash of red catches his eye, brightness almost buried in the beige sand. He digs out a bikini top: C-cups, gotta be, and he imagines, or rather remembers, tits this size, with the unique heft that always stirred him, from bar girls in Subic, or some in high school, not a long list but a few; is there anything else on earth that matches the warm, luxurious consistency, tenderly weighed in his hand?

A few yards on, he checks the rickety wooden boat shed, all peeling one-bys and rusty nails. He pushes open the door, scraping the bottom edge through loose sand, his eyes slowly adjusting to the dimness to take in the tarp-covered little sailboat, the jerry cans and coiled lines, and at his feet, a tiny papery stub—a nice fat roach, charred at one end, but a quarter-inch worth with enough bud inside for a buzz, not that he's interested. It fogged him up too much the last time he and Jan took a few hits, and she had chuckled at his spaciness, which got him compensating with a bit more alertness, which of course she took for paranoia and found even more hilarious. He bends for the roach and steps back out into the glare to tear it up, wondering what else the kids might be into this year. PCP, maybe some other rave club or date rape drug? He hasn't kept up, and there's no need, since Long Island Iced Tea is the poison of choice around here, and trouble enough for most.

Except, of course, for the group of locals idling by now, stringy-haired surfers in unzipped wet suits, faces greasy from sunblock, carrying short-boards and trailing their leashes.

"Hey, fascist oppressor," one greets him.

Chief barely glances his way, knowing the voice from every season of his decade on Carratuck. "Up yours, sharkbait."

One of these stoners lets out a goofy chuckle, and they plod on toward the bright Atlantic, today barely rippling between slow sets of glassy two-footers, hardly a reason to get wet.

For all their piercings and tats, Chief knows they're really just puppy dogs who want to catch a wave, pop a Red Stripe, smoke a jay and get laid, end of story. They talk a line about locals-only on this stretch, but Chief has heard them whine and bicker and fail to appoint one of their own to tell some clueless city kid to find another spot to get drilled.

As Chief scrapes the shed door shut again, his earbud bleeps and he clicks the call through. "Chief Mays."

"Chief, good. It's Sam. Listen . . ."

Chief feels the slow, careless morning already slipping away as he climbs back into the Jeep, still cool from the AC. He tilts his head back and a glint of sun off the surf wash makes him blink; his eyes feel tender from a poor night's sleep. He sighs as he weighs the concern in Sam's voice, and runs him through the short list of probabilities that put them where they are, apparently—with a little kid wandering alone, found dirty, hungry and silent. "Well, it's a single mom or dad, some kind of misunderstanding. They left the kid with a neighbor or someone, waiting on a babysitter that never showed. Happens every other year. You know, or one parent thought the other had the boy, like that . . ."

Chief hears Sam's silence as skepticism, but it's early yet and more than likely that a sheepish, hungover parent will show at the substation or clinic to claim the kid—not the first time, sad to say. Carlson is just too new to know it.

"—just concerned that something's happened, since he seems frightened. He won't talk, he won't write his name or his parents'. It's something you see in people who've witnessed something upsetting . . ."

No one likes being talked down to, and Chief has had to draw the line before with these clinic guys slumming from the city, who think no one will ever know as much. "Understood, Sam, overwhelming experience, post-trauma stress disorder, sure. Upsetting things upset people, especially kids."

"Well, there's just a little more concern here, since we do have a few more question marks."

There's a hiss and snap on the line; a kite snagged in the cell tower, probably, or pigeons, but it clears just as suddenly, and Chief tries not to sound impatient as he pushes back: "Sure, but we get CPS here today and then he's in the system, ferry to the mainland, ward of the court, in a foster house. It's a judge's order to get him out. Sound better than giving it a few hours?"

"A few hours. Meanwhile . . ."

Chief puts the Jeep in gear, steering around another group of families setting up for the day. "Coloring book? Puzzle?" he offers.

Another gap of silence, until Chief finally does them both a favor: "Keep me posted, Sam." He clicks off.

3

This morning Cort has been following a new hashtag, #sleepless43, with silent alerts, and now the tweets are coming faster, buzzing her cell as four of her high school classmates in a quick row join the game—Jenn and Cami in the Hamptons, Deena stuck in Bayshore the whole break, Evi on the far, tony end of Carratuck, from her music exec dad's mansion on a gated dead end. The whole thing is crazy stupid, but harmless enough, so why not? She checks the time in her screen's corner and quickly thumbs, "here"—all that's required, every fifteen minutes on the quarter hour, to stay in the game.

Hands on a Hardbody—that was the old documentary movie everybody downloaded to laugh at how pitiful those rednecks were, standing in some shopping mall with their hands on a Ram Runner or Doredo, or whatever monster truck, to see who would let go last and win the gross, gas-guzzling, planet-killing thing. This contest isn't so different, a virtual version, more like, with nothing but bragging rights to whoever tweets on schedule the longest to prove it. A prize, in fact, would probably ruin everything, since somebody would get the bright idea to team up and tweet from each other's accounts in shifts so they could split up whatever they won, or else figure some automated workaround with a client app, which someone probably has already.

Cinder, a Junior and a year ahead but dumb enough to get left back, started the whole dumb thing and is a famous complainer and kind of a hypochondriac. Her dad is mean, she has a stomachache, or she barely cut her foot on a pop-top or a shell and the doctor at the Urgent Care made her wait. Her eyes are dry, or her ears hurt from her earbuds. Cort can't remember if the "43" is supposed to mean forty-three hours straight, as a goal, or what—but who has time to scroll back?

She double taps her home button and brings up messages; pathetic, because it shouldn't be all about whether or not Tay is here yet—for god's sake, get a life, right?—but she checks texts for the tenth time in as many minutes and twitches her sunburned shoulder beneath her shirt and scratchy bikini strap. Probably she has gone with the wrong suit—this tiny retro madras with little boy-short bottoms—since it does nothing for her broad, too-flat chest, which Tay seemed more distracted by last year than not, glancing and glancing away, as if she didn't see. The boy-shorts ride up plenty, though, and she has caught some looks and had to adjust to avoid the complete wedgie disaster when she steps out of the surf, before she even wipes the salt from her eyes or twists the water out of her hair.

Last year, she met Tay at a full-on run from halfway down the boardwalk, across the dunes from the marina to the bottom of the main beach stairs, so lame, even though his smile seemed really glad before he downshifted back into his cooler, blissed-out surfer self. This year, she knows better, to go with a vague shy wave as she glides up, distracted, with maybe an eye on her cell or, even better, someone else to wave to on her way to him.

For Mom, who hates all boys, Cort has the perfect alibi this year: the chattery, kind of tweaky lady with the crooked lipstick and her big-eyed eight-year-old boy at Roscoe's Market looking for a babysitter, staying in a weekly bungalow on Spinnaker just a few lanes over. The little boy was so cute, with eyelashes a mile long, holding a little GameBox, smiling and saying, "Hilo," like a combination of hi and hello. Cute, but maybe a handful; the woman had left a wacky, stressed message begging Cort, but that was already days ago.

Mom will never check up, anyway, and just needs to hear a story, and the little details here are plenty enough to sound real and make total sense with Carratuck's house-share and hook-up mania. Not so great to lie, but better than sitting on their patio with iced teas all day, listening to Mom's running commentary on every passing person's sad lack of physical charm and fashion sense: "Whoa, sunburned muffin-top—lipo and bronzer, anyone?" or "Greg Norman called and wants his lime-green pleat-fronts back."

Cort glances up to see the local doctor guy who gave her a tetanus shot last year biking by and almost waves, but *BLIIIING!*—incoming! In a little blue rectangle on her cell's screen:

Just got here! East Beach!!!?

She promised herself she wouldn't, but how can she not? So she does, over the broadest straightaway of the boardwalk, by the old Skee-Ball parlor and the ices stand, down a worn beach ramp and past a patrol Jeep and a group of families of kids and dogs, to his hard arms and the light of his deep green eyes, she runs.

A silhouette against the flash and glare from the sea, he stands with his shortboard leaning against a shoulder, a hand draped around the nose, the other thumbing his cell. She slows to watch the light find him as she does, approaching to see the sheen of his half-peeled, soaked wet suit and the smoothness of his broad caramel chest, drops of water shimmering there, and a spike of wet hair hanging over his forehead.

Last second, he sees her, but she is already near enough to bump him with a hip and laugh, so she does, and his eyes squint as his face completely lights with gladness to see her. Her.

"You!"

"You!" They shout witlessly at each other.

He yanks her into a one-armed half hug, the rough shoulder-bump of guys, but with his eyes happy instead of hooded and cool.

And now they are simply regarding each other with smiles like laughter that cannot be stopped, as a group of tweener girls goes by, teasers in tiny halter bikinis and hushed pursed lips at this boy and girl standing like it's just so completely *on*, as his eyes stay with hers, only hers, and he asks, "Where to?"

"I gotta stay low, told my mom I was babysitting."

"Original."

Her cell buzzes and she curses softly, yanking it up for a glance. "Oh, fuck."

"What?"

"Don't ask, it's too dumb." Rolling her eyes, she thumb-types back, like answering roll call in homeroom.

4

Sam's day finds its own momentum, ten minutes or so per patient, no breaks, as he ducks into one room and then the next:

"Paula, curettage in Three. Maybe stitches. Grab that gauze?"

"Do *not* ice it when you get home. It destroys the tissue. Just the salve, okay?"

And the next: "If I can just . . . Hold her still? Wait, wait, okaaaay . . . *there*. All good!"

Most are victims of typical mishaps—a knee scraped on a jetty rock, a finger burned on a hot pot handle, a baby wailing with a grain of sand in its eye—but are there somehow more than usual lately? A few complaints don't quite add up: the heightened noise sensitivity, the severe headache with no apparent cause or history, the sudden-onset restless leg syndrome. Some of these are returnees from earlier in the season, who've shared the same wry observations about Sam's worn look, and Carratuck's hard-partying, "I'll sleep when I die" ethos.

Chief is wrong about the Boy, it turns out. Nothing—book, puzzle, cartoon DVD in the waiting room—seems to interest him; he sits all afternoon in a plastic chair, his eyes fixed on his little handheld game. Sam makes a point of pausing every once in a while to smile at him and ask, "How we doin', Captain?" The Boy's impassive gaze unnerves, though at least his panic has subsided.

But when the sky outside the big storefront windows turns streaky with gold and purple, still no one has come for him; Sam's got a *Highlights* magazine and an old *Blues Clues* DVD ready for the chief, since he has no better ideas, and since police and Child Protective Services jurisdictions dovetail in these cases, as they should. If nothing too untoward has occurred, it's reason enough to think the Boy will be fine sooner than later. If anything has, then certainly County needs to establish custody and a longer-term clinical setting for their own specialists to treat him.

When Chief walks in, wary, Sam keeps his gaze carefully neutral. They confer while Paula straightens up and gets ready to close, hovering within earshot. Sam pitches his voice low, and asks, unnecessarily, "No one?"

Chief glances at the Boy, his lips pursed, musing, "Yeah, no. Nothing. Go figure."

"I'll call CPS." Sam checks for the number on a clipboard hung above a shelf and pulls out his cell.

Chief checks his watch and shakes his head. "Damn. Next ferry's not 'til tomorrow. Might as well call then. Meanwhile, the kid's in good hands."

Sam hesitates.

Chief sighs. "Look, Sam, when I say the system is last resort, I know, okay? I called and put a kid there, year before last. Let's just say foster care did not do well by her. Let's give the parents a chance to get here with some answers."

The logic isn't without merit, but is Chief offering to babysit? Sam barely remembers his wife's name, though it's not so many months since she and Chief and he and Kath had shared an awkward, obligatory dinner at Claude's Clam Shack. Janice, Janet? Whichever, nobody's wife likes to be ambushed with a new responsibility.

For a moment they regard each other silently, stonewalling, only the sounds of Paula shutting cabinet doors and their day aide Andrew shuffling charts intrude. Sam finally offers, "Well, we have some cartoon DVDs you can take with him."

Chief makes his eyes wide. "Hey, you know what? Wouldn't . . . it be better if you and Kathy keep an eye on him?"

"I'm not so sure about that . . ." Sam tries to demur. Kathy would be intrigued by the Boy first, and then obsessed with him and what his story might be, imagining the worst. She might try too hard, smile too big, talk too much to fill the silences. Her fear for him would feed on itself and make everyone edgy, when the exact opposite is required.

Chief clinches it, asking, "Said he was mute, right? Or . . . special needs? So if there is one . . . anything medical . . . or, you know, psychological . . ."

Sam can't possibly treat this boy overnight, though that's the expectation here, and one he needs to counter, quickly and completely. "Chief, I'm just not set up to deal with this boy. He needs familiarity, peace and quiet—"

"For a few more hours until someone turns up for him."

Sam looks doubtful, but Chief claps him on the shoulder with a quick wink. "Thanks, Sam."

———

As dusk finally softens and cools the day, tourists stroll along the boardwalk. Among these, Sam walks his bike and the Boy almost idly back to the docks, hoping someone will stop them, recognize the Boy, and the mystery might be solved on the spot.

He's warned Kathy with a call, but when they reach the boat, she still has to resist gawking at their guest. Wide-eyed, she whispers to Sam, "No one?"

He shakes his head *no* and can't stop her from crouching before the Boy with her big smile and cheery salute, "Welcome aboard! I'm Kathy!"

The Boy takes a half-step back, a twitch in his cheek and his gaze flitting. Her smile relaxes and she lets out a breath, as if to calm herself, too. "Okay, well. Anyone . . . hungry?"

She turns away for the peanut butter and jelly sandwiches she's readied, a staple of her own diet, though without an extra ounce on her lean frame to show for it.

Sam finds himself smiling absurdly at the Boy, too. "Dinette, right here. Kitchen table, on a sailboat."

Eyes averted, the Boy hesitates, but slides in.

Too quickly and with too much clatter, Kathy sets out heavy plastic plates.

The Boy seems to flinch again, eyes darting, but the sandwich draws him, and he calms and chews slowly, almost pensively, while Sam and Kathy trade a glance.

"We're going topside, just up there," Sam points up the companionway steps. "For just a second. Okay?"

The Boy doesn't so much as nod, intent on his sandwich.

Out in the cockpit, Sam and Kathy confer in urgent whispers. The worst has already occurred to her, even sooner than he envisioned, and she can't help but ask, "What if something happened to his parents? You think he saw something?"

He hears it edging upward, from under the surface of her concern: another attempt to corner him into the role of therapist. He quickly borrows the chief's calculated nonchalance, shrugging. "His folks are probably just sleeping one off. They'll probably bang on our door before morning."

She shakes her head. "Must've been one hell of a bender. He hasn't seen a washcloth lately." She looks about to head inside, find one and dampen it, to try to scrub the Boy.

"Better not try, just yet. He's still skittish."

Their gazes drift from each other's, down the companionway steps to the grimy Boy sitting at the galley table, watching them. He jerks his face sideways, hiding his eyes, as if from an interrogator's.

#

Dusk comes to Carratuck from the eastern sea, violet shadow by shadow as lights come on in houses and motel rooms, and the clatter of ice trays and glasses carries across the sandy lanes of Pines Beach and the gently bobbing float of the Bay Haven Marina. There's the low murmur of television, and the faint throb of bass as music begins from the bars and share house patios strung with lights. Mosquitoes swarm in little clouds, folks curse softly and slap at their arms, and the smoke of citronella candles rises and hangs in the windless air, dank with the scent of the tide.

———

Just before closing at Roscoe's Market, Maxine Kinnis sets a cheap electric fan down on the checkout counter, complaining, "Gotta be two hundred degrees in the shitbox I snagged last minute. Cannot sleep a wink this year."
    In line behind her, Ken Oberst steps up with a clever little air-travel kit of earplugs and eyemask, and a bottle of Melatonin, and Maxine eyes these as he chimes in: "I got a halogen security light from next door, no blinds."

———

At Claude's Clam Shack for his nightly Long Island Iced Tea, Doug Raymond ticks off the shortcomings of his Airbnb to a small, sympathetic crowd: "Sheets like sandpaper, neighbors who need couples' therapy, and did I say damp? Mold on the ceiling. I know from staring up at it 'til dawn."

———

Carla Mott doesn't care what Kira or Beth thinks; no help for her headache, she went to bed early, fuck Happy Hour and those guys from SUNY sexting nonstop and the prude label she'll get slapped with by the Pi Delts and their ignorant slut posse who have been posting their vicious bitch craziness every few seconds the last few days, on some Red Bull and whip-it binge, probably, and whining about it nonstop, too, how tired, how they just want to crash already.

So it isn't all the sugar in the White Russians she didn't have at that share house mixer she skipped, for a change, so much as the parade of shames in her nonstop guilt reel, rewinding and replaying, turning her one way and then the other in her twin bed: the tuition her dad pays for her cut classes; the four hundred dollar Kate Spade purse she borrowed and forgot to tell Hunter about and can't use anyway now without her knowing; the loser she didn't quite sleep with (everything but) after all the Jäger in his crappy, clove cigarette-stinky car; the promise she made to Marco to go with to Italy and maybe Istanbul instead of taking her work-study required soph semester interning for that (sorry, but honestly kill-me-now terminally nerd) public policy advocacy liaison dot org; oh, all of it, the entire endless downer season of episodes she cannot pause or fast forward or ever delete.

———

What time is it? In her Surf Beach Sun Motel efficiency unit, Mrs. Frank Talavaro of Weehawken, New Jersey, wakes to see Frank crouched in the dark with a flashlight, on hands and knees, bent over the upside-down kitchen table, disassembling it. His face is greasy with the sunburn cream the clinic doctor gave him, his cell phone blares from the counter—80's rock he down-loaded for the beach, all edgy treble—and he shouts above it:

"Hey, all they have here is a screwdriver, but this table is wobbly. Almost got it. Hey, are there pliers in that other drawer? Remember when we got that media stand from Ikea? Pliers. Vise grips, whatever. What time is it? Maybe a shim. Or saw a little off the other legs."

She has gone still, staring. "Frank . . .?" she asks, as if to be certain it's still his name.

———

Grace Feltch cannot stand the gnats anymore but has discovered that stretched pantyhose can form a kind of homemade mosquito netting over any bed, though she had to buy out Roscoe's entire stock of L'eggs and five rolls of duct tape to achieve it. She smiles, admiring her handiwork, imagining the coming night free of the faint buzzing in her ears and of the lightest disgusting tickle of no-see-ums and blue flies and mosquitoes and other flying insect pests she's looked up on Wikipedia, too.

5

In their aging, modest Cape Cod-style cottage, Chief's wife Jan has achieved a good-natured accommodation with the daily realities of Carratuck—the salt film on all things glass, the grit under bare feet on the hickory planks of their floors, the inevitability of rust. Chief loves any reminder of the luck that's led them to this wild edge of the land; it makes him feel less ordinary, in the way children can still believe they're different—at least until life traps them in a cubicle and rules them with a calendar.

Jan sweeps at the traces of sand idly of late, absently; though tonight as he returns from his day and sets gun and keys on the foyer table, her smile and gaze seem fully present and accounted for.

A dependable enough peace has found them, each safe in the other's charitable regard. They trade a quick kiss, and he has a quick thought of her as another man might: Jan with her traces of rosacea and her floppy gardening hats, her body gone soft but still inviting, her eyes sharp with a ready glint of amusement.

A new edginess hollows his stomach, and he eyes the bourbon bottle in a cluster of others on an open shelf. He will not on a weekday night, of course—that indulgence had become a vice and added pounds and dimmed his wits for too many years, late and loathe as he was to admit it. He turns in place, briefly: what now?

The day clings. The Boy's silence is a question without an answer, an affront, a failure.

Chief checks his cell phone: there's no notification on the home screen, but maybe a text or email from State Police or FBI or Homeland somehow failed to appear there, or sound his alert. He flicks at the apps, scrolls the promos from discount sites, the pitches from charities, the spam, endless. How are we all so easily found?

In the bedroom, he changes quickly into sweats and tee and sits on the bed with his open laptop to search NAMUS, the national missing persons database. He scrolls with impatient taps, annoyed. Without a name or address, he has only the approximate age of whichever parent is missing—useless. Carolyn Koenig, Robert Shulmeyer, David Hurst. Connecticut,

Massachusetts, or New York? What does "missing" even mean? To not be seen in one's usual places, at first. And then, as the hours turn into days and the absence becomes unaccountable, to be seen nowhere at all. None of the reasons are good: kidnapping, death, dementia, or flight. None suggest happy endings.

Over dinner, Jan shakes her head at the story, quick to remind: "Two years ago, that little girl's father missing? Shacked up on a bender with some coed, in the Airbnb right next door. Foster care turned out to be worse. Hard to get it right."

He remembers their own girl Linda at ten years old, waking one morning into a nightmare of abandonment, crying loud enough to bring him in at a run from pulling seagrass by the porch. Now he listens in vain to her voice on her cell for a hint of homesickness beneath the wry quips and complaints of the self-assured New York City college girl she has become, and overnight, it seems.

Stunned by time: for all the careful forgetting of it, who isn't jarred by their own face in a Facebook group picture, or by the obituary of a college friend, or a chance meeting on the boardwalk with a high school classmate, worn beyond recognition?

And if not by time, then stunned by the end of it, looming as ever-present possibility, somehow larger of late. Glimpses return of abrupt bad luck: the storm at sea, human accident, roar of wind and crashing tons of water to drown out human shouts. The old disaster, years ago. And you worry: the more time gone by, the less of it left before the next?

But why think that? Each of the Boy's parents thinks the other has him, simple as that.

He flexes his neck, scratches his jaw, focusing back on Jan and her beautiful, typical, insignificant chatter: "—ran into her in Roscoe's, complaining about getting a permit for the add-on again, Harry up all night worrying, had to pry myself away and then there she was at the checkout counter . . ."

And here, also, are the same bistro-style dishes after all, the thirty-odd-year-old stemware from their wedding registry, the butcher block countertops, the beaded white walls and solid beams of good wood. He holds the heavy cutlery, another gift, grateful for its weight and dim sheen, as if for reassurance.

6

Cort's glad she talked her mom into getting her the fast LTE cell with its customizable home screen notifications, so she can see the tweets coming in (shorter and shorter, with more deeply dopey emoticons, of course) all night long while she whispers with Tay, who has finally given up and joined the contest, with five other new names toward dawn.

"Hang on, I gotta switch ears." Tay's voice sounds rough with tiredness, like someone waking up from a nap.

Cort giggles a little to think she has kept him up, maybe in more ways than one, which doesn't make her a slut anyway, really, just not completely lame. "I would, too, but . . ."

"Show-off, I got 'buds too, but I forgot they were in my Shorty zip, they're fucked." His voice fades a little and then comes back, with a loud digital rustling as he presses his cell to his other ear.

"Am I on speaker?" She imagines him in a tiny room like a closet, humid and musty, much like her tiny "other" bedroom in this weekly efficiency unit shitbox she and her mom rent every August. It's cramped, even with just her single cot and rickety white dresser with faded Alpine trim. The walls are warped painted plywood, the floorboards gritty with sand from bare feet, shadowed by moonlight from the small smudged window.

"Oh, no way, man, they're in like the next room, and these walls are like cardboard. Thinner than."

"Our place too, but with gross water stains."

"Swanky."

"I know, right? The water comes out rusty, too."

"Got mildew? A ship painting?"

"Wait, have you been in here?"

"When?"

"What, when? Ever?"

"You told me, Cort. You described it."

"When?"

"Before I switched ears? Hello?"

She giggles again, confused. "How long have we been on, anyway?"

"Look forward, always. We got maybe two hours 'til daylight. We can make it. Keep talking."

It's crazy, because it's not a question; her eyelids have not once felt heavy, his voice never unheard. Alert, maybe a little hyper, she heard her mother's footsteps a few hours ago, saw her shadow dim the edge of light beneath her door, heard the creak of their shared dingy bathroom's door and the sink tap run, the faint bell of a neighbor's windchime. The living night.

A moth flutters in the porchlight out her window; the surf falls onto the beach two lanes over, seems to pause and do it again. A dog barks somewhere a few share houses down, stops as if thinking about it, then starts up again, too. The island is quiet enough this year—maybe too much, like each sound is pressing back against so much quiet, on purpose, to fill it up.

"Hello?"

"Hello yourself, I didn't go anywhere."

"You did. You just fell asleep, for just a second."

"Did not." She giggles, again.

How wrong can he be? To miss a single word from his raspy sleepy voice? To not hear him breathing into her ears, the rise and fall of the sound of his living almost inside of her?

She checks her battery icon to make sure she's still charging. The cord's a little short, but it still reaches from the outlet and the buds won't pull from her ears if she lies just so. They could fit better; it seems like an easy thing to get right, unless her ears are just weird.

Has he drifted off? "Hello?"

"What are you thinking about now?"

"Ohhhh . . . ummm . . . what are *you* thinking about?"

They laugh.

Her cell starts buzzing softly, intermittently, and she checks the time: 4:45 a.m. The first quarter hour #sleepless43 tweets are coming in from the game. For a few, it's rounding day one, and they compare symptoms, as if they've never had an all-nighter. Evi (evilady26) is already whining:

fuzzy aching like bad period

"See 'Evilady'? She's staying out past Glade Point. Same school. Year ahead, but she's nice."

"See 'MicroMickey4'? Such a pussy."

She scrolls and spots the tweet, one of about twenty now:

cuervo hangover

Tay's tweet comes in:

Aw, nut up GF

Cort smirks and adds her own to the feed:

molly crash

7

With the plexiglass hatch open above them and Sam's little fan whirring, still the air hangs heavily, the damp sheets entangle. Kathy lies turned away beside him, and as he has become accustomed, he tries to be still and float for an hour, letting sleep find him instead of searching for it.

There's fatigue, sure, the heavy ache of it weighing, but more a sensation than a demand, or at least it seems that way, if the difference is other than semantic in this case, or in general. The eyes close, the eyes open. The heartbeat is regular, until you think about it too much.

What the fuck.

Up, quick and quiet, out of the bunk, into track pants, to maybe head out and up to the cockpit just to breathe, see the stars. He pauses, remembering to grab his cell off the bunk-side utility shelf.

When wasn't it so—when didn't he reach reflexively for this addictive little dark rectangle, displaying nothing short of everything? Sometimes more than distracting, it's become an urge—to know, to double-check, to have already read that, to be instanter. Or just as often, to escape. Kathy's take, though, is that these things regress us back to the magical state of intimate play, of solitary child and shiny toy.

His lock screen picture is this yacht, his own beamy Hong Kong-built yawl, close-hauled and heeling on a gusty fall day, shot from another boat. Finger swipe, unlock, blinking at the sudden brightness to check the time: 3:20. It's pixel addiction, all this digitized data, the binary bits and bytes, millions of black/white blunt approximations instead of the infinite curves and chiaroscuro of the actual world.

Paused in the main cabin doorway, an upward glimpse stops everything; lying between spare sheets in the makeshift dinette bunk of thin cushions, the Boy's awake, staring into the darkness, eyes dimly gleaming.

Child is the father. Wordsworth, how random is that?

The ghost of another fear rises, but no, not for now. *Turn away, refuse it.*

Slowly now, nearer the Boy. Smiling carefully, crouching there to whisper: "Hey, buddy. Still up?"

Nothing, only the Boy's eyes flickering away, his stillness like an animal's, sudden and complete, as if at the scent of danger.

"Hey, easy, there. You're safe here, you're okay." What's more to say, knowing nothing else for certain? There are ways in, always, to begin to discover what silenced him, but a word too far or too soon can seal him in denial, in some solitary, unreachable world. Whatever this boy has witnessed, this place is free of danger, this night is peaceable. If only they would let it be so.

The Boy slowly seems to calm.

Sam dares to continue, "Know how I know? I try to remember to listen to the water, the little sounds of it, rocking the boat. Little sounds. It's . . . peaceful . . . hear it?"

They share a silent moment of simply regarding each other. Sam keeps his smile faint.

"Smaller . . . quieter sounds . . . shhh . . ."

The Boy's eyes close, his breaths deepening, fingers uncurling from his little electronic game and a twist of sheet laundered thin and smelling of bleach.

Sam watches, barely breathing himself. The Boy's short, dark hair is clumpy with sweat and oil, his wrinkled, dirty tee rank, his surfer-style jams rumpled. A sideways smudge of dirt or soot crosses his cheek from the corner of his pale, cracked lip to his temple. Beneath his eyelids there's a trace of movement, dreams beginning, perhaps, as exhaustion finally pulls him under.

———

Back inside his cabin, Kathy waits with her inquisitive look. "Anything?"

Sam shakes his head, gaze veiled. "No, but he's out like a light. Why not you?"

She shrugs as he doffs his track pants and slips in beside her, into a bed too warm with the muskiness of damp and faintest sweat, traces of sand-grit.

He meets her eye and sees his own thoughts there. Wordlessly, they climb naked from the bed and she pulls the spare sheets from a cupboard as he whips the damp top and bottom sheets off the bunk mattress and makes a wrinkled pile of them on the cabin sole. Breasts swaying, Kathy stretches her arms above the mattress to fling the clean bottom sheet out to float billowing before settling, until she yanks her corners into place, and he his. The sheet tightens, smooth and clean, and they float the top sheet now to let it drift onto the fresh tautness of this bed they share.

She climbs back in, her smile like a child's at the lightness of fluffed fresh linens. She lifts her lips to his and they kiss, and she pulls away to warn, "Shhhh," and they fight it but she giggles and finally they laugh outright, the sound carrying faintly out into the night where other, silenter boats float at berth.

Laughter fades and starts again more quietly, and fades again into a kind of thoughtfulness as her lips barely touch his, tasting. By his side, her nipple grazes his chest, her hand his thigh, fleetingly, returning him to their first accidental touch, and the next, sitting inches apart side by side on barstools at Claude's. Her hand floating up to tuck a strand behind her ear, the small wobble of a breast so slightly lifted beneath her elbow, the delicate arch of her eyebrow, her reticent smile: all of it hollowed him with a new emptiness by showing him how much he had been missing. So helpless and sudden, the pure wanting a heat in his ears and neck.

She turned him into a boy, nearly shivering to dare to imagine touching more of her—accidentally, of course, both pretending not to notice—but tonight just until the tease of her lips is a question he answers with his, tentatively, as if a guess. Her laughter, again, quick murmured low notes, ends with a faint gasp as one hand holds her wrist and the other glides lightly along the draped curve of her hip.

From wanting to needing, needing to having. All else falling away. He brings her to him, pulling her in with his fingertips sliding the sheet clean along her skin until it's gone and she's cool against him, twisting a little back and forth to sweep her fullness here, her taut firmness there, until the pressure in his chest becomes a moan. Her breath damp on his neck, he rolls and lifts himself over her, hovering as her hands gently on his hips at first finally tense and pull until they're hard against each other, balancing on a small fulcrum of heat with shallow, knowledgeable motions, slowly deepening, slowly hastened.

Both wait for and find the other's urging everywhere, in a gently bitten lip, a shuddering sigh, a gripped shoulder, a foot tangled in the top sheet for purchase. Freed in each other's quickening grasp.

Oh, if he had more to give, he would promise it; she deserves an unwavering, braver heart. But for this sweet moment, the fear—that he has too little of surety to offer—fades.

How it fades.

#day_five

1

"They think I belong here," the Australian kid said, in his broad accent, syllables stretched into twangy dipthongs. "Dorm counselor, a mate." Pronounced "mite."

He stood in the doorway of Sam's campus office, not nineteen, smirking and slouching in mall-bought "alternative" rock clothes: dark skinny jeans, boxy glasses, layered shirts over a silk-screened T, revealing a band name, Weezer or Geezer or Guster. Scalp showing through shorn hair, such vulnerable white. Prickled scrim of blemishes fading along his jaw. His eyes sliding away, bruise-colored skin beneath.

"Yeah? What do *you* think?"

That day's Sam was a blind man, to believe for even a moment that Gabriel's was just another face among the year's patients, one with another litany of longing for lost mother's love, for father's pride, with any of the usual catalogue of childhood hurts, tenderly nursed, tearfully confided.

To have the day back, to be a different man in the moment: what would he not give?

––––

Overhead, light pales the plexiglass deck hatch again. Faint sounds already clutter the morning—the padding of bare feet along the float as somebody heads for the showers, the hollow slap and hiss of a sailor hosing salt from a deck, a radio softly playing.

Turning now, Sam finds Kathy awake, too, facing him, her eyes faintly, oddly amused.

"Hey . . . you're up?" His voice is hoarse, as if he *has* been asleep.

"Before the sun, like I still had early shift at the Coffee Spot. Just laying here. Didn't really sleep at all. It sucks."

No explanation for her complaint occurs to him, and he shakes off a strange, pointless twinge of unease, but admits, "Me too. Found every lump in the mattress twice. Feels like back in med school, on a triple shift."

"Well, I thought *you* were asleep. So I kept quiet."

"Me too. Funny."

It isn't, really. He'll be even further off his game, spacey and edgy, and it'll likely cost him. Already, he's hoping for a light day, with few complications and fewer judgment calls. He's begun too many days here with the same hope, now vain.

Chateauneuf-du-Pape and indica have served him well since spring; he's clocked some hours of sleep on nearly most nights, and happily enough without other pharmaceutical aids, since even the non-benzodiazepines come with a discouraging list of possible side effects and contraindications. Another night like the last, though, suggests they may be the lesser evil, compared to the diminished capacity of too much wine and weed.

He rubs his eyes, sits up.

"Sam . . .?" she begins.

He preempts her. "Sure, I'll go check."

He slips out of bed and finds fresh sweats and T, the mothball scent of camphor from the open drawer, stubborn hint of mildew beneath. He'll need to clean out the drawers one of these days, search out the spot of dampness taking root, treat it before it spreads.

Out in the main cabin, he stops short, seeing what he wishes were otherwise: the Boy awake, lying there with his little electronic game held again in front of his face, like a window into another world. Faintly, Sam hears the beeps and whistles.

"Hey, Admiral! Get some shut-eye?" It's laying it on, but some light cheer can help provide what common sense suggests: consistent, dependably non-threatening interaction.

The Boy glances up and looks quickly away, traces of exhaustion around eyes faintly reddened, the tender skin swollen. Sam steps closer, the question one he needs to ask himself: has he slept at all? Has anyone?

Sam's cell buzzes on the chart table. He grabs it, fast, hopeful. "Hello?"

But no, nothing.

"Hello?"

Nada. He shrugs and hangs up.

———

A half hour later, Sam and Kathy seem to move in a sort of fog, smiling vaguely at their guest. Kathy clears their breakfast of cold cereal and peanut butter and jelly on toast, and Sam thumbs dimly at his cell phone, readying the camera function.

"More coffee, honey?" she asks Sam, her subtle parody of a family breakfast.

He raises an eyebrow at her. She raises one back, a wry duet.

"What about you, sir? More milk?" She smiles gamely at the Boy, whose eyes dart away. She shrugs and pours him some anyway.

Sam lifts and aims the little cell. "If I thought you would, I'd ask you to smile."

Across the dinette from him, the Boy goes still, expression blank. *Cli-ick.*

"Okay, one more for insurance, and we'll get these out to the chief."

But before Sam can aim the cell again, footsteps pound along the float past them, quick panicky impacts, a muffled shout, "This way, here!"

Sam stands, head tilted, listening.

From just outside now, another shout, from a sailor whose boat is just a few slips down, whose name escapes him: "Doc! Hey, you in there?"

Kathy and Sam trade looks of annoyance, then trepidation. He rushes up the companionway and out.

Sunlight stabs at his eyes as he leaps onto the float, met by two wide-eyed sailors.

"End slip, old couple? Went over to borrow some dish soap? Cabin open, TV on . . . I knocked, called out—Man, they look—on the berth in their cabin—I think they're both—"

"Okay." Sam starts off down the float, in a rush quickening to a run toward the big sleek 60-foot Erikson sloop in the outermost berth, a king's ransom worth of yacht.

The two sailors keep pace, one yammering off point, "I guess I just thought I—well, sorry, but maybe you should—"

Sam gives a vague nod and quickly clambers aboard, swinging under the wire rail and hopping down onto the teak sole of the cockpit. The main cabin door is shut, but unlocked, and Sam twists the knob and takes the first step down into dimness.

The rest—galley, chart table, the good mahogany cabinetry, a laptop open—goes by too fast as he crosses the main cabin and blunders on into the small hall to the owner's stateroom, where through the ajar door he sees two pairs of bluish bare feet at the end of a wide bunk, and then the couple themselves, so very still—dead, plainly, even from the doorway where Sam hesitates at first, stunned.

The bodies side by side, barely touching. The blue-white pallor unmistakable, the eyes open and already milky, fixed on nothing.

They were in their seventies, lank and handsome as any in a backlit Cialis commercial, and seasoned hands. They arrived on a windy morning, tacked close into an offshore breeze, smartly lowered the main, and luffed the jib. With a deft touch on throttle and helm, and the wife's long, easy rope toss from bow to float, they eased in to barely nudge a fender.

Hail-fellow-well-met, they'd invited Sam and Kathy over for Pimm's. After introductory chatter, they told tales of all-nighters on watch in the shipping lanes, or running full sails ahead of a nor'easter, sleeping with one eye open.

The man's wife had clocked Sam quickly and asked, "A doctor, huh? No rest for the weary around here, I bet." She seemed to study him a moment too long before the conversation veered onward and away.

By the book, Sam checks their vital signs anyway, and then turns and yanks open a sliding porthole and cracks the ceiling hatches for air. On a utility shelf across from the bed, a little TV is on, a morning talk show of women around a table, chattering and laughing. Sam snaps it off.

And then he sees it there beside the TV—a little amber plastic pill bottle, cap off. He edges closer, close enough to see it's empty and make out the label, "Lotosil," and a prescription date more than a year old.

One of the sailors, whichever one, has appeared in the stateroom doorway now, wide-eyed. "Jesus."

Sam lifts the berth sheet, turns each body a few inches over and pulls up their Ts to check for lividity. He bends and studies the glisten of their open eyes. TOD, probably not earlier than last night.

So no one can say he didn't, he gives the place a closer once-over for any sort of note, but it's Chief's wheelhouse, not his, and he's more likely than not to compromise evidence, should there be a need for any.

The thought occurs, probably unkind, that in the biggest picture their fate is perhaps not an overly-tragic one; after seventy, there are worse ways to go than falling asleep on a million-dollar yacht with your wife beside you—before the routine checkup turns something up, or the name of a day of the week slips away, or you almost make it to the men's room at a rest area off the Mass Turnpike. How much brighter could their future be?

If it's any solace to wonder, it's cold comfort twenty minutes later—when the sheet falls away from the woman's face as she's borne on a stretcher by two auxiliary firemen up the ramp from the float to the dock. Her cheeks shudder with their steps, as if alive; the shocked crowd of weekenders murmurs and gapes. The chief shouts with a pained look of dismay, "Sheet, Tommy! Come *on!*"

A hardened Staten Island FD transplant since 9/11, Tommy looks white himself as he quickly reaches down to readjust and cover her again.

Chief tilts himself back on his heels with his hands in his pockets, shaking his head at the day looming ahead, of paperwork and badgering calls to the mainland for the coroner he's failed to persuade Carratuck's supervisory board to provide. And of course, Deputy Police Chief Ken Ballard's father had to pick this week to die, way out in California, and Chief had to grant family leave; flaky as Ken is, he's better than none, and way better than the auxiliary guys, who need managing and aren't worth the trouble.

Chief calls out a last admonition, "Okay, everybody, nothing here to see!" before turning confidentially back to Sam. There are dark circles under his eyes today, a blurred look to his gaze. "Sleeping pills, huh?" He lets out a small, exasperated sigh.

"We'd all rather say accidental overdose, I'm sure. But both of them?"

Chief nods. "That sucks. Now I definitely gotta call mainland to sign off on forensics."

Sam looks away, more than the sentiment is worth.

Chief shakes his head woefully, watching the bodies being loaded into the back of his Jeep.

"Man, that's hard to see. We had a guy OD on something a few years back. Found him too many days later. I gotta get these two to the Fire Station, on ice." He sighs theatrically. "And call next of kin. Every year I put a coroner in the budget."

Sam nods back, commiserating. Waiting.

Chief remembers. "How's the boy?"

"Still not a word. I just took his picture, before all this, was just about to email it. Maybe show it around, one last Hail Mary before you call CPS?"

"Good. I'll get copies circulating." Chief seems edgy, distracted. His shave is bad, his hair sweat-darkened. He seems to nod as he lifts a hand to the other side of his head. "Yeah, no. Slow down, please. Methamphetamine? Why do you think so?"

Meth—? It takes Sam a small second to realize Chief has clicked his Bluetooth earbud and is already elsewhere, in urgent conversation with someone else. Is everyone somewhere else?

Sam waits, unhappy, as Chief paces a little circle, listening, and then pitches his voice low, holding up a *one-sec* finger at Sam. "Ma'am, hang on now, have you seen your son actually take any, or found any? Can you put him on the phone? He—what's the address?" He gives Sam a helpless look.

Sam gives a vague wave, *later,* and turns back to his boat. Kathy's there, waiting in the cockpit, a hand lifted to shield her eyes from the glare.

Sam slows, seeing just what he hoped he wouldn't: a pale shape hesitating by his main cabin's porthole—the Boy's face, just turning away.

2

"Higher," she says now, or wants to say, or has already said. It's the blue smoke she loves, floating upward in the windless lee of their dune, curling from the thin jay Tay has rolled for them. It's strong bud, and the air on her skin feels tingly, pressure against a dizzy lightness pressing outward from inside. She has an idea to speak again, if she has at all, but the words that occur to her might be dumb, but she hasn't said them anyway, she's pretty sure, so okay.

Tay has a foot lifted backwards behind him and reaches back to hold it higher, bending forward at the waist and lifting his other hand before him in a showy flourish. It's almost the Standing Bow yoga pose she has shown him, but not so much, really.

She blinks at him. An idea from nowhere fills the hollowness of lost sleep, suddenly, urgently important: "The Rig Vedas are a Hindu book. Which is how yoga started, I heard. It's a way of life, even sleep. It says to live in your dreams, or your dreams will live in your life. I read that." Why has she said this?

"Importance of excellent bud, right there." Little snorts of laughter escape him, until he lets it all go and collapses twitching on the sand, helpless, with little yelping howls, tears starting from his eyes.

A strange spasm-like wave contracts her stomach and then her chest and throat, rising and bursting out of her in laughter, too. Spinning now to fall beside him, their shoulders touching as they writhe.

When did they stop laughing? How long ago? Did it just now happen? Why does it matter anyway?

The sky is a white bowl, upside down, split by a green stalk of seagrass.

The black strands of Tay's hair shine and leave a shadow on his forehead in a jagged, perfect sharp row. The surface of his forehead smooth brown like wood with no grain in it, just smooth, deep color. His lips are darker than his skin; his teeth are even and white as the white in his eyes, which have gold flecks in the irises like cats', as they search hers with a question and must see the answer there, even before she knows it though she has always known it, of course, because his lips are softer than she thought and their touch lighter and warm and alive.

What is more alive than the warmth spreading lightly through her from him, which becomes more touching, of everything at once as they lie against each other, pressing gently? The salt sweat smell on damp skin and the sweet taste of smoke still in his mouth?

Quicker heartbeats, shallower breaths begin, and their hands become more questions. Strange, beautiful joy curves her lips against his, but his fingers tracing the curve of her hip move inward and downward to her thighs, stroking and teasing the edge of her shorts.

From somewhere her voice is asking, though not aloud, *what girl am I?* And then, *which boy is he?* It's a thought, only, that can disappear the way it came, as quickly and needlessly, but it won't, because his fingertips feel too urgent, pressing and somehow pulling harder and moving over her more quickly now, until her lips part from his with a soft gasp and she hears her own voice, hoarse and sleepy, "Uhh . . .. hey."

Surprise stops them and they lie there for a still, stunned moment, staring up and catching their breaths.

He turns his head to blink at her, confused. And she shouldn't, she knows, but she can't not, so she laughs—even though she's sorry to—she *laughs*, climbing to her hands and knees and up, swaying to stagger as she giggles at him staring and at herself, so ridiculously, pathetically afraid.

"No, no, I'm sorry . . . not at you . . . me, me . . . Prude-ster, pathetic. Me!" Too stoned, tears streaming.

But how long has this other noise—no, it's her ringtone, the tinny urgent blare of it—been happening?

She pulls out her cell and looks wide-eyed down at the caller ID. Why now, when she's breathless and at the edge of everything at once, this voice again, nagging like doubt, demanding to be answered?

She takes a deep breath, like a swimmer preparing to submerge, and clicks through. "Mom, hi, yeah. No. I'm . . . babysitting. For that lady, I told you? That I met at the . . . market? No, I know. Ummm, two . . . hours? I just said, babysitting. How long? Hello-o-? At the market. Two hours. Two hours, I said. No, Mom, there's nothing weird about the ocean. Take a *nap*." She glances at Tay, makes the crazy sign next to her temple.

Tay sighs and lies back as Cort's cell buzzes again: a text from Jane Felsh:

u quit u lose where r u

She flicks up her page and her thumbs fly over the keys:

fu – up 28 str8

She sends, and suddenly Mom's voice startles her, still alive from her cell, crackling out, trying to find her: "Cort? What is going on? *Hello*?"

3

Chief watches the emailed pictures of the lost Boy jerk and slip from his printer. A little blurry, but who isn't? At 86K, it's an emailable file size in today's instant world, and it's the trade-off that goes with.

In this dank garage for his and Pines Beach FD's Jeeps, his out-of-date color inkjet and desktop computer sit against the back of a rusting tool chest, where he's taped snaps of his girl and wife to bring something of home. Sweeter images, old school, pre-digital, from the days when you dropped your little film cartridge at a counter and picked up your envelope an hour later.

With a beep and a sigh, the print run finishes. The Boy is facing the camera full-on, with a veiled look to his eyes that bends the chief curiously closer, and closer still, but to see what? The Boy's gone mute on a bet, maybe, a dare. It's a game gone too far; kids now get their ideas from reality TV, where ruthlessness rules: "in it to win it," "who's your daddy," "make you my bitch"—it's all ugly meanness and profane taunts now, and maybe even a seven- or eight-year-old like this one has crossed a line no one ever showed him. Little sociopaths are everywhere—habitual liars, shoplifters, animal abusers. Or maybe the parents put this kid up to it, like the Colorado couple who stuck theirs in a balloon basket, sent him up, up and away, and called the news looking for a reality show of their own. Probably, though, nothing near as nefarious.

Chief glances at the door to the utility room, where the auxiliary guys have stretchered in the suicide couple, today's new problem, and packed them in ice. He's called the mainland, the Suffolk County Coroner's office, where they're slammed and glad to accept Sam's prelim for the death certificates, if Chief can alert next of kin and keep the bodies cold for a few days, maximum, until they can spare an aide and send out an ambulance boat.

Chief puts these calls off for now; better to get pictures of the Boy handed out and a parent found, fast, before Sam loses the kid, or the kid loses himself, and everyone has too much explaining to do.

He arranges the twenty-five pictures, printed on 8 1/2 x 11 laser bond, in a stack, slips them into a manila folder, and climbs into his Jeep to head back into town.

Between Hardy's Marine Supply and Pines Beach Sundries, there's a rectangle of water-stained concrete, a pair of straight-backed benches, and a kiosk with a glass pane over share rental and lost pet notices. It's Pines Beach's town square, if any place is.

Chief has his Jeep pulled up and a gaggle of tourists blinking up at him and back down at the pictures he's handed out. These look like Yonkers or North Jersey types, young marrieds partying before the wife gets pregnant and on the wagon, and dad needs to clock in overtime to stay even; the women wear big jewelry, the men wear Hawaiian shirts over wife-beaters and cargo shorts stuffed with small bills and receipts.

Toward the back of the small crowd, there's a foursome who look German, or Swedish—lanky, pink blondes with a fanny pack and a map. One of these women studies the picture and starts to sob, inexplicably, "I'm afraid of losing my child, too. It can happen to anyone. Anyone."

Chief fights the urge to roll his eyes. "Look, I just need to know if anyone recognizes him."

Everyone looks at everyone else. Nobody speaks up.

"Okay. Can I ask you to show this picture around? This boy's folks are missing, and we don't even know his name, or where he was staying."

A new-agey looking Five Towner, probably an ad guy, speaks up, squinting, "Didn't you ask him?"

Chief gives the man a showy, cold smile. "He's not communicating, we don't know why at this point . . ."

Another genius pipes up, "Who do we show it to?"

Chief hesitates. Is it stupid pills in the water? "Everybody, okay? We need to figure out who this boy is."

Another tourist, gold chain flashing: "Everybody? How do we show it to *everybody*?"

Hungover, they've got to be. Maybe Clam Shack ran a well-drink special too late last night, and these vacationers have simply been on a bender and temporarily murdered their minds. "Jesus. As many as you can, okay?"

The tourist hesitates, and then actually shows his copy of the Boy's picture to another standing next to him, already studying his own.

Chief watches, disbelieving. Funny, if it wasn't so weird.

But not as weird as what he thinks he sees now, at the back of the crowd: a middle-aged, silver-haired guy, gleaming eyes observing all from behind pricey wire-rims, holding one of the Boy's pictures. His eyes meet Chief's with a sharp, appraising curiosity.

The crowd murmurs and shifts, blocking Chief's sight line. He steps sideways, but the man is already wandering off behind the Germans, and some sunburned muscle-head has stepped up, actually wondering, "Is there a reward?"

4

"It's just hard to imagine," Kathy pitches her voice low and hopefully out of earshot of the Boy beside Sam, as they walk Sam and his bike along the boardwalk into town. "They seemed cheerful enough. Spry. Had to have some money, for that much boat. How do two people like that decide to just call it a day?"

A list presents itself: a diagnosis, a death, a scandal, creditors? "It *is* hard to fathom."

These deaths have shaken her, of course. Add their unanticipated guest, and no doubt she's seeing the program threatened, too—her summer free of responsibility fading—and is worried that it's just the beginning. It's not what she signed up for since their night five or six weeks ago, when the sex and the wine and just enough of a good joint had him in an expansive mood, and he suggested she quit the Coffee Spot and take the summer off, sharing his stateroom cabin, "such as it is."

She cuts her eyes at him, nodding toward the Boy, nearly whispering, "Any advice for me?"

"You did some babysitting in high school, didn't you tell me?"

"And since." Her mouth forms a slight, girlish smirk, beguiling Sam momentarily, until he hears her tease, "Could say I'm used to it."

Surprise slows him. Already? It's subtext he'd expected a month or so from now, maybe, but not today, and he's got no argument ready to hand to counter the sly inference: that he's in an indecision period, like some college freshman with his head in the sand, unwilling to look at or make the hard choices. But is she really any different? Weren't they both willing to coast through an easy, low-stress summer, taking their pleasure where they found it? Swimming, lobster rolls, some slow dancing after beers at the Clam Shack? To wherever it may lead?

He gives her a long, slow look. "Do we need to talk?"

"Oh, god no. Later, maybe, if then."

"Yes?"

They peer at each other as if through a haze, both a little confused. "Sure, or not. Later."

He slows, watching her. She stops and slaps his shoulder, like a frat buddy. "Just go on. Me and Blue Streak will figure it out."

———

Sam pedals along, zigzagging between dawdling bunches of weekenders staring dully around themselves, and a few small knots of murmuring locals who look up and nod. It's already hot, with a punishing, resolute heaviness that enervates; he fights back, sweat trickling down his back.

Up ahead, there's a good-looking middle-aged couple, dressed upscale but understated—down from Connecticut, probably—smart suburbanites laughing at something one has just said. They trade a nod and easy smiles with Sam, and if the morning were more leisurely and less portentous, Sam would add a pleasantry. But when he glances back as he whirs by, their smiles are gone, their faces taut, angry, as if he has interrupted a spat. What vacation doesn't feature one?

In the square of a peeling motel room window, paleness hovers, and just as Sam realizes he's glimpsed a naked elderly man, the man is gone—someone who's forgotten to pull their shades and stepped quickly out of sight, probably mortified.

More strangeness nags at him: two pre-teen girls who should be giggling and playing, gone still and silent, staring out to sea. A middle-aged man on a bench, plucking OCD-style at his tee shirt, as if at bugs.

———

Striding into the clinic, Sam's just a few minutes late, but he doesn't like to leave too much to Paula, or the summer's new aide, Andrew, always eager to feel exploited and aggrieved at any request that doesn't fit his contracted hours or job description to the letter.

A few feet into the waiting room, Sam slows, seeing a waiting tourist looking straight at him, and then hugely, convulsively yawning. Beside him, another stares at the ceiling with unblinking eyes.

He rounds the admittance counter with a brusque, unanswered "hey" to Andrew, and finds Paula a few steps further down the hall between exam rooms. She greets him with a wry, raised eyebrow. Are all women annoyed at him today?

She pitches her voice low. "Got a couple hasn't slept in two nights." She nods toward an exam room. "In Two."

5

Kathy's the only local at the laundromat today, and must look it, since the women this afternoon are a clique of big-haired Bridgeporters in cruise wear, all little short shorts and gold and silvery kitten heel sandals. They flash Kathy their best quick smiles as they take in her jean cutoffs and faded tee, her tattooed ankle bracelet of thorns and her deeper tan, but they trade sideways looks when they see the Boy in one of Sam's old tees down to his knees.

Kathy had finally got at him with a washcloth, so at least he looks less feral; he cringed at first, moaning and rolling his eyes, but she just overrode him with cheerful, nonstop chatter. Sweat forms its own dirt if left long enough, flakes of dead skin gone dark and stuck to newer pink layers beneath, and these came off in swaths beneath the rough nub of the cloth as she scrubbed. Laughter worked, too; the sound of hers quieted him, as if a sound from long ago he couldn't quite place, an echo of another, happier time. He closed his eyes, finally trusting, as she pulled his tee up and over his stiffly upheld arms, the neckline catching on his chin and making her own eyes fill, to think anyone could abandon this sweet frightened boy.

Even more frightened now, no doubt, with all the ugly commotion this morning.

He still clings to his little game, and he had cried when she tried to take it from him while she tugged Sam's tee on him. Now he stares blankly as she piles his things into a washer, and then he turns slowly in place, eyes finding clothes in a front-load dryer, tumbling past the glass, as if underwater, or falling from the sky.

A voice rises suddenly above the creaking and gushing of the big machines, and Kathy turns to see another young suburban woman in huge sunglasses and fluorescent beach wrap, just arrived with a full plastic laundry basket under an arm and a picture of the Boy in her other hand. "Oh my God! It's him!"

She sets her basket down and points at the Boy, her pink fingernail glinting, glancing at the others for corroboration. They crowd in, staring down at the picture as she brays, "So they found you! Thank God!" One actually aims her cell, snaps Kathy's picture, and begins texting.

Kathy almost laughs, "Oh, no, I'm not his mother, I'm just . . . keeping an eye on him for my . . . for Dr. Carlson, who runs the clinic."

"You're Mrs. Carlson? So—"

"No. Not wife, not mother, okay?" Kathy puts up her own chilly smile.

The woman blinks at Kathy sympathetically. "Sure, sweetheart, I understand."

The other whispers back, too loudly, "I heard he was a big time shrink in Boston. Some patient killed himself, family sued. Why he's here."

The woman with the picture shoots this one a warning look, and they all glance at Kathy.

Kathy almost feels sorry for them, these gum-chewing creatures of mindless domesticity, desperate for drama. She stares right back, her face stony: "No dirty laundry of your own?"

They blink, understanding slowly, these cows. With elaborate dignity, they raise their eyebrows, purse their lips and turn back to business.

Kathy glares after them, and slowly her baleful look turns curious. Are they just dumb, or in a sort of daze?

One loads dry dirty clothes into a dryer and dumps in detergent with a flourish. The fabric softener vending machine completely stymies a third, who tries to wedge a quarter into the bill slot. Past her, out the big front windows, a group of tourists has stalled, and stands looking around as if lost.

Kathy goes still, too, as it hits her: the fog everybody's in seems like nothing so much as lost sleep, weird. And it's bound to make some slow, some mean, and some both, nothing weird there.

———

In Exam Room Two, a wide-eyed middle-aged Massachusetts school board comptroller and his wife present as hyper-aroused, even slightly breathless. The man interrupts his wife often and pedantically, correcting her with finicky details. She falls silent during these interjections, annoyed, smiling apologetically at Sam, who finds her vaguely familiar: someone he chatted with online at the Coffee Spot, or at the grocery checkout? Had she been in before, another complaint? He glances at the chart, but she preempts:

"The second night, we *felt* tired, of course—"

"—well, you more than me—"

"—but neither of us as tired as the couple next door who left. Thin walls. Heard them complaining about it. Nonstop."

"But, it was around midnight, I guess—"

"—not quite, I think—"

"—when we each realized the other was still up—"

"—well, I think I saw that you were still awake and I asked you—"

Sam interjects, impatient with the wandering, pointless narrative, and begins a Q & A, hoping to rule out, narrow down, and finally achieve some sort of diagnosis. "Had either of you had any alcohol?"

The man smiles, pained. "Neither of us drink, no."

What wild, lost youth could have turned these two into teetotalers? Unimaginable.

"Now . . . your medications?" Sam bends to the chart. "Just your Lovastatin, Ed? And Lenore, your diuretic, Duranol?" He glances up with an encouraging smile.

They simply nod, but then Ed begins, "Well, I was on another statin, but they thought—"

"Let's talk about your room, your bed, did you sleep the first night you were here?"

They nod, immediately, no equivocation there, not that it clarifies anything.

"Okay, that's good, but—"

"The bed is wonderful, I think, it has a pillow top mattress—"

Ed can't resist. "Must be new, because they usually indent in a few months, and then you're stuck. All those stories, the reviews online—"

"Any strange odors or noises on the second night? The air conditioning in the room?"

Now they think, or appear to. Ed's leg is jerking up and down, his heel *tap tapping* the linoleum. Lenore blinks rapidly. The hyper-activity could be a clue, but to what?

"Anything at all different the second night?" Sam presses.

Ed and Lenore shake their heads in unison. Until Ed remembers, "Well, sure, one thing: neither of us could sleep."

Sam lifts his gaze slowly to meet theirs. "O . . .kay. Let's run some completely unnecessary tests. Blood panel, urine sample, so we can do our part to increase the costs of health care for all. Okay with you?"

Lenore smiles weakly. Ed shrugs.

———

Minutes later, Sam glances quickly at the chart Paula has prepped for the next patient, and knows the name: Carl Blonner, GTE lineman, in last week, in fact, for a quick tetanus shot after a minor laceration in the field: right hand, rusty nail.

Sam rolls the rattling little stool out from under the countertop and sits. He and Blonner share the wry, simpatico connection of active bachelors, though Blonner might not know that Sam's less of one these days. "Hey Carl, what brings you? The hand okay?"

Ungainly on the exam table, Carl fidgets, his eyes narrowed into a wince. Sam is grateful, at first, to hear today's complaint: a severe headache, gradual onset, with some *Parade Magazine*-style speculation. "Power lines, they're saying now, can eventually affect people, EMF. I don't worry, but, I mean, environmental factors are factors."

A quick neurologic exam turns up nothing. Carl's eyes track, and sensation, proprioception, reflexes, and therefore nerve induction, all look good. Sam draws some blood, proffers a codeine and aspirin scrip, and some casual advice: "Shut your windows, pull your curtains. Try dim and quiet for a change. Maybe get some sleep."

"What I've been telling *you*."

They trade a smirk as Sam scribbles a scrip, tears off the page, and hands it over. "Take one of those. Check back tomorrow if you don't feel better, you know where to find me. We'll run a few tests meanwhile. I'll send Paula in." He gives his quick smile and edges out.

When Sam and Paula confer in the hall, she shakes her head at the coincidence. "Next-door neighbors, Carla and Jim? Up all night, too."

"Maybe they ran late at the Pier View again. Had the karaoke cranked up too loud?" Even as Sam offers it up, he replays the hours, and the sounds he knows by heart, of last night's sleeplessness. "Though I guess I didn't hear it."

"So . . ."

"Yeah, no. I didn't sleep so well either."

She glances up with knowledgeable, amused eyes, but her gaze wanders over his shoulder and her faint smile grows fainter, as her head tilts curiously.

He hesitates, and then his eyes follow her gaze out to the waiting area, where others have entered and sat in the salmon-colored plastic chairs along the back wall: an elderly man in a jacket and tie stares at an upside-down magazine; a woman applies dark lipstick, a crooked slash. Just beyond the plate glass, in the lane outside, grizzled charter hand Dale or Walt dances clumsily by himself, earbud wires dangling, his face tilted skyward, eyes shut tight.

6

Outrigger, Galleon, Spindrift. The Jeep leaves ruts as Chief roars past another lane's beach steps. He knows these by heart, and past a few more he'll be at Barnacle, where a frantic weekender has just phoned in a semi-coherent domestic disturbance complaint.

Two dead old-timers aside, he's seen enough full moon crazy already today, though nothing yet as dire. There was the new kid in Bon Soiree Frozen Yogurt who screwed up the freezer thermostat and slipped in a puddle of melted Espresso Chip and Banana Manna and thought it was all a big joke. Add the shark-boater who charted the inlet forty years ago and this morning ran aground and maydayed, and then failed to give his correct position, sending the bluefishing fleet to the ass-end of the island and back, radioing colorful language. Silliest of all: the FD auxiliary who sat and dialed his own cell phone again and again, cursing when he couldn't get through.

Just ahead, a small crowd of beachgoers has gathered before a big, boxy post-modern beach house, jeering or cheering, hard to say. Chief pulls up and climbs out to see the crowd is staring up at a wild-haired woman standing three stories up at the edge of the roof, clearly naked beneath a half-tied bathrobe. She's not unattractive, but her eyes are frightening, wide with terror, and her face twitches with revulsion. A few of the guys in the crowd seem dazed, just slack-jawed ogling, entranced by the possibility of a breast exposed or a flash of dark triangle between her legs, but Chief only sees crazy and pathetic in the spectacle, and even worse, sad.

Bits of voices find him: "—Chief!"

"—hey—"

"—drunk, you ask me . . . crazy . . ."

On the roof, the woman's mouth twitches, like someone about to be sick, but words emerge, shouted slowly as if to a child, "Make it . . . fucking . . . STOP!" She slowly lifts a hand and points over their heads, behind them.

Chief glances back behind them all, but there's nothing, just fifty yards of empty kelp-strewn beach and the flat blue-gray ocean, which seems to hesitate, and then gather itself up into a waist-high wave that falls apart, gushing onto wet sand.

Most of the crowd laughs, but some fall silent, oddly cowed, perhaps considering it; the sound of the surf *is* incessant, even insistent maybe, once you start to think of it that way, but why would you?

Chief steps closer and calls up to her, "Ma'am? Can we talk for a minute? Can you just stay right there while we do?" Steady and slow wins the race.

Behind the woman now, a man appears, her husband? "Baby?" he pleads. "Come on, now, come on back. You're just tired."

She wavers, and the crowd goes still, until she finally lets out a long breath like a sob, sagging, enervated. Her husband or boyfriend puts his hand out, and she takes it and collapses into his arms.

The crowd boos, hooting catcalls of disappointment and derision.

Chief looks at them all, disbelieving, but what's to do? It's all bozos, all the time this year, and there's no law against it.

Inside their rented beach house for the debrief, the woman grips her robe tightly around her throat and seems sheepish and sensible enough at the moment—over-tired, she explains, from lack of sleep. The man—not her husband it turns out, but player enough to book the whole place for a weekend date—makes his eyes round with sympathy as Chief hands her one of Sam's cards.

"See Dr. Sam Carlson, Pines Beach Urgent Care, if you feel yourself getting anxious again."

"Sure, Dr. Carlson. I've seen him," the boyfriend offers, as if to reassure.

He and his date nod, sober and earnest, but fidgety, as if they can't wait for Chief to be gone so they can go at it on the kitchen floor. Go figure.

Climbing back into his Jeep, he squints out at the crowd sluggishly dispersing. A few frat-types meet his disapproving gaze through the glass, smirking, and he keeps the stare on until they shrug and turn away, murmuring and laughing.

Chief dons his earbud, just as his phone chimes. He clicks through. "Chief Mays."

A stranger's voice, a woman's, shrill and urgent, crackles at him: "Thank God. You have my boy, I think. I heard you have one. Thank God."

Chief leans forward, cupping his hand over his earbud. "Ma'am, yes, we do. Come to the Urgent Care Clinic in Pines Beach. You are gonna have to—"

"Clinic? But—is he okay?"

"Ma'am, I'm gonna need some information. Names, first. How long has he been missing?"

Silence. Chief touches his earbud, tilts his head. "Hello?"

Nothing. Damn. He shakes his head, fishes out his cell to check his connection bars—all good, even as it rings again.

But it's Carlson now, of course, nagging: "Chief, I've had some patients here, they—it's—you get any noise complaints last night?"

"Among others. It's full moon crazy out here. But good news? The boy's mother called. On her way to the clinic to pick him up."

7

The larger question looms, of course, and when Sam reaches her, Kathy isn't shy about asking it: how does a mother lose a child for a day and a night, if not more, and not call the police?

"We'll know soon enough," he assures her.

"Huh. I just got him cleaned up, too. Well . . . we're on our way."

They click off, less than entirely relieved.

Other questions linger, too many, and Sam steals a moment between patients for microscopy and gram-testing blood samples, as good as it gets in an urgent care. He adjusts the eyepiece that gives him back the shadow of his own lashes until he blinks and rolls focus to reveal the lighted circle of cells on the slide, swimming in Brownian motion. In sample after sample, nothing presents out of normal range, nothing but the reminder: we are our cells, and in a droplet of blood magnified a thousand times, we are anybody, nameless as the next.

He moves to the back hallway utility counter, pulling up lab results on the frustratingly slow desktop computer. He scrolls to teetotalers Comptroller Ed and wife Lenore, just in. Gut checks first, always, for small intestine issues and resultant heightened glutamine levels, which can sometimes but not often create excitability. No, nothing. Levels well within range.

Infection: viral, bacterial? No WBC elevation, and none of the rapid-result antigen testing he has available indicate anything.

Tox screen for amphetamine, excess alcohol? Nothing. Heavy metals, other poisons? No, not that anything in their narrative suggests use or exposure.

Scrolling, scrolling.

Next patient, Carl Blonner, local GTE field employee. *Click*: same negatives as above, with a touch of hypercholesterolemia. No help.

Paula's next-door neighbors Carla and Jim's results yield less, though Carla has a touch of borderline proteinuria, suggesting a full kidney workup might eventually be in order.

Charter boater Walt's scores reveal nothing, though a bump on the back of his red neck looks like another basal cell carcinoma, just in time for his quarterly skin check with his mainland dermatologist.

In all, there are simply no common anomalies.

Distantly, the clinic landline is ringing, and he barely hears Paula pick up, her voice low in measured, reassuring tones.

She peeks around the little lab room doorframe, phone still in hand, with news that can't wait. "Sam? Lady on her way, who thought her boy was gone? Found him under the porch next door, playing fort with a neighbor kid."

Sam winces. Good news for her, much less so for anyone else. He checks his watch: 5:26, after CPS regular hours, and well after the last ferry from anyplace else. A deeper worry intrudes, and he shakes it off with a sigh.

He dials the chief to head him off.

"The mother show up yet?" Chief demands. "What's she saying? I'm on the way."

"She's not. She just called, found her kid."

"Jesus. She—"

"Didn't you ask her how long her boy was missing?"

Chief's tone turns chilly. "I'm not too sure how you do it back home, but we like to ask the questions in person here."

Sam takes a breath, waits, lets it go. "Child Services, here tomorrow? It's high season, we have enough on our plate, I know you agree."

"Tell me. People need to get some sleep, if you ask me."

The pieces of the day arrange themselves suddenly, into an even more unwelcome, disquieting, bigger picture. "People need to—say again?"

"Sleep, what I said." After an odd, wary beat of hesitation: "Why?"

Sam begins to pace. "Huh. We're seeing it here—"

"Seeing—"

"Well, maybe a dozen insomnia complaints. And there's the possible sleeping pill overdose this morning—"

Another beat. "So . . . what's it mean, Sam?"

"I'm working on it. I ran everything on site I could, random-sampled urine, blood, even drug-tested. Trace of cannabis, some high cholesterol. But nothing across the board. And there's no other symptoms, white blood cell counts all in range, so I don't see how we're looking at anything infectious. I sent them home, said to check back tomorrow if it keeps up. There's no reason to think it will. Fatigue is cumulative."

"Right. But, same question."

Has he understood nothing? "Like I said, working on it." Sam tries to keep the edge of annoyance from his voice, but fails. "Just . . . Child Services, okay?"

Next call: Kathy again, who's good-natured, as always, but how can there not be issues for a forty-plus woman, childless and suddenly confronted with responsibility for one? Luckily, "discussion" is not Kathy's style, a relief in so many ways. They both know enough to extend the honeymoon phase as long as possible, but it requires a constructive non-engagement with the rest of the world, where the lives of others will inevitably present questions about their own.

Blll-iiing! His cell rings again, startling him. Do we ever really finish a thought, or do others just crowd it offstage?

"Sam? It's Howard, thought you might know why, we've had a run down here. On all the over-the-counter sleep meds. PM aspirin, melatonin, even Nyquil. People are asking for prescription. What's going on?"

Sam's hand tightens into a fist around the phone. "Howard, check your pharmacy stock. And nothing to anyone without a scrip."

"Sure, I know that, will do, but what—"

"I'll get back."

He clicks off and turns in place, gaze wandering as if for a clue, and it falls on more evidence everywhere, it seems. In the waiting area, a thin, sallow man paces, murmuring to himself in argument. Hair awry, in mismatched clothes, a woman smiles beatifically at nothing, her eyes preternaturally wide, unblinking. A little girl shows her drawing to her mother, and even from here he can make it out: a frightening mess of smeared black crayon.

He thinks, and grabs the keyboard and brings up a Google search field, rapidly typing:

CDC

He pauses and looks down the hall again to the waiting room, gaze drifting now to the feet of these patients—in flip-flops trailing beach sand—and to their bathing suits, some still damp enough to darken a beach wrap or a shirt pulled on over.

He backspaces, deleting, and types instead:

EPA

8

"Yes, I'm a physician." On the line with a second EPA flack, Sam keeps his voice carefully level.

He paces the hall past Exam Three, where a wide-eyed, improbably thin teenager waits, and then about-faces and heads back past Exam Two (a bee sting!) and One (generalized itching?).

He glances out at the waiting area again and thinks of asking Andrew to sweep the sandy linoleum, but Carratuck is nothing but a sand bar with houses on it, anyway. Pointless.

"And you are requesting—?" Flack needs a recap, before Sam's even started.

"A conversation, for starters, and then water, air and soil samples tested." He brings the cell phone closer to his mouth, as if it will help persuade. Maybe environmental hazards only turn up during business hours and they're all past ready to head home to family and television, but basic prudence and avoidance of doubt demand he gets a hearing, at least.

"Can you tell us what you think you're looking for out there?" Flack wants to know. He's jotted her name, Suzanne Calder, and her title, "Assistant Field Coordinator," but her qualifications are nowhere in evidence yet.

"No, honestly, not at this point—some sort of agent capable of—"

"—what signs of illness can you describe, exactly?" She's working down a checklist, of course, and it makes sense; they need to cull the cranks from the initial incident reports, or else fly helicopter HASMAT teams everywhere, all hours, every time a stoned high school kid makes a prank phone call or some conspiracy theorist thinks we're all being poisoned.

"No physical illness, but behavioral changes. Insomnia. A dozen official cases, and we've had a run on over-the-counter sleeping pills at our local drugstore, as well."

"So . . . no underlying physical illness. Any . . . fatalities?"

Is she disappointed? "Do I need to have some?"

"Sir, I'm doing what I can to help you with your situation. We—"

"Two deaths, waiting on forensics, but it looks like Lotosil—sleeping pill—overdose. Insomnia would certainly be a contributing factor."

A pause, the soft clicking of typing. "Can I get your name and location and the best number to reach you?"

He gives it all again, carefully polite. "I hope to hear back soon. Thanks." He adds hopelessly, "Suzanne," and clicks off.

Why should it be otherwise? From their point of view, he's got people with trouble sleeping, and two deaths with no real proof of a connection. If he were them, he might hesitate too, before hanging his ass on a limb and spending hard-won funding to send a team.

Paula, of course, is suddenly there somehow, as if materialized. "Sam, people are getting anxious. What have we got here?"

He gives another wan smile, all he has. "Not as much as I'd hoped. I'm on it."

He would retreat down the short hall to his office to gather scattering thoughts—if not to flee—but in the waiting area, behind Paula, a woman in a plastic chair tilts her head back, closes her eyes, jaws widening, nose wrinkling as she yawns.

Beside her, a little girl swings her feet back and forth, flip-flops scuffing the lino, and she, too, pauses to tilt her head back and yawn.

Sam stares.

A weathered local, another charter owner, no doubt, joins in, shaking his head with a sigh.

Sam's jaws ache to open, too, but he stops. An unformed thought, forming.

Yawning.

He moves, driven quickly to the desktop computer in the back hallway nook to pull up the browser and search before he even sits and leans in, the words returning to him from the grad school lecture everyone tittered at:

Mass Psychogenic Illness.

No pathogen required, behavior communicable as any virus. No toxin needed, just our suggestible selves. Yawning. Laughter. Delusion. Hysteria.

He leans closer, typing, *clickety clickety*, searching with eyes scanning rapidly back and forth, back and forth, like a dreamer's in REM sleep, as hits appear, underlined blue links:

"War of the Worlds radio broadcast, hysteria . . ."
"Virgin Mary Sightings, Corado, Peru"
"Tanganyika Laughter Epidemic . . ."
"Chupacabra Panic Spreads, Quezon, Puerto Rico"
"Motor Hysteria in Nunneries"

"Tourette's Symptoms Outbreak, LeRoy, NY"
"St. John's Dance"

He clicks the last, reads on, remembering it as the *Choreomania,* or "Dancing Mania" phenomena from a grad school seminar. Odd, inexplicable cases, in Aachen and Strasbourg, hundreds of years apart, of thousands dancing erratically and uncontrollably. Otherwise known as St. Vitus's Dance.

Click. Tanganyika Laughing Epidemic. The afflicted were girls, villages apart, laughing for as long as a week, some finally hospitalized. He pictures them: long, thin, dark arms reaching for solace, their choked gasping, panicked eyes. Sent from their school to their homes, where calm seemed restored, until other villages in the area reported more children afflicted, and then siblings, parents, neighbors, until the cases numbered near a thousand. One must have begun it, certainly, but investigators never identified exactly whom.

Click. The incident in LeRoy, NY, most recently, presented multiplying localized cases of Tourette's syndrome, with subjects babbling gibberish, cursing, convulsing. Again, as in all these cases: no discernible physical etiology. Social media, or suggestibility? Academics debated, as they will.

How much easier, after all, to cause lost sleep than to cause these extreme physical symptoms? Need the suggestion even be conscious? Can't the wakeful wake the sleeping? In this age of anxiety, of constant and instant stimuli, why can't a tipping point be reached, Circadian rhythms falter?

He leans back, exhaling, relieved to have a precedent and a diagnosis, and one that confirms what he already knows: in the end, the cumulative effects of deprivation always prevail—eyelids grow heavy, heads nod, sounds and sights fade, and off we drift.

Sleep, of course, will defeat sleeplessness. It has never not.

#

Linda Habst's son is a tweaker now, and why not? He's had all the gateway stuff, come home late from school or a night at the movies with his homie posse stinking of pot smoke and giggling like a girl, and who else could have drained the Smirnoff level below the mark she lightly penciled?

Now he sits on the futon in his room for the week, his hair dirty and his teeth yellow, his skin bad and his eyes wide and glazed as he stares into his laptop screen, playing his interactive Internet multi-roleplaying game (another addiction, right there!) World of Witchcraft *(or Warlock?) for like the forty-third hour in a row.*

"Kev, honey? How about a sandwich?"

The gaze he lifts to hers is cold and depthless, which says one thing and one thing only, plain as day: pure crystal Methedrine drug abuse, the scourge of young America.

Or LSD, for sure, if not "roofers," the rave-party date drug these kids eat like Pez. She'll search his backpack again, check the balled socks in his underwear drawer, buy the urine-testing kit. She will find and destroy it—whatever powder or pill has sent her son spiraling further and further beyond her reach, forever, into the unbearable agony of so much frantic despair, and loneliness too.

"You asked me three minutes ago. Go to sleep *already, Mom."*

———

Glass television screens are sturdier than Marion Holk-Menges ever suspected. A swung broom handle only scratches the one in their rental unit, and a second blow only leaves a hint of spiderweb cracks across its black surface. The metal stem of the patio umbrella, though, produces a satisfying thick crunch of smashed glass, and flying gleaming bits.

In his boxers, Pete, her husband of eighteen years, circles the room, hands fluttering, "What are you doing? It's off, it's been off!*"*

Marion doesn't pause, battering the set with the patio umbrella in a slow, halting rhythm, "I can . . . still . . . hear it!"

———

Kenneth Balk has secretly watched a few of those reality shows about hoarders and even recorded an episode on his digital set top box because it somehow scared and fascinated him at the same time, so he's been meaning to strap and dolly the old Frigidaire from behind his bungalow around front and call Pritchett Hauling to take the damn thing away, even though let's face it, they're the only game on the island and know it; it's extortion, plain and simple.

But tonight an idea comes, but then it disappears before he can remember it (he's a little foggy after however many all-nighters and now the ocean and the crickets out in the salt marsh are just nonstop in a whole new way), but then the idea returns and kind of expands into a question, a simple one that seems more and more urgent until finally he wants to open and close the Frigidaire door behind him to find the answer:

How quiet is it inside?

———

A weekend fisherman's ear has been burning inside, as if something has crawled into it and is stinging him before it dies and explodes into putrefying bits of pestilent insect. Clinic doctor guy said no, but it's a green fly, has to be—he's looked it up, they can do that; they're always in a cloud around the chum bucket, tickling the sweat on his forehead when he guts and scales the day's blues and flounder, biting and leaving welts until he can free a hand to smash the fuckers into smears.

After too many nights in a row lying still and pretending to ignore the maddening, prickling sensation in his ear, maybe it's not the best idea in the world, but it's all he's got: his house key isn't long enough to really to get in there, so maybe this fishhook, straightened with pliers, can reach.

———

Against the southerly beaches of Carratuck, the moonlit sea pauses and sighs and lifts itself, before falling back, and lifting again.

9

At just past eleven, the night seems to press in against the bedroom window, deep and barely illumined by some far neighbor's deck lights. Chief wonders briefly where Jan is, and what's keeping her, but he's not sorry for a few minutes alone.

He sits at her vanity in his boxers, typing quickly and quietly into his laptop. The Homeland Security website is easy navigating, and the Board of Supervisors-mandated seminar on the mainland now seems a pretty silly use of the taxpayers' dime, since pointing and clicking pretty much cover it.

Click. "Office of Domestic Preparedness." *Click.* "Emergency Responder Guidelines."

He leans forward here, scrolling and scanning.

AWARENESS LEVEL GUIDELINES FOR LAW ENFORCEMENT OFFICERS

I. The law enforcement officer should:
    1. Identify what hazardous or WMD materials are present in an emergency incident or event.
    2. Be familiar with the means of delivery of WMD agents or materials. Know locations that could become targets for persons using WMD agents or materials.
    3. Recognize unusual trends or characteristics that might indicate an incident or event involving hazardous materials or WMD agents.

Well, thanks, everybody, but it turns out there's some actual deduction required here, working backwards from "unusual trends." Too many people are sleepless for it to be coincidental, check, but that leads right back to "means of delivery," which is not kids dumping No-Doz in the water supply, you'd need a truckload. Something stronger? Carlson's patients are showing nothing in their blood. Something brand new, as yet undetectable? Lots of know-how required there, which begs the next question: what kind of strategic significance does Carratuck Island have for anybody who might possibly have means and motive? Why not your lone wolf, an active shooter or a Unabomber type, essentially, but with some new weapon? More likely a group of some kind, organized and more capable, with some shared, insane agenda.

News stories come back to him: subsonics in the Cuban Embassy, diplomatic staff practically driven mad. Sarin gas in the Tokyo subway.

He grabs his cell, thumbs through his recent outgoings, clicks the one again and listens to the DWP's emergency voice menu, sighing and pressing keys until he hears the beep and leaves his second message requesting a call back.

The day has drained him—an overdose of too much inexplicable ugliness to dwell on, especially flat-out burnt from no sleep as he is.

Some off odor from somewhere reaches him, an earthy funk, sharper than low tide and drying mud and rotting clams. What is it? The septic tank out in the yard? How many years has it got?

The beach is one lane over, the surf muffled, but still the low breadth of the sound like some vast breathing thing never does go away. What would it be like if it did? Everyone curious and then awed, wandering from their beds out into the night to see the moon shining on miles of kelp-strewn mud and gleaming rock, fish flopping stiffly, eyes rolling. Time to run, of course, before it all comes rushing back in a towering, filthy wave of death and debris, but run where?

His cell buzzes beside his little laptop, pulling him back, and he grabs it and clicks through to hear his Linda's bright, untroubled voice, bell-like: "Hi, Dad!"

The world fades, so suddenly, so completely, as if nothing else exists but his daughter's words in his ear, in a pretty spot-on imitation of the Wicked Witch of the West: "I'm *melllll*-ting!"

"What's wrong with your AC?"

"August, Manhattan, Dad. Need I say more? It's wheezing and dripping. It's trying. Me too. All of the above."

He thinks to invite her out, but the thought turns on itself, darkening, as too much comes back to him. Way too much to be sorted out before she sets foot back here.

"Do you need another unit?" This one wasn't cheap: a portable, wheeled job with a ribbed, plastic flex hose and a window kit.

"Nahh. I just needed to complain. To whom better? Whom better to?"

"I answer to either. Either." The second choice with a long "i." "Potato, tomato," he adds, riffing.

They laugh. He loves being laughed at by her. It's their joke, that he's hopelessly popular-culture ignorant and cheerfully unfashionable. He invents malapropisms and plans their use, carefully straight-faced: "Pokeyman," "iSongs," "Netfix."

"Tell Mom I'll be out first weekend in September, after the hordes clear out."

He thinks fast, unwilling to let her go. "Didja see that kid sing on *The Choice*?"

"Gotta go, Chief. Be cool."

"You okay? It's late, you staying up too late?"

"Yes." To which? "Later, Dad."

"Peas." He listens another beat. "Hello?" She's already gone, of course. He hangs up, staring off in daze of fondness.

Some off odor out of nowhere suddenly hits him. The septic tank out back? How long has it got?

"Jan?" His voice rings off the hardwood floors and windowpane.

He stands, head cocked and listening, padding slowly in his boxers to the doorway.

Jan's on the sofa in her plaid robe and white sweat socks, glass of pale Chard on the coffee table, bent over her own laptop, another item that needs an upgrade.

"Didn't you hear me? Jan?"

Her eyes seem to focus again, and her face seems thinner, drawn, annoyed, as her gaze finds his.

"What?"

"What are you *doing*? Aren't you coming in?"

Her words seem rushed, the question oddly urgent: "Did you know you can arrange your favorite places in folders? And put those inside other folders?"

"Jan?" he asks her.

But she has already returned her gaze to the bright screen in her lap. "Hmmm?"

10

Tonight Cort has snuck out to join Tay in the doorway of a rickety boat shed and share another skinny from his stash. They've both turned their cell alerts down, though agreed to remind each other to stay in the game—romantic as it isn't to have to tweet every fifteen minutes. Part of her secretly hoped he would suggest they quit, anyway, but half his surf posse has already joined, and now he's into it typical guy-style, to "school those morons."

Shadowy light reaches them faintly, from a far house's perimeter lights, and she stares at his shy sideways smile and sleepy eyes as he fills his lungs and turns to her, smoke curling, index fingertip to thumb-tip, offering.

"Oh no," Cort mock-demurs, "I couldn't possibly." She takes a half-hit, already seeing the darkness pixelated with color, and continues her story: "So Mom was staring at the TV like she never saw one before. So weird. So I climbed out my window, Rapunzel but without all the hair. Ground floor, too. So . . . nothing like Rapunzel. Like I was saying."

They laugh. They are always laughing, it seems, and through her half-lowered lids she is always dazed by the whiteness of his teeth.

"What will you say if she finds out you're gone?"

"Couldn't sleep, walk on the beach, don't want to answer a lot of questions about it, like these."

"Yeah, that makes . . . no sense."

"I know, right? It's perfect."

When did he lean in and kiss her? She can't remember now, because her eyes are closed and she has devoted herself so completely to the warm give of his lips, the sweet pressure, the wanting that is beyond and bigger than her and pushes her against him, gently at first, and then pulling, a hand behind him, until they are gripping at each other, almost as if struggling, which they are, aren't they? Against everything cruel and loveless and stupid—those voices disappearing, the polished cinder block hallways of bullies and boredom; the cookie-cutter, split-level half-million-dollar prisons ruled by parents heartbroken and stunned at their own sudden age, so bitterly jealous of theirs, enough to punish and deny and demean out of spite.

This is payback, sweet for every diss, all the stony turned-away faces and the muffled giggles behind her in homeroom and science from Madison and her crew of spoiled princesses, unable to settle on the verdict: geek or slut, virgin or whore, all we can ever be because of boys.

All of it, so over. She is *seen* now, held in hard tight arms with his leanness against the length of her, by half-shut eyes even in this dark, seen as somebody maybe even beautiful, as smart and funny enough to make him laugh, finally and forever *seen*.

There's no nagging voice on her cell phone, or in her ears, but suddenly in her memory and imagination one grows louder, unwanted, fading, then back again, asking not *what girl is she*, but *what boy is he?* One who will brag to his friends about what base he got to, how soon, how sweet it was that the dumb cunt let him feel her up and put her hand on his dick, over his jams, but still? Or the one who will shake his head at what a prude she turned out to be, because even now she is pulling back her head to part her lips from his, gasping, afraid, "Ohhh . . . hey . . ."

"What? What's wrong now?" He's annoyed, the edge of a whine in his voice.

She pulls back. "Is this it? Why I'm here? All you want?"

"Why are you here, if that's what you think?"

When did he become this guy? The same one all over again, hurt because she doesn't trust him enough to give a blowjob on their second date?

She backs away, angry now. "Wait, that's not fair. It's normal to wonder."

"And it's normal to want each other."

"But is that all it's about?" It's a war inside, suspicion spreading like a virus versus what she really knows, or would if she had an hour of sleep. She almost knows better.

"You're paranoid! How does that make any sense? So kissing you . . . doesn't mean anything?"

She shakes her head, as if trying to clear it. "Why are you being like this?

"Why are *you*?"

Oh, how could this *not* be? What does she even know about him, really? Is a smile a reason to trust? The way he looks in a wet suit or on a wave, flinging back his wet hair with a toss of his head?

For a brief moment they stand there, close enough to touch again, but too far away, really, to ever reach each other. It's easier, somehow, to give in to this pain than to suck it up and apologize, to admit she was wrong or over-reacted, or is just being weird. This ache is small enough, manageable; later she will have given too much to shake it off, so now is best, this night, this ending.

His eyes dart downward, and she follows his look to see his cell in his hand, screen brightening and fading, a bluish shining, that stupid game again. A sound comes from her throat, almost a laugh, but more like the start of crying. Was he always holding it, always half-someplace else, on with his goofy crew, only pretending to be with her?

He actually holds up a finger. "One sec, lemme just . . ."

She tries, breathlessly, through the shadows and the heavy loose sand and up the beach steps to her lane, but she can't outrun his voice, traveling through the dark at the speed of sound: "Cort!"

11

"It's one of those things. People get an idea. It goes around, and psychoso-matic symptoms spread." He clings to the best examples he has, a mantra: "Nausea, panic, cases of hysteria."

With the Boy finally tucked in below, it's later than usual, but he and Kathy try to recreate their ritual, last nightcap out in the cockpit, in the soft air of the late summer night. Usually they sprawl on banquette cushions, her head on his shoulder, sipping wine and trading hits on a fatty, gazing idly up at the shrouded moon, but tonight they face each other across the sole, leaning forward with elbows on knees as they confer. She's watchful, face impassive, all common-sense Yankee skepticism. Her folks must have been hard cases, Libertarians in no-nonsense L.L. Bean gear, autodidact agnostics.

A drunken shout echoes across the float from the pier gate where a few tourists wander by, well past closing time, back to their share house, razzing each other: "Moron!" "Up yours!" "Oooh-*woo*."

Kathy lifts a bemused eyebrow at Sam, at the revelers out so late, as if to prove his point.

He offers the clearest example: "Sometimes it's as simple as a rumor in a school lunchroom—one kid hears somebody got sick, others imagine they are, too. And imagining can make it so."

"So we're just crazy, or some of us more than others, anyway."

"Not at all. Simple example: laughter. Simpler? Yawning. Involuntary reflex spread in a group."

Kathy looks thoughtful, and then, of course, helplessly yawns, finishing with a soft little laugh as Sam follows suit.

As if on cue, a cascade of faint, loopy laughter sounds from a few boats down. Kathy and Sam trade another glance.

"So . . . there have been other cases?"

He pauses. "People get afraid and lose sleep. *War of the Worlds*, the Orson Welles radio show? Anthrax scares. Escaped convicts. The panic in Puerto Rico, *chupacabra*."

She squints, bemused. "'Chupa—' who? But what's everyone afraid of here?"

"Actually? Not sleeping, best I can tell."

Kathy gives her head a tiny shake. It's a ribbon of thought, twisted once, ends met.

He sighs. "It's also all I've got, and without more, nobody official's in a hurry to come check it out."

"So, okay, say you're right. What happens?"

"Well, good news there. Sleeplessness for no physical reason? Always goes away. Always." He keeps on, clinching it with a show of kindly understanding, his voice warm: "But you always can get on the next ferry, Kath, if you decide that's what you want. I don't think anyone needs to, but anyone can. Probably not me so much, you understand."

She nods slowly, weighing the irony: it's easier to stay when you don't really need a way out. Even easier if you have one.

Her gaze shifts down the companionway steps to the Boy awake in the dinette bunk, eyes gleaming in the dimness. She drops her voice: "Sam, he's up too. You should try and talk to him again. He seems . . . traumatized?"

Two possibilities present themselves: one where he patiently explains the dangers of beginning a difficult, lengthy treatment he can't finish, and the other, which he chooses for simplicity's sake, and because it's just as true: "He knows he's safe with us tonight, Kath. Child Services'll be here tomorrow. They know what they're doing."

"Come on, Sam," she presses. "I'll just go on in to bed, you can try. You were a psychiatrist, you could at least—"

He gives her a smile, stubborn but not unkind. "I'm just . . . really not anymore, Kath. And it's just until tomorrow."

She watches him silently, appraisingly, waiting.

She's put a good-natured face on another night with their guest, and it's shifted the ground.

He nods, finally, and stands.

———

In the dimness, the Boy's eyes flash toward Sam as he nears, and then away.

"Hey, Captain. Mind if we talk? Or if I do?"

Nothing. Sam hesitates, and then sits near the Boy in his dinette bunk.

"Wish I knew what to call you. I guess Captain'll have to do. You like boats?"

It's still a cloying, patronizing approach, but too much, too soon can bring too many unimaginable consequences, with too many regrets sure to follow. Of course, too little, too late brings its own attendant sorrows.

"How's the bunk? It's funny to sleep on the kitchen table, isn't it? But I like the way it folds down."

The air around the Boy seems charged. His eyes remain downcast, his pale lips pressed together, a stubborn line.

Sam takes in a breath and seems to hold it as he asks, "We'd sure love to know who your mom or dad are. They'd want to know you're okay."

The Boy begins trembling, eyes everywhere, breaths quickening until he's nearly gasping.

Sam backs off quickly, raising his palms. "Okay. Okay, Captain. You know the most important thing of all? You're safe. Everything is fine here. It's just us . . . and the little sounds we talked about. You can hear them if you listen. You hear them?"

The Boy seems to calm, little by little, slowly.

Sam murmurs, "Hear them, the boat, the water?"

Suddenly, inexplicably, the Boy's eyes find Sam's with the cold certainty, once again, of an accusation.

Sam pales and stands; it's a look he recognizes from eyes he remembers, of the desperate, the failed and forsaken.

He backs away, speechless, and with a half-turn ducks into his cabin, where Kathy's already in bed, *Destination: Tuscany* cued up on her eReader.

She looks up inquisitively.

"Your turn."

———

Through the main cabin, Kathy moves quietly and quickly to the Boy. No hesitation, she simply puts her arms around him and brings him up against her. He doesn't resist or respond, but she doesn't falter, just gently clinging, accepting his stillness and silence.

"It's okay. You just sleep. You're okay. Shhh . . ."

Somehow, she has guessed correctly; he needs gentle decisiveness, freedom from the confusion of choices.

He blinks slowly, as if absorbing her reassurance, and his eyes begin to close. They open again, briefly, but weariness seems to overtake him and trust to allow him, finally, to yield.

She listens to his breaths slow and deepen, and feels his little muscles relax as his body sags, and she carefully lays him back down, tenderly brushing hair back from his forehead. She watches him another moment, relief glistening in her eyes at his, now closed.

She stands quietly, steps to their cabin doorway, looks back, and then slips inside, leaving the door ajar.

From their bunk, Sam looks up inquisitively. He has simply been wait-ing, it seems.

"He's fine now. I guess we're all gonna be," she offers.

He exhales. "Good. Thanks."

"Sure."

Both go still with uncertainty.

Finally, she switches off the light. They turn away and close their eyes, lying in the dark, listening to the night's customary sounds: the faint ringing of a halyard against a mast, the gurgle of an eddy against the hull, soft groan of a plank ripening with moisture. When will they stop—these ceaseless motions of air and water, of everything keeping them from their own stillness?

Slowly, she opens her eyes again.

Beside her, Sam opens his.

———

Out in the main cabin, the Boy lies in the dinette bunk, clutching his little game, the dim light of it flickering in his face like a small warming fire in the dark.

#day_six

1

Fidgeting on the sofa in Sam's campus office, Gabriel Thomas craved a smoke. His hands found each other, one bending the fingers of the other back, flexing, rubbing, making a quick fist, together a steeple. His hands had a repertoire.

"I'm dreaming, but I'm awake," he said, Aussie-style: "awake" like "awike." He laughed a little, almost bitterly, grimly.

Sam tried not to lean forward. "What are you dreaming about?"

"Oh, shrink porn, man. Water and fire. Mirrors and hands." He laughed again. "Doesn't matter. It's that I'm awake, see. My best mate Jimmy knew—he's in a Sydney jail now, another Abbie statistic. But he knew—the dreamtime was coming through a hole in the world . . . what Jimmy said . . . before he went crazy 'cause no one would listen—"

"Do you feel like no one listens to you?"

So Gabriel had haunted Sam—in small ways at first, with notes, phone messages, off-hour office visits, a glimpse of a face in a window on the quad, or turning to look as Sam's car pulled out of the faculty lot. Upturned in the rain of a late winter night, under a streetlamp, spectral.

"You know my office hours, and you have your appointments," Sam reminded him.

Laughter, always somehow knowing.

———

Light is an enemy now; colors possess a paler aspect, bleached by it, promising nothing but hours upon hours of the ache in our tender eyes.

Sounds, too, signify nothing but more of the same as the day begins: faint radio, footstep, clang of block on mast, over and over again in a dull predictable pattern of no significance.

He turns. Kathy's gone, out in the main cabin with the Boy, of course. Alone in this close little stateroom with its sagging painted plywood ceiling, its mahogany walls and sole in need of varnish, there's nothing to look at.

Already the day feels wronged by glare and stiffness in his quads and ankles as he climbs silently from his bunk; this ache of too many hours of unending stimuli become the omnipresent pain of consciousness without respite. The air around him has achieved a different, stubborn density, and every movement demands enervating will and effort.

What now, after another night awake, when the one before was to be his last awake, everyone's last night awake? Cast off, make for the mainland and some far, safe harbor? But how many others are staring up from their share house and motel room beds, facing the day and the fear that it may never end, after he promised them all otherwise?

He kneads the back of his neck with one hand as he stands in his boxers, running the tap in the stateroom head's sink, gray brightness through the porthole making the side of his face throb. In the smudged mirror, the skin beneath his eyes doesn't bear study—indigo, with faintly yellow, jaundiced margins; like a tweaker on a binge, sweat dried in his hair, uneven stubble, stinking white paste in the corners of his lips. A whiff of his own fetid breath has him grabbing his toothbrush and scrabbling through the drawer for the toothpaste, but the sound of his cell reaches him—*BLIIIING*—on the hall utility shelf just outside the head. He steps out to snap it up.

"Yeah?" Did he say it, or only think he did?

Inexplicably, he hears a wave of static, indistinctness made audible. It isn't possible—digital signals are either dropped or not. But a sound emerges from the white noise, growing louder and louder now, the last voice he wants to hear, wheedling and smug. It's the same outback Aussie accent, garbled and underwater, but sharp with treble, the end of an interrogatory: "—sleep?" Pronounced "slape."

Sam's eyes flick sideways at the cell at his ear, his hands trembling, gripping the cold edge of the sink, heart pounding a rush of blood to his ears.

Slowly, his lungs fill again, a tremulous breath, another. He pulls the now-silent cell from his ear to check the recents. There's no one, no call, no connection to anyone or anything but the state of his own nerves fraying from the sounds and sights that won't stop entering his brain for even one blessed, beautiful second of silent darkness.

Memory flashes him dreadful glimpses: a sight line through a dim doorway into more and more of an empty room, to the darkly spattered sneakers and cargo pants of someone small and thin lying against a wall, their hand on the bare floor, palm up, fingers curled on nothing.

It's him, still him, always *him*.

Movement turns Sam to see Kathy and the Boy standing there now, staring. The Boy trembles wide-eyed, lifting a hand to point terrified behind Sam at water rushing over the edge of the sink, pouring out into a puddle inching across the floor.

BLII-INGGG!—the cell in Sam's hand rings, and he flinches as he spins to slam off the tap. He hesitates—*BLIIINGG! BLINNG!*—dread like ice touching his heart, and then he lifts the cell to his ear.

"Sam?" Paula's voice crackles out at him. "It's *spreading.* People are just not sleeping."

2

Sam's bike stops with a little *wfff,* wobbling there as his foot floats to touch down and balance himself while he stares at the line of patients snaking out his clinic door.

How is it possible? These faces are too many, maybe twenty now, blurred ovals swiveling toward him, some dimly recalled from prior visits. These are the Sleepless, but all actually look as if they have just awakened—shirts buttoned wrong, makeup smeared, hair sweaty, faces haggard. The colorful cheer of vacation-wear appears a ghastly joke; the bright Hawaiian shirts and fanny packs, short shorts and clingy tube-tops highlight the pallor beneath sunburns, the smudged darkness under eyes, the bloodless lips of the exhausted. Some sit in the attached plastic chairs along one wall, with pencils hovering uncertainly over admittance forms; others stand leaning or bent, as if beneath the burden of their own weight.

Inside, med tech Andrew sits at the admittance counter, eyes wide and downcast as he checks patient forms. "These are wrong. These." He shakes his head, angry. "These, too." Sam steps behind the counter and glances over the paperwork, seeing illegible scrawls, cross-outs, shredded spots from erasures.

Paula approaches from the back hall now and joins him, an eyebrow raised at the crowd.

"Doctor Carlson, that's you? Can we get a sleeping pill?" One tourist has raised his hand, like a grade-schooler for a hall pass.

"Or just find out what's wrong, at least?" another chimes in, and from the back someone unaccountably lets out a yelp-like laugh and goes silent.

Sam straightens to regard the crowd, winging it: "Folks? Who slept last night? Hands?"

No one. Even Paula gives Sam a tiny shake of her head. A small prickle of panic climbs his neck.

"How do we all have the same problem?" This guy has a long horse face dotted with acne, hair dried stiff with salt, a dingy collar half-up.

There's some iffy hygiene all around; a sweetish, sweaty odor prevails from so many unwashed bodies, from dirty hair and rumpled clothing worn too long.

"I got a kid cryin' nonstop!" insists a woman, her shirt on inside out, label sticking up.

"Three nights, I'm starting to see things. I mean, I hope I am." Unfortunately, this confusion comes from the most credible so far, a clean-shaven guy, early thirties, in immaculate khaki walking shorts and a white linen shirt over an unwrinkled tee.

Sam gives him a sympathetic nod, but it's unwelcome news. Hallucinations can certainly begin after three sleepless nights, and with a host of other attendant worries: paranoid ideation, hysterias, obsessive compulsions, dissociative states, generalized delusions. It's a potpourri of whatever fears, furies, and urges our dreams keep in check—since we unconsciously process all these while we sleep. All good, since no one gets hurt that way. Probably not so good otherwise.

Sam is tempted to let out a taxi whistle, but instead makes a show of cupping his hands to his mouth, megaphone-style, to shout, "Hold up! Please?"

The crowd falls silent, staring with mouths like dim slots.

"Everyone I've examined for insomnia so far? Nothing. I don't see any physical reason why you're not sleeping. Meaning, of course, that you will, sooner than later. If we make it through the day awake, we'll be out like lights tonight. The body always wins."

"Okay, same question, then. What's wrong with everyone?" Horse-face again, with an aggrieved edge.

Absent evidence, there's only deduction. "Look, it's rare, but it happens. Behavior can spread. We've all seen it. Simplest example?" He tries again: "Yawning."

A few oblige, of course, and then a few others, faces twisting, eyes shut, but fewer care. It's exactly the wrong example, probably—a prelude to sleep, not anything even remotely preventing it.

"Or say someone feels nauseous at a picnic," he continues. "Then someone else thinks they do too. So you hear about a neighbor who's not sleeping—next thing, you're worried about sleeping, too, and can't get any yourself. And so on."

Group behavior can be odd, that's the point, but the derision and disbelief that bursts from this crowd still surprises:

"No picnic last night!" This one looks like another old salt, with a pale, bald pate and a tobacco-colored face, probably a fishing charter owner.

A junior wise-guy type pipes up, eyes wide, fingers splayed on his chest, "I'm not sleeping 'cause somebody I don't know from Adam ain't?"

"Hey, I think I *do* feel nauseous." A voice from the back, prompting guffaws.

It's a chorus now, a cacophony, every weekender and local suddenly an expert:

"It's the ocean, something from the ocean. How far are the shipping lanes? Who knows what they—"

"Bird flu—"

"Electro-magnetic fields, power lines. Have you ruled that out?"

"Lyme's."

"If it's something toxic, or some kind of pathogen, we're not taking the chance. We're leaving."

Sam makes a show of shrugging. "Every test, every blood panel and urinalysis, has come back negative for toxin or pathogen. If I were you, I'd hate to cut my vacation short when all the odds are you'll be asleep, tonight. All of us."

Chief enters, as if on cue, looking stern but worse for wear. The crowd turns to him. "Officer, maybe you can tell—"

A leathery-looking woman joins in angrily: "Chief, what the fuck—"

Chief puts his palms up: "Look, folks, I'm not the doctor."

Wise-guy pipes up again, "Yeah, but you gotta know something. What about those murders yesterday?"

Chief glares, nearly sputtering, "Those—where do you get that? It was an overdose, that's all we know. And all you need to."

A Manhattanite in a punky tee isn't buying, turning his tipped brush cut back and forth. Sam recognizes him as a patient from days ago, how many he can't recall, or with what complaint. Earache, insect bite? "We need more cops," Soho insists. "People are way out of control, we should call the mainland and have them send—"

"Hold on now! You want to call, then call! They'll put you right in touch, refer you right away, give you a direct line right back . . . to *me*. And here's what I'll do: tell you what I'm telling you now—to listen to what Dr. Carlson here says, or go home—"

Alarums sound in thick Long Island accents, calling for retreat: "Works for me. Fuck this. We're on the next ferry out."

"We're gone."

Wise-guy again: "—sure, like I'm gonna see a dime back on my rental—"

The crowd seems to hesitate, *en masse,* calculating the slim odds for a refund on their Airbnb, or motel room, or share house.

"Seriously, what about some pills? The market's sold out of the over-the-counter stuff." This from an ad agency art department intern, probably, his hip, boxy glasses smudged.

Sam shakes his head. "Look, I need to examine you, one at a time, before anyone gets a pill. Sorry, that's the rules. I'll need admittance forms completed by each of you, and then Andrew will bring you back."

Sam points to Andrew, who glances up at the crowd, a bit hollow-eyed too, daunted.

Paula shoots Sam her questioning glance, and he whispers to her sideways. "Buy us some time. Meanwhile, somebody'll nod off. Then a few more."

Outside, across the lane for an impromptu conference, Chief seems worn himself, one ear reddened as if he's been slapped, stray hairs of one eyebrow askew, quivering, his breath sour. He listens to Sam's theory with narrow eyes, lips pursed with distaste, before he finally interrupts, drily, "Good, great, sure, follow up on all that. Meanwhile, no harm in DWP testing the mains, see if some kids or somebody's dumping anything into the water. And power lines for EMF."

Sam glances back at the clinic, at the gathering crowd, their manic laughter, their rumpled clothes and private, spiraling little dramas. Misdiagnosis won't help any of them. "No sign of toxins, like I said. And last I looked there weren't more than a few houses anywhere near the high voltage lines. Not that the science is there anyway."

"Less than your grad school seminar theory?"

"It's what we have. And it's good news. It means people will go back to sleep."

Chief gives him an arid look: "Sure, great to hear. And until then, we . . . what? I keep the peace, and you—?"

Will he ever back off? "Treat the symptoms."

#

Spinning, the circular blade bites into the wood. The shrill, grinding noise of the hot metal sawteeth ripping feels like a blade in the brain, especially after an all-nighter; so subcontractor Dallas Penske has stuffed bits of torn Kleenex in his ears, club-style, as he gets the jump on framing out this cutom job, now just foundation and studs amid the last dunes on Tern Lane.

Stu and Mike, fuck 'em, called in too sick after days of whining about being tired, for shit sake, more likely hungover, but no shut-eye. Join the club. Twitchy like from a sugar high, last night he logged in around four and ended up trolling for some names from high school. But no way Carla Habst could be this hot, still. How old is anyone's Facebook picture, anyway?

He chalks another two-by, sets it on the sawhorse, and cranks up the saw. He starts the cut and a flash across the beach makes him glance up to see splinters of light dancing from the chop out past the surf, and there's sudden warmth on his face, wetness, really, and his hand is jerking because it's burning but when he looks it's blood flying hot into his face from a flap of skin at the end of a finger, and the saw skittering off and out of sight, all of which is already going dim, with the sounds of the day fading as they get further and further away too.

———

Thrash metal, they call it, and what's amazing is the sound of violence it imitates, like the metal of a crashed car shredding and twisting—the screeching that comes from the electric guitar microphone parts, or pickups is what they are, when they put them right up to an amplifier and the amplified sound gets amplified and around and round in a vicious loop. You see it at rock concerts, like Lynyrd Skynyrd however many years ago, but that's at a rock concert, okay? Not all night long louder than this fucking rain, from the slum next door to the restored Cape Cod summer house you saved your whole working life for, where these weekender stoner kids figure they paid the freight and can do whatever the fuck they like, play their e or i or whatever Tunes as loud as they want.

You'd think asking politely to turn it the fuck down would help, but no.

You'd think offering up the logic of why it would be smart would convince, but hey.

Maybe a little item would help, if casually displayed during their next chat? Like the one from out in the storage shed, under the bungee'd tarp in the padlocked cabinet, wrapped in rags soaked in Cosmoline, beside the box of 12-gauge Fiocchi shells?

———

Drew Bennis bends, fitting his pipe wrench on the cylinder housing's hex bolt. Tighten, tighten the wrench. Good. He wipes sweat from his eyes, already blurry enough, and straightens up to give his back a rest—of course, just enough to ding his head on the low engine room roof. "Fuck." Whoever designed this ferry had midget mechanics in mind, typical of the egghead types with their T squares and mechanical pencils and compasses who never changed a gasket like this one, leaking diesel like a sieve. He's downloaded and double-checked the schematics twice, not that he had to, but if this gasket keeps dripping the whole engine will overwork, overheat, seize up, and that's all she wrote.

He bends again. Just twist that wrench counter-clock, twist. She'll give.

White Danskin top is what Agnes what's-her-name wore in mechanical drawing class, sitting at the desk just in front of his. Catholic, dark blonde hair, peppermint shampoo smell, Danskin top thin and tight enough to see her whole bra through it, the back strap bumpy where the eyelet clasp things met. The top creasing diagonal across her front when she turned for her books, so you could see the shape perfect, her little gold cross swaying, her sharp eyes glancing up and holding his.

Whoa, fucking hex bolt. Wrench lost its grip, bolt corners gone smooth. Stripped, damn.

Well, no biggie. Gasket a little leaky. No biggie.

3

Cort's bare feet scuff through heavy sand, sun heating her shoulders, brightness throwing rainbows at the edges of her eyes as she walks aimlessly along the surf leaping and spilling, windblown and breaking to the sky's edge.

She thumbs her cell blindly as she walks, glancing down torn again at the text Tay has left this morning, after the dozen or so that came in last night:

still sorry—need to sleeeep. don't b mad. And my parents are wack - weird 2. Meet me? pls

What now? Forget him, or run back to him and risk everything, because what does anyone ever have if they don't? Does love ever live otherwise?

Heat has already driven everybody indoors or into the water. Old guys with white chest hair stand up to their droopy waists inside the break, swaying against the push and pull of the spilled waves, staring at the edge of the sky like they've always been there, waiting. Like maybe somebody's ship will come in.

The sky looks white, bleached, almost. The world between each blink seems like a short, random video clip. A woman sits alone, twirling a curl of her hair around a finger, over and over; a sunburned guy walks in circles, talking to himself; a little kid bawls while two others smash his complicated sandcastle back into sand.

Just past Claude's Clam Shack, where the lane narrows and turns inland, a burst of reggae blares and stops, a peal of laughter rings out from a share house. On the patio, trashed-looking in a saggy bikini, a girl lights a cigarette and closes one eye against the curling smoke while she whoops wearily and flounces back inside as the reggae blares again. A party starting, or ending?

Cort trudges on, down a boardwalk ramp along a patch of sunken forest—thorny bramble of twisted, peeling branches buzzing with deer-flies—through the green dapple and hot, still air out onto shadowless redwood planking.

Her timer chimes and she pulls out her cell again, thumbs flying blind again to type:

still here u f'kers – 44 3/4

She sends, because at least it's some connection to something in this boring place with no one now but too many dopey families with babies and dogs and staring geek boys in slipping jams with their bony sunburned chests and chicken arms.

She slows to scroll back and check, and sees she missed a tweet war between two from back in Bayshore, Jane Felsh and Sarah Rubaker, now accused of cheating because she missed the fifteen-minute mark.

JanesterJane flames:

UR OWT!!!

Cort can imagine SaRuba90 rolling her eyes, her face stony, as she typed:

I absolutely did tweet in time and if your time on your page is wrong, it isn't my fault.

Cort snorts laughter; has Sarah become British?
Jane definitely hasn't:

UP URS LIER

Someone she doesn't know and didn't notice before, KatieMatson87300, chimes in, whiny:

too juve, sorry. I didn't lose, but Im quitting. Anyone else have a life?

Cort almost smiles. Her thumbs fly again:

less & less

She looks up as the boardwalk tops a rise over a low dune, emerges from behind a bank of sea grape and tufts of seagrass into the day of ordinary bickering, laughing tourists carrying coolers and umbrellas to the beach, seagulls yawping and diving at trash, rap blasting, a dog barking at a family, boys younger and dully gawking, the flying shadow of a kite.

She could cry; her eyes want to from not closing for two nights, unless they did and she can't remember, which would be even weirder. She could cry, though, mostly from the total confusion over Tay, the what-ifs of it, the chance of truth being lies or vice versa.

She stops and feels a surge of something rising in her throat and realizes it's only laughter. Manic, is what, she's in some absurdly emo bipolar phase of all-nighter mania.

Just ahead, a big lady in pouchy shorts and some sort of peasant blouse has on giant ugly sunglasses that seem to swivel Cort's way as she lifts a photograph. It's always something, right? As if Cort has a dollar to spend on a homeless project, or her signature on a petition means anything, and she tries to slide past but the face in the photograph slows her down, because it's the little kid, *him*, with his big dark eyes but no smile now, just a stunned blank look—the little kid she's supposed to be babysitting.

4

"Hey, no, spread out, okay, folks?" Chief shouts above the surf, and points across the kelp-strewn width of beach that today's volunteers seem so reluctant to patrol.

Drugs, TV, alcohol, video games, porn—Chief can only hope one or all are why this group moves in a slow, dazed bunch along the tide line up ahead. Unfortunately, worse and more likely, everyone's a little spacey since this insomnia deal hit. But is it rocket science to fan out and cover a little more search pattern for an MP?

Sam Carlson's group behavior theory is no help, and typical of an MD who was a shrink: it sounds neat, but where does it leave you? Shrinks always find the perfect, clever little realizations—it's really your mother you're angry with, or your father—or don't you see how you're just recreating the same problem here that you never solved over there?

His earbud chimes and he clicks through. After his emails and voice messages, it's County finally getting back, a lieutenant he knows on the line now: "Chief, hey. It's Marvin."

Chief scrimps on the pleasantries, maybe a bad idea, but it's a way to convey some urgency. "Marvin, any luck on the personnel—"

"—working on it."

Stay loose, stay easy. "Look, I don't call you guys lightly. I need a search team for the parents. And Child Services for the kid. Sooner than tomorrow's ferry."

Typical of County's attitude toward Carratuck, the leftie chuckles. "Hey, Gilligan, come on, dial it back. Folks get robbed and killed over here, we're kind of busy. Not to mention shorthanded from budget cuts."

Chief rubs his eyes, debating. Will the truth bring help any more slowly? "Hey, Marv, listen? People are . . . strange, not sleeping. Flaky, edgy, like. Out of control. You know I wouldn't be saying anything if I didn't think it was something serious . . ."

A pause gives him hope. Maybe he's rung a bell? Maybe people on the mainland are experiencing the same weirdness and there's an easy explanation: sunspots, or some new airborne pathogen.

But laughter bursts through his earbud, loud enough to wince at. "Not sleeping, out of control? Sounds like Pines Beach. Man, I was there for my buddy's batch party, 24/7 the whole weekend. I needed a nap, too."

The prick. See if he gets comped a room for his anniversary ever again. "Hey, look—"

"Tomorrow's ferry, Chief. Best we can do."

Chief shakes his head, frustrated. These mainland prima donnas have all the slack in the world—full backup, EMTs, IA, IT geeks and gophers, MP specialists and their assistants out looking for lost cats, *pro bono* psychics and profiling shrinks, for god's sake, and it takes them a day to spare anybody?

"Tomorrow? Seriously? You guys can't—" His earbud chimes and he sighs, frustrated. "Hang on, this could be—" He flashes the line.

"Chief, it's Brian Hennessy, DWP. We got nothing out of range here."

"Nothing?"

"Sorry. We ran it hard—trace elements, parts per million, full stats."

"EMF?"

"Ran a gaussmeter by the high voltage lines. All in range, no surge."

It was always one for the tinfoil hat crowd, anyway. "Brad, thanks for getting on this."

"Brian."

"Hey, right." But Brian is already gone.

Chief's earbud chimes again, but when he clicks though a new voice startles him, a woman's: "Chief Mays? You said to call if anybody recognizes the Boy in the picture?"

5

Sam sits on a metal folding chair in Room Three, willing himself to keep still and not look too directly at the thirteen-year-old who sits now on the wax paper-covered exam table, picking at his bleeding cuticles, a foot twitching.

The eyes of patients, today, are wrong somehow, darting and hooded as if harboring a secret, but dull with dryness, reflecting less.

This one isn't much more than a boy, with a studded eyebrow and a swirl of tattoo on his arm. Manhattan, private school, son of an internet marketing guru or media conglomerate exec, Sam guesses. The kid gives a raspy, weary little laugh. "I keep thinking of some things I wanted to do, but I knew better and I don't want to. Keep thinking of them. Kid who told on me for pushing him, spike his juice box with powder from a bag on a shelf in the garage. Dog next door wouldn't shut up, yap yap. So I scotch-tape a dog whistle to an electric fan. I used to dream about doing them, not so great, but then at least when you woke up nobody got hurt or sad or disappointed in you about it, so okay. But now . . . I don't wake up because all I am is awake, really, these days. Nights. So, what if I go ahead and do something because I think I'm dreaming, but I'm not?"

Sam shifts in his chair, unhappy at still more of the same: darkly obsessive thoughts, the circling narratives, the blurry gazes. But does he feel any different?

"I can give you something to help you sleep. But . . . your parents? Maybe talk to them? Do they know how you're feeling?"

The kid's gaze lands on Sam for a long, strange moment before he simply bursts into laughter—a low, rising howl cut off by a series of ugly, derisive snorts. Sam watches silently—for what?—and then stands and slips out of the exam room, his face burning like a taunted boy's.

———

"It's the light, it doesn't stop, or the sounds. They hurt now." This patient is a middle-aged woman, sweet-faced, slender, redheaded, her voice abashed somehow, as if she's embarrassed by her plight.

"'The world is too much with us . . .'" A light touch and a prescription pad are all he has. He clicks his pen and pulls the pad onto his clipboard, but sees her curious look and explains, "Sorry. It's Wordsworth, freshman English. Not really apropos, after all."

"I should look it up. I don't really remember. But I remember less and less." She tries to smile, tries to shrug.

"You'll be okay." Won't she? He scribbles a scrip for sleeping pills, one with the least side effects and contraindications, Ambesta, and tears the page from his pad to hand to her.

———

Moments seem to repeat themselves as Sam moves quickly from room to room, a rhythm developing: a minute or two for each patient, the Q & A now automatic:

"I can write you for four Ambesta. See your doctor for more when you get home."

"Trouble falling asleep, or staying? Or both?"

"How many nights?"

"Any new sounds, odors, anything taste strange? The water?"

"Try these. Ambesta, a few nights' worth."

"Hammer thumb, in Two, Sam."

"Take one before bed. Ambesta, should do the trick until you get back on track."

"Stove burn, wrist, some third degree."

Accident cases, too, are stacking up more quickly—a radius fracture from a bike spill, a glass splinter from a dropped bottle, dizziness from Indocin overdose. Most are not so unusual, but in the current context of events, they could well be caused by the impaired judgment and diminished motor control of sleep deficit.

A few are actually repeats, back for a few more sleeping pills. It's a mixed message: the pills work, but they need more. Did the old sailor couple develop too much tolerance to their own prescription, and finally OD trying to achieve any result at all?

He hesitates in the hall, trying to add the patients. The numbers would peak, of course, before they fell, as with any communicable illness. Here, the turning point would depend on the physical need overruling the psychological, every hour more due.

From the entrance, a burst of noise and motion yanks him back. Two shirtless, lean, sweaty guys in toolbelts and shorts stagger into the waiting area with their hands joined in a two-man carry for a third, who lolls between them, arm in a tourniquet, blood leaking from a hugely bandaged hand. The others make way with dim disinterest, and even Andrew stares a beat too long before yanking out a wheelchair, helping them lower the bleeding man into it, and turning to shout toward them, "Paula?"

———

Without a hand-specialist surgeon and pricey real-time laparoscopy imaging and gear, there's no way to reattach the severed finger, no matter how clean the cut; small blood vessels need to be grafted and rejoined, nerves reconnected and conduction results verified—it's all well beyond Sam and the capabilities of Pines Beach Urgent Care.

When Sam has fully stopped the bleeding with a pressure compress and dosed the guy with enough fentanyl, he seems amiable enough about taking his fingertip to the mainland in the little med cooler Sam has packed for him, to have a specialist perform the procedure there.

"You've got a day or so to get back to shore and have surgery to reattach. The ferry tomorrow should be fine," Sam tells him. "But keep it on ice. Don't be taking it out to show your friends at the Clam Shack."

From nowhere, Paula's preternaturally calm but insistent voice reaches him. "Sam?"

Again? He turns to see her pointing out into the waiting area, where Chief stands beside a darkly tanned teenaged girl in cutoffs and cowboy shirt over a bathing suit, barely distinguishable from her friends—but for her worried, skittish look.

Carol, is it? Cora? Sam shakes his head. She's here, but the name is lost again, for the second time in the blur of this day. Or was it yesterday?

6

After so many months riding his bike to work and the beach and back, Sam's uneasy with the close glass, unyielding seats, and jerky motion of the Jeep as Chief guns them out onto harder sand.

In the back, Cort seems nervous, but at her age it takes more than a sleepless night to dim her hair and eyes or fade her tan into pastiness.

Chief tries for a wry note and misses: "Cort here told her mom she was babysitting last year, too. Favorite alibi. For all-nighters in the Jensen boat shed with Tay Garner. They oughta put a padlock on that." He steers them bouncing along West Beach, around groups of beachgoers who seem oddly sullen, quiet, blinking at them as they go by. One family's eyes follow them with a kind of desperation, the look of the marooned.

The girl leans forward from the backseat, wiping at aggrieved tears: "My mom used to not want me to be happy, but this year she just doesn't even care. It's all vodka and TV. I'm really sorry, anyway, I just met the lady in the market, and I was going to and then, you know, I guess I . . . didn't, right?" She focuses on Sam. "So how is he? Okay? Is he okay?"

Sam takes in her borderline manic affect, probably another acute insomnia symptom—plenty to go around, another that will abate when everyone finally sleeps, and not soon enough. "Well, he seems okay. Do you . . . remember him being quiet when you met? Silent?"

Cort blinks at this, as if trying to recall someone from long ago. "Opposite of, really. Talking to himself, playing. Said hi."

Unhappily, it only confirms what by now is obvious—that some trauma has precipitated this Boy's silence. No need, though, to make the point to Cort, who seems plenty thrown as it is.

Sam nods at her. "Okay. Thanks, Cort, for everything." A closer look at her makes him ask: "What about you? You look tired."

"It's my friends, there's like a contest? Who can stay awake the longest."

Sam trades a fraught glance with the chief and looks back at the girl again. "How do you know if someone cheats?"

She stares out her window, shrugs. "Tweet every fifteen minutes."

"How . . . long have you been up?"

"Not so long, two days, I guess."

"Meaning . . . two nights without? It's not really good for you."

"Some friends longer. Nobody can remember who started it."

"Parents must be thrilled." They share a vague smirk, but Sam's mind is already circling: is it a possible cause, somehow, or yet another symptom? The new meaning of "viral" is possibly more than apt, but would it change anything to know for sure?

Chief steers them over a dune to a fire access way beside a lane of peeling mid-century bungalows. He pulls them over and stops outside a shabby little studio rental, an ugly cinderblock box with aluminum sash windows and a fenced patio under a water-stained green umbrella.

Chief turns in his seat to regard the girl. "Cort, we're gonna have to ask you to wait out here." She nods again, wide-eyed, at once frightened and grateful to remain behind.

Chief's woeful gaze slides to Sam's and then to the rental's door.

The three climb out and Sam and the chief approach the unit slowly, almost reluctantly. Sam's mind is racing with too much, too soon: the bloated faces of the elderly OD'd couple return to him, and a new image appearing, fleeting—a woman prone in tangled sheets, a pill bottle over-turned on a rickety end table.

Finally, again, he imagines the sprawled blood-spattered legs of someone he can't see yet as he approaches another doorway, this one down a dim hall he will always walk with dread as familiar as an old grief, since it is a memory and not some imagined thing at all.

A shard of sunlight from Chief's watch stabs his eyes as Chief lifts his hand to knock and finds the front door ajar, creaking open a few inches at his touch.

They do not look at each other now, each of them steadying himself for what may lie inside the dim interior: a dead woman, most probably, and perhaps not alone. But what can prepare them, if not other deaths—crime scenes, accident sites, hospital rooms, patients, relatives at the end?

"Hello? Ma'am?" Chief calls out, barely loud enough. The door creaks again, complaining, as he pushes it gingerly open to reveal the inside of this single room efficiency.

Light leaks from the edges of a single curtained window, slanting in shafts of dust motes. Slowly, their eyes adjust to take it all in: the unmade beds, clothes strewn, toys, flies buzzing around leftovers on a kitchenette counter. A single bird feather in the middle of the floor.

Sam lets in a small sniff of air, judging the thick, dank sickly-sweet smell of the place, but as they take another step inside, they can see no one through the ajar bathroom door, or tangled prone in the dingy bedsheets, or anywhere in the dim single room. Chief moves slowly to check the far side of the bed along the floor; Sam approaches a furry cheap-looking teddy bear perched on a high bookshelf, as if watching.

The idea makes him go still, and then he reaches up and pulls the thing down. It's heavy for a stuffed animal, short stubby arms held out to hug, smelling of dust. When Sam turns it over, he sees what he suspected he would, half-hidden in the glossy nap: RCA-style outputs. Huh, a nanny cam. He flips it over again and studies the little button eyes, one of which now barely conceals the little lens beneath.

Sam brings it over to the TV, a boxy little Sylvania (nothing to put in the brochure), and leans over the back: sure enough, red, white and yellow RCA cords dangle obligingly from auxiliary inputs, just waiting to be connected to a source.

Sam glances over at Chief. "Nanny cam here, may be something."

Chief looks over, mild surprise. "Yeah? Let me see . . ."

Sam ignores him, already bending to hook up the video cord and flick on the TV. He turns the teddy bear over and over, and finally finds the strip of plastic sewn into the fur with the directional symbols.

On the little TV, snow flickers, hissing bursts from its cheap little speaker, and then, from the side of the frame, suddenly looming, the face of a woman fills the screen.

———

So many visit Carratuck for the best reasons—the gleaming sunlight, the kindness of the sea cool on their skin, the sound of their children's laughter. Some, though, come to escape to the last of the land, as Sam well knows. To face away from the past, out to the straight edge of the sky's end, the line there as sharp as the one between before and after. She was another of these refugees, strange to him as any, though it seems now more kindred after all.

It was her, he remembers now, on a shaded bench. On one of these narrow lanes between houses from to bay to beach, she was a woman crying. How many passed, rolling coolers and long-handled wagons of groceries, carrying a toddler, a beach umbrella, glancing at and away? How many spoke to her, how many ignored her? Was it a week ago now? Sam had slowed his bike and finally stopped, lowering his creaking kickstand to climb off and unhappily approach, slowed by the previous night's exertions and palliatives. What had he seen? Mid-thirties, limp salty hair, with a slack, worn face streaked with tears.

"You okay?"

She looked him over and laughed, derisive. "Me? You look like you had a long night."

He shrugs. "Carratuck, summer. The island that never sleeps."

"Just, please, go away?" she said. But before he showed his palms in defeat and turned away, her eyes seemed to take in the dark glint of his own, and his hers.

The ones we turn from haunt us most, merciless to the end.

———

On the screen now, she appears blurred and dim, with familiar bruise-colored skin beneath her eyes and her eyes preternaturally wide, blinking too rapidly as she stares into the lens, talking to herself: "It's gonna be a brand-new girl, seems nice but we gotta be careful, who doesn't? Just in case . . . right, baby?"

Her hands flash by and her wrists fill the foreground as she adjusts the teddy bear cam. The rattling profusion of bangle bracelets don't really hide the long dark scars that run the length of her forearms, inside of elbow to wrist, and Sam tenses as the Boy appears in frame now, in the background, ignoring his mother while he plays listlessly with his same little electronic game. *Doi-oing! Whoa-oh!* Cartoon noises leak from it, tinny maddening music.

She turns away and moves to him. "Can we stop for a minute, baby? Here, I found this, for you." She pulls a feather from her beach bag and bends to hand it to him. Smiling too wide, too desperately. "Will you keep it?"

He glances up, slack-jawed, bleary-eyed, to grasp the proffered gift, barely regarding it before setting it down and returning to his game.

Now his mom's cell rings, stock marimba ring tone, and she snaps it up, anxious, stepping back, forgetting the nanny cam altogether as she turns away from her son, her voice bright, eager: "Hello? What? You're . . . *not* coming? Before I go crazy, for god's sake, please. Oh, sorry, I must sound like forgot my Zoloft. Wait, I *did*! I need to go to sleep, or something, or take a swim, to wake up. But . . . it's Cortney, right? Cort, okay . . . Look, I'm desperate . . . please . . . oh, but . . . well, ill? Oh. I see. Okay . . . no worries, all good, right, okay, but . . . sorry, okay, sweetie."

She hangs up and spins slowly in place, looking around as if for escape. She begins to cry, in soft choking sobs, and her hands flutter to her hair and begin to pull at it, on either side of her head. Her face twists into a quivering grimace like a hideous smile as she steps past her boy, leaving him in the foreground as she paces.

The tinny maddening music from the Boy's game seems to grow louder, sharper, tempo increasing.

In the background now, fully visible in her sweatpants and a wrinkled tee, his mother lies down on the unmade bed, closes her eyes, and goes still there, as if in a pageant or play. Her eyes snap open again and she turns over onto her other side now, facing away from the camera. Suddenly, she leaps up, does a half-turn, muttering unintelligibly, and then lies down again with a theatrical sigh. Improbably, she leaps up yet again and rushes across the room to the efficiency kitchenette, where she digs frantically through the drawer.

She's cartoon-style frantic, tossing items behind her as soon as she finds them; they flash by—a corkscrew, a potholder, pliers, a spatula. Her boy doesn't even look up, entranced by his little electronic game again, staring down as he thumbs at it.

His mother stops, finally, and turns from the drawer, a box of Saran Wrap in her hands. She smiles down at it, as if at some novel labor-saving device, but then she kneels and yanks open a lower cabinet and starts all over again. She slides out pots and pans and cookie tins with a clatter, until it seems she has found what she needs: a roll of gray duct tape.

She stands breathless with it, collects the Saran Wrap, and crosses the room to an open closet, where she knocks aside wire hangers to kneel against the back wall.

The Boy turns his head to look at her and she smiles tearfully at him, her voice tight: "You play now, sweetie, okay? Play your game now."

He bends dutifully back to the chirping little screen in his lap.

She rips a length of duct tape from the roll, tears it off with her teeth, and now opens the box of Saran Wrap to tear off a yard or so of it against the box lid's serrated edge. No hesitation, thoughtlessly, she wraps the clear plastic around her face, blinking rapidly, and duct-tapes off the top around her hairline and the bottom edge around her neck with a quick overhead circle of her arm. She tightens it with a last twist at her throat.

She goes still, waiting.

The plastic tightens around her mouth, loosens, tightens, her eyes no longer blinking but wide and terrified, darting as if desperate for something to look at last.

A hand flutters now, restless, rising, hesitating, rising again, struggling against itself as its fingers begin to twitch. It jerks downward against her side, her arm locking hard at the elbow and beginning to tremble, as the other lifts and falls back again.

The Boy glances back at her, a quick, furtive glimpse, and then he focuses downward again on his game, the feather unnoticed there beside him as he thumbs the little buttons, faster and faster with new desperation.

Behind him, she goes still suddenly. Dead, holding her breath?

Her hand flashes upward to rip at the plastic, once, twice, until her fingers grasp a twist and it tears in a ragged patch from her face as she gasps in air, her chest heaving, tears streaming.

Suddenly annoyed, she rushes out of the closet and past her boy into close-up again, hissing angrily, "Well, whoops, nobody needs to see this, anyway." Her hands flash into and past the foreground, the camera tilts and—*pffft*—goes dark, and then bright with snow and white noise.

Sam and Chief look at each other now, neither breathing, a new dread taking hold. They turn to look at the closet door behind them, its cheap wooden slider doors shut now, revealing nothing.

Sam hesitates; he has no immediate jurisdiction over this new, imminent horror. It's Chief's move to make. Chief sighs and moves slowly to the closet, pauses nearly imperceptibly, and then slides a door open, scraping on rusted rails.

It's empty, but for a few wire hangers swaying.

From the front doorway, Cort startles them both, wide-eyed, face blotchy with tears. How much has she seen? A wail emerges, of guilt and self-loathing, becoming words finally, as Sam and Chief stare at her: "I should have been here like I said I would . . . I should have!"

Sam puts placating palms up. "Hey, there's no way you could've known—don't—"

She shakes her head at him like he's just too dumb to get it, and then she simply turns and runs—past the Jeep and into the dunes bordering the beach.

Sam shouts after her, "Cort!"

She just keeps on, lost to them beyond the dunes and a row of houses. The day suddenly seems endless, all the days.

Chief shakes his head. "Looks like we're gonna need more volunteers." He turns to Sam.

"What about this game they're playing? Not so different than your theory, or could be a part of it?"

What if it is? Every thought dead-ends. "And do what?" Sam asks. "Confiscate everyone's cell phones? Even if you could, there's more than that happening here."

Chief's look is deadpan, cold. Is Sam up to the task here? Any task?

Enough at least for Sam to return Chief's look, and to remind him: "Child Services?"

"Shorthanded, they promise somebody tomorrow." Chief shrugs, his gaze sliding away.

Another night now looms, of the Boy in his makeshift bunk, just staring off, lost in his strange, animal stillness.

Sam's phone buzzes in his pocket. He yanks it up and swipes it, an aggrieved voice crackling out at his ear: "It's Howard. We're getting low on Ambesta."

Not good. "Substitute Lotosil, or Sonosol. No problem. Just no more than three per from here on. Okay?"

Howard's silence is contrary enough, unmistakably petulant.

"Hello?" Sam presses.

"Sure, okay." *Click.*

Sam avoids Chief's inquisitive look and turns back to the Jeep. A deeper weariness begins, with a steady downward pull.

7

"It's a scorcher today. But that sky will knock your eye out, not a cloud!" Kathy opens and shuts the little fridge, gathering jars and bread, filling the hours with chirpy chatter and snacks, fighting the heavy slowness that threatens to engulf her the second she stops.

In the dimness of the galley, she imagines the Boy sitting silently at their dinette table is much like any boy, waiting for his mom to cut the crusts from a sandwich while he grasps his glass with both hands, sipping, watching, barely listening to her.

She fusses at the counter, pulling a knife from the chock, lining up the square sandwiches. "Food of the gods, breakfast of champions, PBJ. I used to think peanut butter and jelly sandwiches grew in rows, like potatoes."

Her back turned, she doesn't notice him silently, thoughtlessly climb off the dinette bench and drift away, drawn up the companionway steps to pause there like someone listening for some distant sound.

"PBJ *farms*." Kathy laughs as she cuts the sandwich—but then sucks in a breath, feeling the thin sharp pain of the blade along her thumb. "Damn!"

She drops the knife and yanks up her thumb: a fine pale line oozing blood, not so bad, really. She runs cold water on it, back to chattering, "Well, they didn't call me klutz for nothing. We'll get you that sandwich in a jiffy. More milk?"

Finally she turns, expecting see him waiting there, wide-eyed, a film of milk all that's left on the side of the glass he grips with both hands, a telltale mustache of white on his upper lip.

Of course, he's crept off into the head, and she crosses the two steps to the door and raps twice, not that he's likely to reply. "Hey, you okay? Scared me!"

She goes still to listen and hears nothing, only her pulse beginning to pound harder and faster as she pushes open the door into the cramped empty little room and begins to understand that she has lost him, somehow, impossibly.

She shouts, "Hey!" the name of the nameless as she races up the creaking companionway steps and out into the day, where the placid marina greets her mockingly with the slow bobbing of yachts in their slips, the creaking of rigging, the lapping of the tide.

She leaps down onto the float, spinning left, right, scanning for human movement, but there's no one, just a crusty sailor coiling line a few boats down, one who never fails to ogle her on her way to or from the showers.

"Hey, Walt, seen a kid around here?" She keeps her voice even, so desperately even.

Walt looks at her sleepily as she turns in place. "Sure, last night, one you and Sam came back with. He yours?"

She ignores him now and keeps spinning, shielding her eyes from the glare until she sees him, finally, a thin silhouette against flashing sun on water, nearly lost in its brightness.

She runs, feet and heart pounding, past dock boxes and coils of line and hoses and yachts, the seconds and yards interminable. "Don't move! I'm right there! Don't move!"

He doesn't, just staring into the water, as if waiting for something to surface.

She grabs him, holding on, breathless, gasping, shrill. "Are you okay? You're okay. Oh, you're okay."

His eyes never leave the water, and he lets himself be held, more entranced than afraid, it seems. Until he pushes back and offers her his little electronic game, a dead black rectangle.

"What?" She laughs. "You—need batteries? Come on, we've got some somewhere."

He somberly offers his hand, and tears fill her eyes as she gently takes it and they start back to the boat.

What makes her turn back slowly to study the bright shifting surface, and then the row of boats and the float whose length she has crossed to the dock ramp and beyond, where motion makes her look again?

By the dock gate, a silver-haired man watches them impassively. He turns away, but not before hiding his hands in his shorts' pockets, and not before Kathy catches a glimpse of inexplicable oddness: gloves. Some kind of latex meant to protect against germs or toxins, yellow, tight, unmistakable.

Sterile gloves.

———

Chief and Sam cut back through town, the patrol Jeep bouncing over a berm and onto the narrow service lane behind the storefronts bordering the marina. The shut passenger window gives Sam's face back to him, a spectral reflection of a haggard man with distant eyes focused on too much elsewhere, on a boy and his mother out for an adventure before anyone else is up. On the stillness of the hour and their low voices as they step out into the damp, dim lane. The low, patient boom of the surf waiting a few lanes away, just a short boardwalk and a ramp away. Her last smile down at him.

A flash of movement brings him back, Chief slamming the brakes, swerving them almost sideways to avoid two kids running, shouting, "bright!" but no, it's "fight!"—the ageless clarion call from grammar school, for all to crowd hooting around a brawl.

Chief is out the door without a look back, leaving Sam to follow at a run between two shops out into the wider marina, where a shoving, shouting group surrounds the ticket booth, dockside before the clanging, hollow hulk of the ferry, "Sea Mist 1."

Bits of chatter reach him:

"—overheated, idling right there."

"No *way*! I've been waiting!"

"Back off, huh? I have an emergency, okay?"

"Who doesn't?"

The salesclerk looks familiar, a balding, stone-faced middle-ager whose name Sam has never learned. He quickly closes the rickety service window shutter to hang an oaktag sheet scrawled with Magic Marker:

FERRY CANCELED – ENGINE REPAIR
NEXT TOMORROW 7:45 pm

There's a burst of complaint, incredulity, and derision as he fits and locks a padlock on the shutter and then turns, hesitating, looking for a quick way through the crowd and out of sight.

Chief raises his voice over the din: "People? Come back tomorrow, the other ferry'll be here from the mainland. Everybody got it?"

Another group of families appears from around the corner, upscale vacationers from the pricey beachfront rental stretch of Pines Beach, crowding in with aggrieved faces. A few have cell phones pressed to their ears, spreading or receiving the news, voices already rising in argument, a few in outright anger.

Sam turns at more shouting. He edges past a group of teenagers, sidesteps a family bristling with coolers and umbrellas and half-zipped luggage, to see the combatants: a mom whose face is contorted and patchy with rage, dad alternately beseeching and finger-pointing with a squinty, hateful glare. Their little girl tugs at her mom's legs, stretching a single incomprehensible syllable of bewilderment into a wail.

"I paid for the whole week! We won't get a dime back if we go!" Dad's dark wet mouth gapes with incredulity.

Her eyes bulge, her voice climbs, shrill. "Stay, I don't give a fuck! We're not! I'm right here, online, first thing tomorrow!"

Chief steps forward with his palms up, but they ignore him.

The hapless clerk tries to edge through the throng, also ignored.

Dad stabs the air with a finger. "You've lost it—take a nap, okay? There's no—"

"Just listen to yourself, always the fucking expert on everything. All night, you keep moving around, moving around, you think I don't know you do it on purpose? A little cough, a scratch, a little innocent sigh. Always something, *why*?"

"Easy now," Chief begins, but now a stocky vacationer in a Hawaiian shirt and flip-flops points at an older couple in golf clothes, all rayon pastels. "But *this* guy's ticket from today is good for tomorrow? He's good to go?"

"So buy them, like I did!" Golf Clothes shoots back.

Hawaiian Shirt points at the shuttered ticket booth. "They're. Not. *Selling them*!"

Golf Wife chimes in now, mimicking, "But. Tomorrow. They *will*!"

Hawaiian Shirt's wife blinks at her, eyes swollen. "But see, right now, some have and some can't have, and how is that fair? My kids are scared and tired and need to go home."

The women step closer, as if about to exchange pleasantries. "I'm sorry for that, but . . ."

"Oh, you're sorry! It's always easy for you. You were always bitches, stuck-up, judging. But you know what?" Her little girl starts wailing, grabbing at her knees. "You were all cheap inside. I know how you got where you are."

Golf Wife gasps and lifts a hand to slap her, but Hawaiian Shirt grabs her arm. Golf Clothes shoves him away, another tries to stop him. A melee begins, ineffectual, absurd, just ugly.

Two teenage kids in dopey calf-length jams trade looks and test the hasp on the ticket booth window padlock, while two others bookend the wary clerk, who has tried and failed to edge away unnoticed. One grabs the man's shoulder even while he tries to cringe away: "Keys, man. It's not fair."

A tourist steps in, bald pate sunburned an angry red, blinking furiously. "Whoa, now, back off."

The kid takes a wild swing, face contorted, connecting a glancing blow the tourist ignores as he lunges for him, grabbing and gripping him bent in a schoolyard bully's headlock.

Chief gives a taxi whistle, wading in, pulling combatants apart. "Enough! I need you to step over this way, right now. Let's have a talk."

Sam watches them slow, stop, move away, like chastened bitter children. The crowd backs up, muttering.

A gaggle of college girls comforts one of their own, who gawks at them, her tear-stained face hectic with outrage: " . . . another *night?* No, no, fuck this."

"We wouldn't mind cutting it short, either. Nantucket can't be this bad," a patrician Connecticut-type opines, his tall, sleek wife nodding beside him.

"You know what it is? It's the fuckin' noise, seagulls all day, crickets at night." This from a sage high-schooler.

His friends guffaw, swaying, staggering as if dizzy with mirth. "Take a chill pill!"

Eyes seem to glance at Sam, away and back again.

He backs up a step. The clinic's just a few blocks away; there's no percentage in being buttonholed here. He moves sideways to fade behind a gawking family, a woman with a yapping dog, a clutch of girls giggling like drunks, to make his way quickly back.

8

In his waiting area, the dozen new tourists are more than a harbinger of worse to come, but worse here already: faces sallow and drawn, skin under the eyes bruised like shiners. They laugh and chatter in little groups, loud with manic bonhomie, like fans waiting in line for a rock concert.

One woman's face seems jaundiced, her hair matted, clothes awry. She flirts and rolls her eyes like an ingénue at two charter-boat crew who ogle her openly, nudging each other like junior high schoolers. A middle-aged man sits alone in nothing but white briefs, blinking politely at everyone. A handsome young couple cling, lost in each other's mouths as they kiss wetly and obliviously, tongues and lips busy, faces shining with saliva.

Eyes front, Sam rushes through.

"Doctor—hey—"

"Excuse me—"

"Something to help my little girl?"

A palm up to acknowledge them all, he rounds the admittance counter and steps into his tiny office, already dialing his cell.

411 has the nearest office of Centers for Disease Control in Boston, close enough. Sam quickly navigates the voice menu, gives an assistant the gist, waits a brief moment, and then shuts his eyes in gratitude when an authoritative voice comes on the line:

"Yes, hello? Doctor Carlton?"

"Carlson, yes." Sam exhales.

"Doctor Laris, Stan Laris. Okay, now you have cases of . . .?"

"Severe insomnia. Dozens, it's creating a situation here. A few days, getting worse quickly . . ."

"Insom—any underlying illness?"

"No, not so far . . ."

"You have a means of transmission? Coughing, sneezing? Any other physical symptoms . . .?"

"No, but accidents . . . impairment . . . motor control, judgment, cognitive deficit. No etiology, blood and urine panels show nothing out of range. It's hysteria. We need a team here. CDC has responded to these events before."

"So no evidence of underlying . . . but, environmental causes? Have you ruled them out?"

Sam paces. "Like I said, blood panels and urinalysis show nothing."

"Now you're out on . . ." A rustling of papers, faint clicking of a keyboard. "Carratuck Island?"

"Yes, we—"

"So we're taking about rudimentary testing, neighborhood clinic-style. EPA can be a bit more thorough, no doubt. What sorts of accidents, just to start to gauge the severity?"

"Burns, a finger cut off, bike spills—" He sighs at himself.

"Bike—"

"—a couple OD'd on Lotosil, another missing person, probable suicide . . ."

"Missing, probable. Well, now, this is a beach resort, pretty busy this time of year . . . ?"

"Of course, but it's the *number* of incidents we're seeing . . . Increasing, rapidly, with symptoms worsening. Impaired judgment, confusion, delusions, some panic beginning. Some violence."

"Violence?"

"Tempers are flaring. An assault."

"Have you had a summer without one? You have noise keeping people up? What's the weather been like?" More rapid clicking of keys. Pausing, clicking.

Is Laris already Googling him? Seeing the DUI, the settled lawsuit? Enough to dismiss him so quickly? "Look, not the problem. I'm dealing with psychogenic illness here. Anomalous, I understand that, but not the first case, and well within CDC jurisdiction."

"I'll bring it up. Meanwhile, EPA, you should try them. Hey, sorry. Can you hold? It's nonstop Zika today. We're just slammed, and never not shorthanded."

"Same here, I have patients waiting now. You have my information, can you get back?" Sam squints at the sudden, complete silence. "Hello?"

Nothing.

"Hello?"

He grits his teeth and stabs his cell off, turning in place.

Another voice intrudes; aide Andrew has somehow found time to hover in the hall outside Sam's tiny office, gossiping on his own cell phone:

"—a pediatrician, used to be an epidemiologist, met him at Claude's. Guy worked in *Africa*, okay? Said any contagious disease has to be stopped at the source, because otherwise people will just keep getting infected. Treat the *cause*."

Annoyed, Sam moves to the door and steps out to confront Andrew, but he's already pocketing his little cell and moving off.

"Sam?" Paula is there again, suddenly, a hand on his arm as she pulls open the sample drawer, rummaging through it. "We're nearly out of samples, and Howard called, *his* stock is running out. Ambesta, Lotosil, Sonosol, any of it. People are lining up."

"Jesus. Have him order more, stat. Next ferry."

"Not due until tomorrow, *late*. They had to pull a replacement off Block Island and track down the other pilot."

"Right. Then . . . water ambulance, county police boat, whatever works."

His last words become an idea. If actual sleeping pills are effective, then why not? Even safer, since an overdose will kill no one. He blurts it: "Placebos."

Paula squints. "Sam?"

"Tell him to hand out placebos."

He pauses, images of generic-looking pills flashing—Lovastatin, Dimetapp, Losartan—none right, all too recognizable, with too many possible side effects, interactions, contraindications. Wait, supplements? No, they're capsules, too unlike sleeping meds. But maybe—

"Vitamins. Sure, Ds." He lifts a hand, as if to offer a few. "The small round tabs, I know Howard stocks them at pharmacy. Say, three apiece."

Paula hesitates too, at this threshold never crossed. The lie of it galls her, contrary to every instinct to provide honest treatment. Finally, she nods and crosses to the admitting desk to speed-dial the pharmacy on the landline.

Sam shuts his eyes a moment, but a sideways pull of vertigo opens them again. He turns in place, his hands twitching. What now?

The Boy, of course. With the ferry out, County will have to spare or charter a boat to send Child Services. It'll be a day's delay, easily, given the speed at which they typically fail to move.

He sighs and moves to the landline on the opposite counter, dials, and tries and fails again, this time at a dry, clinical tone as he fills Kathy in on the day.

"Sam, what does it all mean?" she finally wants to know.

"Mean? They send another ferry, not the first time, I heard. And the longer we go without, the sooner we sleep. A good night's worth will fix everything." His voice sounds squeezed, like someone about to laugh.

"The EPA? Or the other—?"

"—lumbering bureaucracy and last refuge of the inept? Our case has

been kicked upstairs, where it's being vetted and discussed internally."
His tone is too bitter, manic, and he shakes his head ruefully at himself.

Her silence unnerves him. He fills it with a rushed sign-off: "I'll be back
soon. Keep our young customer happy?"

"How will I know if I'm succeeding?"

"See you soon." He clicks off before there's even less to say.

#

Cold and flu seasons certainly create an influx of patients prescribed the same medications, and we pharmacists, especially those of us possessing more than the requisite pharmacology background, prepare with plenty of backstock and with each patient's individual, updated medication lists ready to hand to check for and avoid risky interactions and contraindications. This surge in demand for sleeping medication, though, is quite unexpected, if not entirely unforeseen, and requires some improvisation, on the fly, which could easily and understandably create a somewhat stressful experience, for anybody, somewhat.

As in: too many fucking customers. Printer jammed, no time to fix it, so no bottle labels. Oh, fat guy in plaid shorts, is that why you forgot which pill is which, and how many to take at one time? So that's why you've been vomiting and damaged the lining of your esophagus? Sorry. Old lady sadly dressed teen in a hoodie and leggings? Your sleepy meds didn't play well with your Heparin? Whoops, oh gosh, stroke. Really, how in fuck-all do Sam and Paula expect me to be responsible for all these total bitch assholes from Hewlett or Great Neck or wherever? Oh, they're tired. They're exhausted. Who isn't? I try to make sure no one will croak from a BP spike or turn purple from anaphylactic shock, because (I know I'm not a doctor, thanks, but) I didn't go four years fast-track at Fordham Pharmacology Institute and take home a shit ton of debt and a sheepskin to be ordered by Sam Carlson's piggy old nurse to fill scrips without complete, current medication lists for each patient.

But Carlson says it's on him, fully answerable, totally responsible, no worries. So I guess whatever, okay. I guess.

Which doesn't mean I'm not sorry to tell these late-to-the-party dimwits, confused or pissed off as they are, that I'm all out of the Ambesta, the Lotosil, the Sonosol. They argue, they pace in angry little circles, they swear, but what can they say when I shake the bulk bottles of nighty-night candy and turn them upside down over the counter—like a clown hobo turning his pockets inside out with a sad face—see? Or like a magician, more like, though unfortunately unable to make anything appear in place of the nothing that's there.

Next up, though, is one I feel worst for: a sleek enough redhead but with an office tan and her eyes red from crying and her hair stuck to her neck with sweat and with rain since it just started to pour—air so wet it finally just gave in, like it does around here. This one somehow believes that the meds I do not have to give anyone I will give to her because she has the same scrawled white page off of Sam Carlson's scrip pad that everybody has. And it's sad to see her hope against hope, a kind of denial that falls apart finally, turning into the stunned look of someone realizing some huge betrayal, like all their money is worthless, counterfeit.

So it's rain or tears on her face, which is contorted with fear now, and if her scrip was for anything I had or had even a substitute for, she'd have it and be halfway home already. Which she is nearly is, rushing with a panicky sob for the door clutching her useless prescription while I answer the phone, which I realize has been ringing nonstop.

Speaking of Paula, it's her again and I listen and ask again, for avoidance of doubt and all, because now I really don't want to be responsible if it all goes sideways, as if it could any more than it already has.

So I say okay and hang up, reach for the back shelf, and find the vitamin stock and pull down bottles of D vitamins. And then I think to call out to the redhead lady to fill her scrip with these, but she's gone, a last glimpse of her out the door, and more are forming up anyway for their three apiece of Hail-Mary hope, good luck, fingers crossed. I'd try some myself if I didn't know better, but I do, and tonight no one on god's green earth is gonna stop me from taking an Ambesta from my own hard-earned personal inventory.

Outside now the rain quickens, hissing and spattering as dusk falls and down the other nearby lanes soaked, sagging shapes, solider darknesses amid the darkness, emerge to watch with covetous eyes and follow the lucky ones leaving the pharmacy with their little paper bags.

One man with a little bag can wait no longer; he rips it open to shake a double dose from his pill bottle and chews and swallows down the rough fragments. He turns his face to the maelstrom and trudges on.

After a while, the light ahead is a single lamppost; the rain is a tunnel of lighted stinging drops; his feet feel nothing beneath them. Even the chill of the water running in rivers on his skin is gone as his knees find the wet wood of the boardwalk, and then his side and his back as he lies smiling up, closing his eyes on everything, finally.

Behind him a dim form appears, out of the din and gloom, to find him there like a pile of wet rags, a hand protruding from a black soaked sleeve, still clutching the prescription pill bottle. This man bends and pries the bottle from the sleeper's hand and trudges on himself, shaking out pills, chewing them also, to hasten their effect.

Behind him, still another dim form appears, keeping pace.

9

Now the sky and sea are plunging gray and white and Cort's feet pound the hard tide line, jarring her spine as her heels hit, spattering drops lost in the downpour, the hiss and roar in her ears like the sound of the white noise on that little television in that little room where she was supposed to have watched and played with and cared for that little boy, but never did.

Tears sting her eyes and she lifts the back of a hand to wipe uselessly at them, and she stumbles on a greasy pile of rotting kelp and goes down, a sob torn from her throat. Her face is sideways hard against the wet sand that disappears beneath white foam as the wash rushes up and soaks her fully.

She spits and gasps and climbs swaying to her feet off the clinging sand and continues down the beach, but she needs to lie down, really, if only there were any warm, dry sand where the sunlight could sink into her skin again and leave floating orange blotches burned on the black inside of her eyelids, even just for a little while so she could stop thinking of names of people that will never think of hers anymore: her dad who never did anyway, so what?

Janey, Cami, no way. There are no girlfriends to really call, not since Sioux accused her of trying to poach her boyfriend and the others took sides, as if she could move in on any boy who got everything he wanted from Sioux in her eyeliner and micro jean skirt and white tee over black bra, even out in the parking lot during lunch, or behind the handball court on weekend nights where low bushes hide the picnic-table area.

Where is there a voice now? The kind concern of anybody's words to say what she needs to know and believe somehow: that this lady's tragedy is not because of her, that this lady's desperation would have driven her into whatever she did, sooner or later, someday anyway.

But the same thought comes back again and again, a sharp twinge that makes her whole body clench as if she's flinching. By putting her worst, most selfish self first, hasn't she, sorry or not but forever, been a part of this death?

But no mother's craziness is her fault, how could it be? These single moms with their clown makeup and push-up bras and blatant gold-digger hair-flipping and giggling. Or the others with their pills and cigarettes, stringy wrinkled bitches who hate everybody and fuck disgusting men and cry about it with their scrawny shoulders shaking and their skin ugly and blotchy and flabby, skinny as they are anyway, skinny ugly. They sneer and smirk and roll their eyes and exhale cigarette smoke and sigh like actresses in old movies, but they're no one but dangers to themselves and their own children who are so alone in the world with nowhere to turn, but worse, because if you are not loved then the ones who don't love you will come for you, always.

Running is right, in her jean cutoffs over her suit, wind through her thin shirt and tangled hair, running until it's all a blur she's moving by, with air burning in her lungs and a cramp like a wound in her side, running until the stab of pain bends her gasping, hands on knees, the edge of the sky tilting downward and the cell in her pocket buzzing, buzzing like some poisonous flying thing trying to escape.

She yanks it from her pocket and shields it from the rain as she stares down at Sarah Rubaker's tweet, and the others now sliding into being from the top edge of her page, one after another, judging, ridiculing, shunning.

UR OWT!

loser

!!!☹!!!

wakey wakey

10

From the last gawkers at the marina, Chief has recruited a few of the same preening, fratty guys he's seen all week, blinking like bulls, all pumped arms, goopy hair, and surfer-meets-rapper chatter—"yo dude" and "biyatch ho"—as if any of it, from their clothes to their bad imitations of macho bravado, reflects even the slightest reality of their lives. Raised in Long Island tracts of mid-century split-levels, these sons of mid-management insurance or stock account execs are headed straight for more of the same, and the fewer bumps in the road, the better. Now they shuffle dumbly along the beach, reluctantly, holding soaked cardboard over their heads, in makeshift ponchos of plastic bags, trying against all hope to stay dry.

A few of their posse are late-comers from town, stumbling down the dunes to join in, murmuring and jostling, and Chief thinks he clocks flashes of hands trading cash for . . . pills? One even gulps back a few.

"Hold up." Chief stops the group. "What is that?" He points to a fist one spiky-haired poser tries to jam in a pocket.

The kid's lip quivers, like a defensive child's. "It's *prescription*. For sleeping."

"Yours? Let's see."

The kid pretends to shrug and hands over the little amber pill bottle he tried to hide. "They're not printing labels now. It's only six."

Chief squints down at the unidentifiable bottle. What the fuck is Sam doing? New disasters loom: a criminal economy of sales or outright theft of anybody's pills, overdoses from stockpiled meds. Sam will have to answer for it all, when the world rights itself again.

Chief hands the bottle back. "Do *not* be selling, or trading. It's controlled substance, got it?" As if he could tell whose was whose. He wants to laugh at himself.

They nod slowly, as if trying to figure it out themselves.

"Let's keep moving." He points them forward.

It makes sense to start the search at East Beach; if the tide was incoming, the current would have taken her sideways, easterly somewhere along the flatter sections of the barrier island, floating beneath the surface until expanding body gasses brought her back up. He almost sees her, her hair moving slowly, her hands hovering, dim light streaming from above.

Not a good way to go. No matter how inevitable it seems and how resigned we think are, the body fights at the end, clawing at nothing, trying to scream, and the face Chief finally sees—if it's not too much later—is always nothing short of terrified.

Sand shifts fast, and sooner or later the gleam of a bracelet or a ring will likely make somebody see a hand, and they'll discover her a few inches under wet sand, with it caked in her mouth and nose and ears, wet grains stuck to her eyes still open on the last thing they saw—just the blurry pall, and maybe her own hand reaching into it, as if for another to pull her out.

A name would help; he could track down next of kin and maybe find her sleeping it off at her sister's in Bayshore or Far Rockaway, or at her own walk-up in Williamsburg. But Chief has left messages for the realtor who rented the unit to her and heard nothing back yet.

He points the group eastward, and they move forward at a ragged pace, finally spreading out, becoming vague in the whiteout swirl and shift of the pall that has descended on Carratuck. His feet throb, one angrily at the ankle joint, and his eyes feel dry and tender, as if tears would be a relief. The sound of the surf has shifted into a pulsing, fuzzy headache. Out beyond the break, the dark water's surface is mottled with raindrops, fleeting ripples lost in the windblown chop.

A shout sounds suddenly, from off to his left, out to sea, improbably.

What now, what else—somebody else drowning? Why not? Chief spins seaward, and by the time it truly dawns, he's yanked off his gun belt and flung down his cell phone and is knee-deep in the uprush to struggle through and finally fling himself forward for a few fast strokes of crawl. He ducks under a looming breaker and emerges gasping, treading water and turning and searching.

The drowning man's not far, really, the bobbing dark roundness of his head, his flashing hand. Just a few more strokes, a hard kick to edge behind him to grab him around the chest, to keep him on his back and his face clear.

"Okay, easy. Got you. No problem."

The man spits and gasps but luckily doesn't panic or try to climb out of the water by climbing onto Chief's shoulders and sinking them both; Chief's seen it back in the Navy; the only hope left is a chokehold hard enough to knock somebody out but not kill them, and from there drag them in—bad odds all the way around.

Chief barely gets a look at the guy, just quick glimpses of a fleshy, sun-burned nose and red eyes, and now just thin hair plastered to a balding head. He's bigger than average, and in shape, from the firm girth of chest and bicep under Chief's arm.

There's no rip here, so how far east has this one drifted? Chief's still got his hiking shoes on, filled with water, and his own clothes fight him like deadweight around his body, trying to pull him sideways and under. A choppy, stinging splash fills his nose and he coughs and then sucks in air too soon, choking.

His feet reach for purchase, find none, one arm flailing when the ocean suddenly bulges up and shoreward, and they nearly tumble in the rush of whiteness. Chief loses his grip around the man's chest, but his foot touches down and he shoots out a hand to close around the man's slick forearm and yank him into standing depth, toward the paler width of beach.

They stagger out, stumbling in the backwash, to lie gasping in the soaked sand. Chief's lungs burn, head pounding as he lies still, waiting for strength enough to speak or stand. He turns his head to the sideways world down the beach, where his search volunteers have continued into the gloom of rain and dusk, no look back, as if soon to be lost themselves. He rolls onto his side to kneel, facing the swimmer whose life he has just saved.

"You'll be . . . okay. You . . . shouldn't swim alone."

The swimmer regains his breath, finally, looking at him, smirking. "I'm on vacation. I'm *supposed* to be swimming."

Chief squints at the man, at the red knot of burst blood vessels in one eye, his unfocused look, his mouth slack like a drunk's.

The man plucks up a seashell, holding it to his ear, grinning. "Hear it? The siren song of the sea? The she-devil in Davey Jones's locker! Singing mermaids!"

He staggers away, laughing. Dripping, still gasping, Chief stares after him.

When he looks down to retrieve his gun belt, the leather holster is half-filled with damp sand, his revolver gone—stolen by some unseen thief while he struggled in the surf. He turns in place, mouth open, a sob of fury and dismay half-stifled.

The rain, the beach, houses, more beach, surf. Turning.

No one.

11

Soaked, Sam's tee and shorts cling, heavy on his skin. Through the dark, the rain comes at him almost sideways, windblown, stinging. The wet sand deepens and tugs at his bike tires, but he presses on slowly to Bramble Lane.

Barely a shadow, a low shape darts and stops and darts again in the tilting periphery of his vision, and he cannot blink it away, even with the quick hand he lifts from the handlebars of his bike to wipe at his rain-spattered eyes.

He would slow, but can go no slower without stopping, so he stops, touching his toes down for balance as he peers into the darkness. A dog stares back, trembling too, fearful but drawn slowly forward, short fur rippling.

"Hey, boy. Hey." Have animals been infected, too? What would their pain be like, of awareness uninterrupted, of constant movement, noise, light, endlessly?

The dog whines, stops and half-turns away, turns back, whining again. Sam approaches slowly, a hand extended, palm down, low. "Easy. Easy there." A metal tag glints, dangling from a black collar Sam can barely see against the dog's soaked fur.

How far has this one wandered? Sam shields his eyes from the downpour and looks around; he's on a remote stretch of lane between dunes, and his eyes strain to see another glint of light—from the open doorway of a lone beach house, flickering distantly between gusts of rain, like a broken beacon as the door swings open and shut to no rhythm but the wind's. Not a hundred yards off.

The dog starts slowly toward it, pausing to look back, as if leading. But why follow? If that's his home, he's not far enough to be lost. But the door left open to the storm? The dog quivering with fear?

Sam sighs and starts forward, half-rolling, half-dragging his bike along through the wet pelted sand. The house sits atop a dune tall enough to require steps, and these are tiered railway ties with broad landings, a few too many to drag the bike up, so Sam leans it against a rickety wooden erosion fence and follows the dog up to the yawning doorway.

"Hello?" The wind swallows it, so he shouts, "*Hello?*" his voice ringing off the hardwood floors and wainscoting.

A hand out, grasping the edge of the front door before it swings again, Sam steps into the doorway, hesitating to listen. Close by, the surf sends up its broad, menacing sound, basso thunder and seething hiss. Rain streaming from the eaves, the gurgle and clatter of runoff in roof gutters. No one.

The high foyer light is a wooden chandelier, a ship-timber theme repeated in the gray hardwood planks of the floor Sam steps slowly across. Ahead, another half-open door seems a reproach, the hallway dimming along its length to another door shut tight, no trace of light beneath it.

Sam peeks slowly around the edge of the first into a clean, well-lit living room of white denim slip-covered couches, hurricane-style lamps, wood barrel end tables of distressed staves: Pottery Barn Cape Cod, spacious but inviting, neat as if ready for company.

He glances back to see the dog has disappeared, suddenly, unaccountably.

It's dim at the other end of the hall, which is just exactly that, of course—a hall to a door, where they all seem to lead, the point of a hall, after all. He wants to laugh and yawn at the same time, a twinge at the joint of his jaw. A hollowness within slows him, a flutter of viscera. There's a gap in the drumming of rain, filled by a moan of wind.

His hand twitches for his lost flashlight, but he takes a breath and a few resolute steps to the shut door and raps on it, knuckles first—thin, unconvincing impacts—and then simply bangs the heel of his palm hard against the wood.

"Hello?" He shouts it. Why waste anyone's time here?

The doorknob feels warm in his wet fingers and turns easily, the latch mechanism releasing smoothly. He tries a soft push first, to just glide the door open.

It's loose, but stuck, too, somehow. Something heavy up against it, other side.

A muscle lurches in Sam's chest, a quick gripping, as if against some larger force trying to pry his arms wide, trying to open him. But it's just another door right here, in a world of others.

A firmer shove still fails to budge it, and Sam finally puts his shoulder into it, nearly slipping in the wetness of his own soaked boat shoes.

The door gives, grudgingly, a fraction of an inch.

Again, cursing softly, "Fucker." Harder now.

Something on the other side slips, flops heavily over, with a thick, dull slap on the floor.

A prickle crawls up the back of his neck, the tightness in his chest twists outward, and he leans with his full weight to push the door harder against the weight of whatever prone thing is now sliding away, an obstinate inch at a time along the floor.

A sight line opens, narrow, into darkness complete. He lifts a hand to feel blindly around the edge of the doorframe for a light switch, but a heavy waft of cloying odor, palpably warm, feels like someone's breath on his face, and he yanks his hand back.

Gas.

Back up, now, away. Call Chief and let him find whatever there is to find. Let him call in the auxiliary guys, Stuart, or Tim, that he says are so useless, or what's-his-name, the EMT. It's their jobs, best luck to them. So just turn now, blunder away back to the bike, and pedal hard straight back to the boat and a warm berth, where sleep may yet come.

He moves quickly back down the hall to the lighted foyer, eyes searching. For what?

There, a faux-antique wooden boot bench with a hinged seat. He lifts it and rummages past the rubber boots and umbrellas to find what he hoped for: a serious, four C-type battery flashlight. He flicks it on; even in this bright, shadowless foyer, the trace of a beam snaps out, dancing along the wainscoting.

Good enough, it seems, when he returns to the ajar door at the end of the hall and sends a broad beam inside, downward first to see the striped child's mattress someone must have propped against the door, barely pushed aside. He aims the beam higher into a shadowy kitchen. He hesitates, seeing stacked baking tins, nesting bowls, pricey stainless cookware hanging from a pot rack. Behind the chunky stove, a row of prep knives gleams darkly from a mag strip. A cook's kitchen.

He shoves the door wider, enough to step carefully in, a hand covering his mouth, beam already finding a bay window behind dual prep sinks, sealed with layers of gray duct tape. Quick now, to pull a knife from the block and slash sideways at the duct tape, parting it, yanking the frayed edges of the gaping split back to crank open the side casements and breathe in great lungs full of rich, wet night.

To the stove, now, a chunky stainless, commercial-style affair with oversized, gleaming knobs set full-on, burners hissing like snakes. He snaps them off and stops there, a glimpse worrying the edge of his vision, still safely at the edge of his vision just so long as he doesn't turn his head to look.

He turns his head, points the beam floorward, and takes a step around the edge of the broad kitchen island.

Fear would be familiar, something to which one may become accustomed, but this dread is a cold fist around his heart, a brutal, insolent grip.

His first recognition is of squares of solid colors, and he blinks to see they're pillows—on which lie three prone, naked human forms, white as bone. His eyes follow the beam's swath over details, refusing them even as he understands these are a family: a young pre-adolescent girl, a father, a mother—though her body's hands are not covered in quilted oven mitts like the others. Like the others, though, a quilted sleep mask covers her eyes, and her ears are hidden behind furry-looking earmuffs.

Her hands are bare, one wrapped loosely around the wrist of the other and the other upturned, as if awaiting receipt of some object, a key or coin, a talisman to grant her passage.

Only after he has done his best to shut it from his memory can he let himself admit he recognizes her, can he let his eyes wander again up her angled white neck to her lifeless face to her dull, lank red hair. Red.

The woman he quoted Wordsworth to. The world no longer with her, late and soon.

A dim, small white square on the countertop draws him closer. He bends to it, pointing the flashlight beam to see his own rushed scrawl on the wrinkled, wet page from his prescription pad: the prescription never filled, somehow, with neither real nor ersatz sleeping pills. No matter which now.

His gaze darts to the young girl and to the downturned cell that lies beside her, the edge of its screen dimly flashing. He moves nearer, bending to flip it over and see the home screen notification center, pushed Tweets appearing white on black, each new one pushing the last downward, one after another, all #sleepless43, until one stops him with a lurching in his chest, an ache in his throat:

asleep is the new dead

12

On hands and knees, rain streaming down his face, Chief inches forward in clothes soaked cold and heavy with brine. He pauses and sweeps his Maglite's beam into the dimness ahead, spotting a black gleam.

His hand closes on kelp and shoves it sideways. He's found a horseshoe crab shell, a black stick of driftwood, a piece of broken glass worn smooth. He's a beachcomber, that's all; it's a hobby of the idle, absently sifting the sand for some fool's hand-me-downs, cast-offs, forgotten objects.

His girls, Linda and Jan, would imagine his side of the story worth telling, and invent it if he didn't: he was saving a man's life, after all, when his gun was stolen, and it could not and should not have been any other way. No backup, blameless, brave, in fact—that's Dad, Navy hero, cop, hard case with a soft heart, the family man devoted to his community, to the values he swore always to protect and defend.

Suffolk PD might believe it. If no one got shot, if his weapon is never used in a suicide or murder, or robbery or maiming. If, if. But then why steal it?

How can he admit it? Someone simply ran off with his department-issue, fifteen-round, semi-automatic Glock 9-millimeter handgun while he braved the surf to pull out a man who laughed in his face. The truth is his to nurse in secret, like an illness that will slowly, surely kill him. It's started already, the hollowness of humiliation spreading from his stomach, poison in the thrum of his pulse and the blood in his veins.

If he could just lie down, even in this wet sand beside the roar of the ocean with the rain pelting his face, if he could maybe just for few moments let his eyes close, then maybe he could dream a new dream—a beach filled with dozing, sunbathing parents and kids greeting him as he rides by with his blued Glock in his holster and an elbow out the open window and his wry little salute: "How're ya?"

He blunders to the Jeep, hand slipping on the door handle, yanking open the driver's side to climb into the seat, saltwater and tears and snot and rain dripping as he sits watching the storm streak the surf white and black, blurred through his windshield.

A gust rocks the Jeep, but his stare is fixed, a resolute refusal to look elsewhere or to think of anything else but water in all its forms, and how living in a place surrounded by it puts you so completely in it at some point, over your head, figuratively if not literally.

He's not sure, though, exactly when the little cell phone in his lap began ringing, its little screen flashing, a buzzing, busy little rectangle. His Bluetooth set, of course, is gone, yanked off his ear in the maelstrom, and he needs to swipe the screen with a wet finger and lift it to his face, motions nearly forgotten—the thing had become such an appendage.

He wipes at his face, clears his throat, but still his voice sounds choked, ragged, broken, as he lifts it to his face: "Hello?"

———

When he has seen all that Sam has summoned him to see, Chief drifts stunned from the kitchen into the hall and stops, and to Sam the moment seems to begin and end again before Chief takes another half-step backward, his head quickly back and forth as if in denial of some unimportant fact, but his voice somewhere between a sob and a whisper. "They knew, they knew, they knew . . ."

Chief's gaze is wild, unfocused, darting over the walls and floor, the look of someone desperate to escape. Sam grabs him by the shoulders, dimly realizing he's soaked through, too. "Knew what?"

"That it will never end, none of it."

Sam tightens his grip. "Fuck all that. That's nonsense, okay?"

"How did they not try and get out, get off Carratuck, get anyplace else?"

Sam shakes his head. "You know deep sea diving. You trained. It's like hypoxia, the disorientation takes over, total confusion. Which way is up, or out, which way to town, where there's no ferry. Maybe they tried. But where are their glasses, wallet, children? Maybe a kid runs off, refusing to go. Do they wait? Maybe they're too afraid. They start to believe there's no place to run from it."

"How bad will it get? What if you and I—?"

"Teams'll be here tomorrow. I'll pull some strings, get CDC, full event response, forensics, counselors, everybody, here tomorrow. But tonight, just you and me, that's all who can know about this, understood? You don't call Tim or any of the auxiliary or fire guys, you don't tell Jan, I don't tell Kathy. Word gets out, it's just panic. There's nothing to be done tonight. Understand?"

Chief tilts his head at Sam as if he has just spoken in some utterly foreign language.

"Got it?"

Slowly, Chief blinks at him, his eyes finally focusing. He nods.

13

In a daze of déjà vu, Kathy turns from the Boy again as he sits at the dinette. The shut, close cabin seems to slightly turn in place and stop, as though from a bout of dizziness.

She remembers the Boy's empty, haunted eyes staring at the water from the end of the float, and it chills her to think this child may be an orphan and has likely witnessed more than any should.

She wasn't old enough when she watched her mother drift off coughing and shuddering and then wake up terrified in her last minute, pleading. Now that terror is hers forever, gift of the dying, and she hopes against hope and reason that this Boy wasn't given it. But then why is there nothing but his wide eyes and the faint sound of his breathing through his mouth as he watches her desperately fill these hours with bright, idle nonsense and thin cheer?

It's painful to think these months haven't been so very different—filled with frivolous diversion.

She has an idea, suddenly, ridiculous and from nowhere, that if the Boy would only speak, everyone would sleep again. Sam would laugh, of course, but would she see a tiny glint in his eyes, as if at hope, no matter how silly? And how crazy is it, really, to think in some way the world hangs on the first words of a boy whom tragedy has silenced? In some way, anyway, it *is* true, maybe not literally, but as if in a kind of story or fable of a cursed kingdom.

She yanks open cabinets, a drawer, busy. Finally, she spins, holding up a sealed package of hot dogs and a box of cereal. The Boy points: *hot dogs*.

Kathy gives him a tearful smile. "After my own heart."

Clambering down into the cabin, soaked and breathless, Sam slows beside the Boy thumbing his handheld game at the dinette table. He meets the Boy's quick glance with a murmur: "You okay, Admiral?"

Sam watches the Boy's dark lively eyes that follow everything but always return quickly to his bright little screen. Did his mom walk him halfway to the beach and turn him bewildered but mercifully away, down some other lane, while she kept on?

"Sam, you're drenched!" Kathy exclaims, but he's drawn by a glimpse of the Boy's flashing screen—a princess in a castle, waiting to be rescued, no doubt. His eyes fill to see it.

None so lost as children who witness.

Sam turns away with a quick, apologetic smile. "Just going to dry off and make a quick call. Anybody hungry?"

He doesn't wait for a reply, but steps into the stateroom. He wipes his face with a flung tee shirt and paces, scrolling his contacts for Dr. Malcolm Hale's home number. His finger trembles over it as he hesitates. Hale was his psychiatrist for much of the required therapy that any psychology professional must undergo, and through the sudden loss of his client, later, when continuing in the field no longer seemed like such a given.

He closes his eyes and rubs the lids, trying to focus, but a sheet of improbably hard rain drums on his deck and a gust has rigging *ding ding dinging* against masts.

He imagines a relaxed, murmured tone that doesn't sound panicky or scattered, but it all deserts him when he leaves his message:

"Professor! Sam Carlson here, hope you're well. Been awhile, I know. Can you give a call back when you get this? I could use some advice on a . . . situation. I'll try you back later, too. I'd just like to—"

"Hello? One moment." A rustling on the line, a creaking sound. "Yes, I'm sorry, who's calling?" Hale sounds annoyed.

"Doctor Hale, it's Sam Carlson, I'm—"

"Ahh, of course. How are you, Sam? Out on Carratuck, I heard. A clinic?"

"Yes, Urgent Care, a day facility. Barely an ER, really." He plows on, absurdly, too edgy for silence. "Sunburns, jellyfish stings, that sort of thing."

Sam hesitates here, hoping Hale will prompt him to continue. Is his call so unwelcome?

He wades in: "More lately, it's why I'm calling."

Ten minutes of pacing, positioning, framing and cajoling meet kindly skepticism: what proof has Sam got that these fatalities, the missing suicidal mother, and the dozens of sleepless share a single cause? Or even the same multiple causes?

Hale shifts from mild doubt to musing speculation: "Of course, these days sleep deprivation is a complaint I hear more and more. But why not? We're barraged, everywhere, by screens flashing more and more images, faster and faster, overt and subliminal, wearing down our resistance to suggestion. Why shouldn't it affect us in unprecedented ways?"

Sure, but who cares now? Sam remembers the man's prissy, patronizing moue, his shifty eye contact, the cheesy titles of his lectures. A vain spinner of his own image, adept at the intrigue of departmental politics.

Sam tries for a measured cadence, as if to casually steer the conversation back: "Kids around here have made a game of it. Maybe elsewhere, too, I don't know. Whoever tweets every quarter hour the longest wins." It sounds so utterly harmless, from a bygone, innocent time of short-sheeting and prank phone calls.

"Symptomatic, I'd say, of the same ongoing hyper-arousal. Too many choices, distractions, self-images defined by the constant mirror of connectivity . . ."

Sam tries to steer them away from what sounds like Hale's next pop-psych magazine pitch. "Sure, but, so, in terms of the acute situation here, and treating the increase in patients presenting with insomnia?"

Hale refuses to understand, and grunts, exasperated. "Well, certainly you prescribe on an individual case by case basis—"

"—Understood, yes, I have been, and sleeping medications have been efficacious—" Should he tell him he's run out, and is now treating with placebos? No, Hale might find it too questionable, and possibly alert someone, and once word got out, they'd have no chance to work. The old joke comes to him, naturally enough: *just because you're paranoid doesn't mean you're wrong.* "But I'm not sure that's getting ahead of the problem."

Hale circles back. Or is this the first time he's asked? "But—epidemiology, environmental toxicology?"

"No, tests came back negative for pathogens or toxins. That's why I'm certain this is some form of hysteria."

"Have you tried CDC? They've investigated those situations in the past, albeit reluctantly."

Sam sighs inaudibly. "Sure, they need a little more to be convinced that it's not EPA's problem."

"Way of the world. So it shall ever be. And absent any other sign of somatic illness or proven connections to these murder-suicides you describe, horrific as they sound, neither agency would consider it their purview."

It's true, but also a convenient way for Hale to ingratiate himself and encourage confidences—by suggesting CDC and EPA or any other medical authority wouldn't first rebuff Sam over his spotty history, which now, slyly, predictably, becomes subtext: "But how are *you* feeling, Sam? To have discovered these deaths . . . first on scene—"

"I see plenty of connection between them. These people were just desperate for unconsciousness. The oven mitts and eye masks, the blacked-out windows, all crude attempts at sensory deprivation, until they had no other way—"

"It's a theory, certainly . . ."

A pause here, a masterfully timed caesura, and then Hale's tone modulates into one almost kind, even concerned, as he gently presses, "But, Sam, forgive me? How long since *you've* slept?"

Sam lets out a long, slow breath. It's a tightrope—too forceful a reply can sound defensive, but he needs to pre-empt Hale's suspicions firmly and quickly. "Of course, you're right to ask. I'm not trying to be argumentative or resistant, okay? But—"

"—you've had sleep problems of your own, since you lost that client and became one of mine. You know the list with extreme deprivation: from impaired judgment to waking dreams, nobody's immune . . . issues can surface. I'm hearing some of yours—guilt, Sam—over the student, and now this family—"

"Right, but having said all that, I've had plenty of sleep." The truth won't serve anybody here.

Sam rubs his temple, widening his eyes, feeling the onset of a deeper headache. He sees again the grainy, jerky haggard face of the Boy's mom, and imagines the last walk to the deserted beach, hand in hand. Night's last hour, probably, darkness just beginning to pale.

"Sam?" Hale's voice yanks him back, oddly melodious. "How many prescriptions would you say you've written?"

Sam shakes his head, gripping the phone, torn. Will it help to hear it? "Maybe forty, a little more." Obviously, it's a fraction of the number of people experiencing symptoms.

"Forty . . ." Hale has to repeat it, of course, like a slow student moving their lips when they read. "You have professional nursing staff there with you? In the clinic?"

That prick. No way to persuade him now. Blundering on: "I'm going to have to ask you. I *am* asking you. You have more touch with CDC. Call them and corroborate what's happening here?"

For a moment there's nothing but the sound of the rain, the edge of a squall lashing the boat, the frantic beating on the deck over his head. And then Sam hears it, faintly, but unmistakably over the line: the faint *clickety click* of rapid typing.

"Well, here's what I suggest, Sam." Hale adopts a soothing tone. "It's late, and no one can get out there tonight in this weather to investigate. If things haven't improved by tomorrow, I'll come myself for a look. But meanwhile, why don't you try and get some rest?"

Sam stands, turns left, right, trapped into begging. "Why not make the choice now? Support me in this?"

Hale feigns a good-humored chuckle. "Support you? You want a life coach, Sam. A motivational quack. With better hair and teeth."

Wary, Sam listens for another beat, to nothing.

Hale clinches it: "How many did you say, again? Prescriptions?"

Sam shakes his head in disbelief and disgust, at himself, at Hale. It's the job, too, that turns professionals into bad listeners, often weighing affect over intention, context over content, subtext over statement. The denotational undervalued. How infuriating for a patient, finally.

But the idea blooms, beautiful. How easy will this be, after all? Just go along to get along: "They're in on it. You, too. Listening now, every thought, everyone's. Please, no, it's okay." He pauses, dropping his voice to a vicious whisper of accusation. "You. You let this happen," he adds for good measure, hopefully just enough to present a credible imitation of spiraling, paranoid ideation. It could work, given Hale's ego and a showy opportunity to play the hero.

"Sam?"

Sam clicks off, exhaling.

A thought makes him almost laugh: he's not sleepless at all, but dreaming, even now, of sleeplessness. Why not, since his dreams too often have brought him the bloodstained, torn face of Gabriel? He turns in place in the dim cabin of his boat, as if turning away from it all now, again, but still he sees the dark narrow hallway to that open doorway, the massive blue shoulders of the cop, his eyes black and glaring with gleeful fury, stepping aside and gesturing like a maître d': "this way, Doctor." It's the money, always, they hate his money and his degree, and why shouldn't they? In that room, beyond the half-open door, lay the end result of it all.

14

Chief has pulled the Jeep over down the beach from his house, lights off, buffeted by the storm, to slouch in his seat while his little cell screen gives him the everyday world he needs so badly to see—multi-colored, peppy web pages of scandals and sports scores, celebrities and Washington gridlock. His eyes leak fat treacly tears at it all, so blithely innocent and utterly normal, and suddenly he imagines Linda's voice, almost hears it, jaded as only a twenty-year-old's can be, melodic, wry.

He wipes the wetness from his face and FaceTimes her, adding a little distance to the screen, taking a slow breath to steady his hand.

"Dad?" Her voice crackles through, the screen bursts into light, a tilted jerking image, shadowy legs and feet, a crowd of them, glimpsed before the rectangle rights itself into a window on a Manhattan street. Linda's face fills the little frame suddenly, with the sound of hooting, cars honking, the blazing trail of a streetlight or headlight. Behind her, other faces crowd in, indistinct, bobbing, turning one way and then the other, awed as if surrounded by a world never before seen and wondrous to behold, though all Chief can see is more of the same. A shout goes up, indecipherable, with shrieks of delight, incredulous laughter.

He wipes his face again and puts up an absurd, ghastly smile, his voice a croak: "Baby?"

"Can't see you, Dad, too dark! Too hot to sleep! 's crazy! Everybody's out! Whoa—what?" Her face drops from the frame and returns again, as if she has bent and straightened, the broad planes of her face working, her eyes gleaming slits as laughter bursts from her.

"What's—" The image blasts into gushing black and white pixilated picture static, like a TV tuned to nothing, and then Linda flickers back on again, time-sliced, stop-motion-style, turning sideways with a hand half-lifted as if to point. But the snow appears again, hissing now, oddly high-pitched, shrill as feedback.

"Hello?" He grips the cell in both hands now, shouting into it, inches from his face. He yanks it away, speed dials again, frantically shoving his index finger into the screen, again, again, to hear only the sad triple tone of a dropped network signal. He lets out a sob of frustration and shoulders out of the Jeep to stand facing seaward, unseeing, lost.

A wave leaps and spills, spray windblown in the rain. Chief shuts his eyes and lifts his face to the maelstrom, as if when he opens them again, it will be on the brightest, most ordinary day imaginable.

The tumult of darkness shifts, scrims of white shallows roiling over his soaked shoes. Yards out, just beyond the head-high walls of waves, a dark oval bobs, a thinner shape lifted above, waving—a hand?

"Chief! Hey—!" The sound of this voice is a weakness behind his knees, a prickly chill crawling up his arms and neck. He leans forward, into the wind, eyes straining to see no one now, even as a second cry sounds from the pall off to his left, another voice, unforgotten after all:

"Chief, don't leave us!"

Another calls out, half-sobbing with fear, from off to his right, "Hey, no!"

He moves into the wash, thigh-high, the force of it rocking him, peering out into the empty violence of the storm. At the dark shapes of drowning men, too many to be saved, too many to be drowning, too many to be there at all.

Another arm swings upward from the maelstrom, in heavy soaked white cloth flapping, a uniform.

Another voice rises and fails, from farther out, unreachable, unreal: "Please! You can't! Don't! Don't shut it!" Stolen by the din of another wave.

What voice now, what cry, what glimpsed faces from another life hover fleetingly in the blustery chop to disappear? Andy, ensign from Chicago. Doug, a warrant. Dan, Pete, Steve, engine room guys, heavy ordinance spec. Heroes as surely as if they chose it. Gone then, irretrievably, irrevocably, gone now.

Chief presses the heels of his palms into his eyes, fingers clutching his forehead as he sinks to his knees on the wet sand. A blast of rain turns his face sideways; a shrill wail like a child's rises from his throat, hovering, tremulous, before it subsides.

———

He enters the house quietly, leaving his soaked shoes by the door, dreading the kindly, trusting eyes of his wife, the undeserved welcoming warmth of home, the late dinner prepped and waiting, table still set. If only it were so.

But every house light is on, and in the center of the living room, Jan is on all fours—sponges duct taped to her knees for padding, scrubbing the hardwood planks where she has rolled back the big faux-Turkish rug from Ikea. Bottles of bleach and cleaning supplies surround her; when she lifts her gaze to his, her look is glazed, and then oddly defiant, half-hidden beneath a thin veil of listless hair.

"Mildew somewhere. I can smell it. I've already gone over the kitchen floor, but now I wonder if it isn't the coat closet, though maybe the base-boards along the other wall, or the sub-floor, even though I'm not sure it makes sense to pull up the floor until things dry out a bit, when we can really track it down, like we did last time with that mold starting up in the laundry room—we don't want that again—how awful was that?"

He nods as if it's all completely understandable, as if they haven't drifted on this tide of unendurable wakefulness to utterly separate, foreign shores. He blinks away the sudden wetness in his eyes as he moves to her and gently urges her up.

"It's okay."

She smiles curiously, in dim surprise as he brings her close, swaying a little.

"It's okay," he repeats, lamely. Why did he not ask Sam for a dose for her? Self-loathing hollows his stomach, tightens his throat. Is he up to the task? Any task?

"I'll be right up." She pulls back, and he nods again, as if all were well.

He moves on, and all he has strength for are these careful silent steps to the worn sofa and plaid throw in his study, to lower himself down, turn his face to the wall, and find a spot of painted drywall to stare at with unblinking eyes while the echoes of this endless day and dread of the next assail him.

15

There is nowhere else for Cort to lie to face this darkness, to listen to the rain pouring as if it will never stop, but in her bed in her little room, alone. Even the dimness hurts her eyes, which she can't close, not without seeing the face of the sad, manic woman on that little TV screen, not without wondering if she could have saved her from herself—played a game with her boy in their bungalow while she took an hour's beach walk and maybe found a better way to look at her life.

Tay doesn't text, hasn't texted, which means what she's most afraid of is true, of course, and always was, that he only wanted what all boys want, only her stupid lameness wouldn't let her admit it, like all the slut girls, and Cort's sorry now that she ever judged them, ever smirked or rolled her eyes at a story in the hallway or lunchroom—though now there is a lady who is gone, not just a boy bragging to his idiot posse.

There is a lady gone. Did her choices disappear, until she did too? Did she have no husband or boyfriend or mother of her own? Did she trick herself, going out too far past the break, pretending not to know she would never make it back?

In her hand, her cell's screen brightens with more game tweets, her notification center updating more and more often. She scrolls idly, with a sharp little inhalation to find "Tayser10003" among the players, like clockwork, his tweets now just punctuation marks, as if brevity has become part of the contest, too.

She should send him a funny text to let him know she's cool anyway, no biggie. A wink smilicon, dumb, or a link to a Funny Or Die. But which girl is that, anyway, prideless, chasing? The one okay with getting used and laughed at?

A blast of rain spatters her window, and she looks up at the drops running, edged in yellow from the porchlight. She finds her own face reflected there, loveless and unloved—the face of a girl she doesn't want to be—cheekbones too broad and flat, eyes too close together, hair dull and limp from a crooked hairline she hates—tiny coarse hairs she has tried to trim with cuticle scissors.

But what can save her from her deeper ugliness, which maybe killed a woman and made a little boy an orphan, which he probably is, or where was his dad anyway? Missing dads are dead dads, to anyone that cares—dead in any way that matters.

The world's hold on her loosens. Mom's voice, always angry or filled with her own sadness, and Tay's voice rough and laughing, sleepy-sexy, fading now; her ex-friends' voices also are memories, but of shrill accusing. Fainter.

Loosening. Rain farther away, the room slowly turns as if she's spun in place and flopped down on this bed that softens as she settles more deeply, as the night itself seems to loosen beneath her and let her through.

Downward now, floating pleasantly, while in the dark vague drifting blotches of color begin to form, behind her eyes almost becoming identifiable shapes, when dreams begin.

Finally free, slowly falling.

Wait—the fear finds her and already her hand has reached out so she won't fall alone into more aloneness, and her eyes snap open again and she's gripping her cell.

She thumbs it awake, bringing it to her face, her own small light in the darkness, to bring up her feed. She swipes away sweaty hair to read the last #sleepless43 tweet from usernames she knows. Another of the other girls out at the swank end of the island, in borrowed beachfronts, Cami Melvine's already complaining:

I quit yesterday so why am I still here. so sick of it. dreaming awake did I write this already or think just about it or am I doing it now

Kimi Gardner, too, staying near Pine Haven:

I give up but it won't give me up. Ha ha. im crying.

Chris Kasten urges everyone on with smug enthusiasm:

48 sucks – but 52!!! can fly - xray vision - immune to pain

New usernames appear, at first it seems like a few, friends of friends discovering the game and tweeting with the hashtag, but when Cort presses "more" at the bottom an entire page comes up, and she scrolls that downward, too, revealing what must be hundreds now, from everywhere, it must be:

!!!I'm so in!!!!!

brought to you by Jolt

36!

Yaaaay

From Madison, whose only talent is snarky whining:

I don't feel good I need to stop

Cort stares at these flat, witless words, dimly alarmed; she tucks hair behind an ear, bends closer, sniffling. She flicks to Messaging and types quickly:

Mad you ok???

The light of the little rectangle of her screen seems to dim and brighten, dim and brighten, like something alive and breathing the darkness of her room, but there's no reply from Madison, who would not ever have signed out or turned off or even left her cell for a second.

Madison, Sioux, the others, do they already know she got felt up and then freaked and ran like a prude all while she pretended to babysit for a woman who maybe killed herself?

But that's just ugly, when it's Madison to worry about now, her scary tweet and now nothing, as if she's simply disappeared.

She punches up FaceTime. She's turned down her volume so the hollow *bbrrr, brrr* old-school ring won't wake Mom, who seems as sleep-deprived as everyone else lately, anyway. It sounds twice, and then Madison, it must be Madison, the streaky flash of a face swinging out of frame and then a shaky-cam close-up of a mouth twisted into a shriek of laughter and a shout:

"—outta here!"

"Madis—?"

Dead, hung up, or dropped, the image blinks into blackness. Cort stabs the redial, but Madison lets it ring and ring, a dull lazy sound, more annoying than urgent. Nothing, no one. Cort quits.

Is it everybody? The lady leaving her kid, Madison gone to crazytown.

She looks up. The thin strip of light beneath her door has darkened, a board creaks with the weight of her mother's footstep.

16

Sam waits in his cabin, listening to the rain drumming on the deck above, faster as squall lines rake the marina. Each thought leads only to the missed signs, the late response, the blind stumble past the hands that reached for him and the voices that called, until there's no thought to follow but back to the desperate longing for fatigue to finally set him, everyone, adrift in sweet luxurious sleep.

Kathy slips quietly inside, leaving the door ajar. Sam looks up and she nods, her hard-edged beauty harder, the lines of her face sharper somehow, even as her eyes seem duller with fatigue.

"He's out, finally," she murmurs. She turns away to undress and slips quickly into a robe. She sits on the edge of the bed, perched, and adds, "He picked hot dogs over cereal. It's something."

He doesn't smile. "Well, it's progress."

"Nothing for you?"

"What do you mean? We all had—we—"

"Mac n' cheese? Salad? That was last night."

"Well, sure. I had something at the clinic, though." He looks away with a vague shrug. Has he not eaten anything but the two or three Power Bars chased with Evian, out in the hall between patients? Hunger just another hollowness, one more forgotten thing.

She studies him, and he bears it, stonewalling. It's nothing to do with dinner; she doesn't want to understand, of course, why he isn't in the main cabin, encouraging the Boy to recall everything about the thing that stole his words away.

He dodges, dropping his voice to a whisper: "I brought these." He brings out a sample pack of Ambesta—two doses, bubble wrapped, innocuous beautiful pink oblongs.

She worries: "What if he wakes up?"

"I'll be up." It's reassurance, hopefully.

"Maybe you shouldn't be. Maybe you should take one. Or part of one."

He looks at the meds, part of him wanting only to give in, to end the endlessness of this day. He understands the urge too well, and barely battles back the impulse to tell her everything—the red-haired woman and her family, the chief's fugue state, the island's quickening descent into so much fear and confusion. But what solace can he offer? He shakes his head. "Too much going on. Something happens, I get a call, I don't want to be out of it. But you go ahead."

She doesn't look comforted. She cuts her eyes to the door. "But if you do get a call? *I'll* be out of it." A final hesitation, and then she decides: "I'll pass for now."

She slides in beside him in the dimness, murmuring, "Sam, he was staring into the water today. Like . . . waiting?"

Throbbing behind his eyes, in his throat: the bitter needless waste, the cost of it.

"Do you think she took him to the beach?" she presses.

"I don't know, Kath. Even if he was talking, he might not be ready to remember."

"And if he is ready, and needs to?"

Woodenly, fighting his own anger: "You tell me. Shall I go and slowly, carefully, win his trust and begin to open the wound—that's just what it is, Kathy—and then hand him off tomorrow, bleeding, to someone he's never met, so they can start all over again?"

He sees the flicker of surprised pain in her look and softens his voice. "Child Services will be here tomorrow. It's what they do."

"Well, not a day too soon."

He shakes off the sting, wondering if he should take her hand, look her in the eyes; it's what she wants, of course: sincerity, even about uncertainty. If only he knew how to begin. "I know. Thank you, by the way. Not what you had in mind this week, I'm sure. But when this is all over, we'll take some days . . . just us . . ." It's a start, weak but well meant, and more honest than the Sam of a few days ago, with his blithe reassurances.

But before he can go on, she gently disengages her hand with a thin smile. "Yeah? Hurricanes and karaoke at the Pier View? That what you're thinking? Some boogie boarding?"

His smile is shaky, best he's got right now. "Sure, all of the above." So much more waits to be said, but once asked, doesn't it always ring hollow, too little, too late?

He needs to become an honest man, a kind man. He needs a drink, a hit off a J. He needs to turn away the thought of the others he failed—too workaholic, too slow to commit, too skittish when pushed—the tearful, shouted endings and the quieter, woeful partings. He needs a night of true velvet darkness to close his eyes in, a darkness beyond all thought or memory.

But there's still the incessant rain and the *ding ding* of wind in the rigging as she slides into bed, barely mussing the covers beside him, and turns out her small lamp. Her eyes don't close, even for a second.

Another squall line passes, drumming on the deck above, a crescendo of pattering, then a diminuendo, like a million fleeing tiny footsteps.

She springs up again, suddenly, and grabs a tissue from a box on her night table. Jaw set, she rips it into pieces, as if a page of unwelcome news, and then twists the larger bits and jams them in her ears. She lies back down.

He lies carefully motionless, just staring out the porthole at the deluge.

———

Later, how much later he can't guess, Sam slips silently and carefully from their bunk to pad to the main cabin doorway.

Flicking sideways away from the small light of his little game—impassive, incurious, cold—the Boy's gaze finds his.

Sam steps back, before he even realizes it, into the shadow of his cabin, retreating as quickly and soundlessly as if he were never there.

#day_seven

1

Snow had fallen heavily over the campus the day hollow-eyed, reticent Gabriel returned. Shrugging out of his huge parka, he sat silently, snow in his hair melting in the steamy heat of the little office.

The peeling radiator hissing and murmuring. His pale hands worrying each other.

Sam waited with a quizzical smile and finally leaned forward. "Well, suppose we start this way: why do you feel like you're here today?"

"I'm here for everybody." No hesitation, just a simple certainty, unequivocal, from deep within some elaborate private construct.

"How so?"

A shrug, a glance away. The planes of his face sharpened, eroded.

"Are you sleeping?"

"What? Right now, you mean?"

"No. In general, lately."

"Not so much. I'm afraid, I guess." Pure Brisbane: "afraid" pronounced "afride." "Guess" like "gis."

"Of what, do you think?"

The radiator sighing, the little digital clock rearranging its numerals.

Was it impatience? The stifling heat of the tiny office, the late hour with darkness fallen hours ago? "Do you feel threatened . . . or . . . do you feel . . . responsible for something? Like something is your fault?"

Another glance away, his dark eyes veiled. "Not yet. But ideas can spread. Maybe believing that even makes it so. And it's how they come true. Maybe . . . some shouldn't be talked about."

"Which ideas are those?"

Gabriel's hands had gone still as cold statuary, his eyes widening and his mouth opening a little. He shook his head, mute, as if a thing named was a thing more frightening.

"Gabriel?"

When did he stand? His face twitching like some aged broken man's as he backs away.

"Gabriel, wait—"

How we flee. How Gabriel had fled—out the door and down the empty, ringing hall into the dark quad, one sleeve of his clutched parka dangling behind like a dead man's farewell.

Sam had gone after him, of course. To the edge of the lamp-lit icy sidewalk in front of Eton Hall, calling, the echo of his name fading even as he faded into the swirling darkness.

———

Daylight, like a sledgehammer, lands again and again with each throb of blood in Sam's forehead. Vertigo begins as time gaps and repeats so that the spinning of this close cabin stops and starts again. Air also touches the exposed surfaces of his open eyes and blinking does not relieve the smaller, steadier ache continuing there, as irrefutably as fact.

He turns, and blurs sharpen into Kathy's lean shoulder, her face and her red-rimmed eyes returning nothing, frightening to see; her focus is hard elsewhere, on a memory or a waking dream so vivid that this world has fled. Sam reaches to touch her hand gently, to bring her back.

Her pupils focus slowly, barely moving and shrinking to take him in. She doesn't smile, so he does, though one lip seems pasted to his teeth. Voice thick with phlegm, pinched from the soreness in his throat, he whispers, "Hey."

Recognition dawns in her eyes, but dimly, joylessly. She nods, barest acknowledgment, as if meant to discourage conversation from a stranger. It's worse than that, he knows. In the haze of exhaustion, she has let the undying doubts of mid-life turn him into a cad who's toying with her affections, with no honest intentions for the future.

"You okay?" A poor start, by any measure.

"I'll check on him." Her flat whisper sidesteps his question and accuses all at once.

She climbs out of bed; unaccountably abashed, Sam looks away from the lean body with its smooth upturned bottom and sinewy back that once stirred him, that once he found any excuse to see—a voyeur in his own cabin, or in the shower, or at night, tugging the sheet ever so slightly lower while she slept. He hears the whispery sounds of her quickly dressing and waits until her footsteps fade.

He slips out of bed and into a pair of sweats.

In the dank little bathroom, his watch reads 7:10. When did he put it on? It looks slightly fogged, as if condensation has formed behind the glass, or maybe on the surface of his own eyes, which in the mirror now regard themselves grimly; are they vibrating ever so slightly, a telltale nystagmus, or a vestige of REM sleep? The idea becomes a sort of Mobius strip: do they appear that way because they are? Suddenly, he yawns convulsively, his jaws stretching around a mouthful of tepid air, the pressure in his ears like a basso rumble even as another sound reaches him: knocking, faintly.

The top of the companionway looms suddenly, the dark small mahogany door, the tarnished brightwork latches, the *tap tap, tap tap,* of someone there. Sam swings open the door to see a little girl, Sandy Winter from a few boats down, blinking up with seemingly lashless eyes, darker tender skin beneath. "Sleeping pills? My dad wants to know if you have?"

A balance fails in Sam; his heart lurches and his head pounds to imagine a child's bewilderment at so much exhaustion, the pure innocent fear and confusion at still being awake after the stories and the tucking-in, the warm milk and the murmured endearments. Another kind of nightmare, more terrifying than any dream.

"Tell him to come over, honey. I might have, but I'll need to talk to him. Can you go get him?"

The little girl's hands ball into tiny fists, and her eyes glint dully with malice. She turns and moves slowly and wordlessly away, climbing down to the float with the stiff care of an osteoporotic. In the dimness of the cockpit of her family's yacht down the float, Sam sees a vague form stirring, a shadow—her dad, of course.

Sam waves and doesn't wait for the man to wave back before he ducks back below.

In the close dank dimness of the head again, the moment stutters and his eyes look back at him, or seem to, and his watch seems cloudy as if condensation has formed on the inside of the glass as he checks the time: 7:10.

No, because wasn't he just above decks, talking with a little—

BLLIII-IIING! His cell seems to blare, shrill. He reaches out the head door to snap it up off the hallway utility shelf.

"Yeah?"

He doesn't want to recall the voice of the kid leaking over the line, barely older than a teenager's, because the voice is from another time and place left carefully and completely behind, but apparently not after all, because now it asks, "Hey, hear this?"

"Hey" like "hi."

On the line now, there's a heavy *sssssshhhhht-click*—a weapon locked and loaded.

He can never be quick enough to yank the cell away from his ear in time, to not be deafened by the gunshot, a sound so sudden and so impossibly loud that it seems to echo forever, if only for him to hear.

He yanks the cell away, gasping, too stunned for fear—until it begins anyway, a prickly sweat of dread that now slowly turns him to see the Boy and Kathy standing there, side by side, just outside the open head door, staring at him.

He blinks, dazed.

Her voice seems to rise out of static: "—talk?" She nods topside.

2

Above, the marina is all dampness and glare and noise—water lapping nonstop as if the day weren't windless and oddly still, halyards *clang clanging* against boom and mast as if somebody's bungee has come loose and there's a gale blowing. Steam rises off the wet decks and dock in the sun that hammers his head like a fist.

To the south, Sam glimpses whiteness rising and shifting into the sky, a bank of sunlit fog obscuring the tips of masts and spars, rolling in from the channel to finally turn the sun itself into a throbbing circle.

He and Kathy sit across from each other on the cockpit benches like a couple out for a daysail, both blinking at the brightness.

In the dimness below, the Boy waits; Sam can see him at the dinette again, so sweetly, sadly patient that he can understand how Kathy can't understand it: how Sam could leave the talk this boy has needed for days to others, to strangers, after they have shared these close quarters and lived the length of so many hours together.

"Try again, Sam. You can reach him. Something's wrong. Before something goes wrong."

Sam shakes his head, searching for focus, but he notices too much: the white sky closing on masts and stays, sun alternately dimming and glinting off channel water, Kathy's gaze which seems vague and resolute at once, as if she is reading her lines from cue cards or has memorized them and needs a beat to recall.

"It's just a few hours. Child Services . . ."

She studies him, shaking her head. Deciding, apparently. "Okay, then. Take him with. I'll be packing my things."

"You're . . . what?" It adds up, finally. His reticence about the Boy fits too perfectly with what she believes is his reticence about her; it's wrong and unfair, but even now the Boy is watching from below, and every argument feels like equivocation, too scattered and haphazard to firmly, quickly grasp and offer.

What was he about to say? His mind is worried about itself; hers worried about his, probably, too, and vice versa.

What's needed is bended knee and ring, too far beyond them both on this torpid, punishing morning. After the accumulated ceaseless hours have weakened and numbed and confused, doubt comes too easily, trust and faith too hard.

How can he even begin to know? What part of the urge to cling to her, to promise her everything, is fear—of nights looming without another voice to hear but his, or worse, none but those remembered? Or is it another fear, that she will see perfectly the blind man he has been?

The last distance between us, always the longest.

She sighs. "It's time. I always thought you were half here. Now I know it. You lost a patient, so you're hiding until you get your nerve back. Until then, I'm pretty much just . . . a party gal. Fisherman's daughter, coffee shop waitress thought she won the lottery. Lazy *and* stupid. Maybe they'll take me back. When things get back to normal."

Does every failure guarantee another? The world tilting, he's sliding backward, reaching out too late. "Kath, you're just tired, we all are . . ." He makes a move toward her, already knowing better.

She steps back, shaking her head. "I know you believe your own lies—but don't try to talk me into them again. I'm just someone who doesn't threaten you. This is all a vacation, and that's not good enough for me anymore." She turns her gaze from his first. "You go on ahead with him."

"Kath—"

She flinches, her eyes quick and furtive. "Don't, okay?"

———

The Boy ascends into the light, his eyes calm and unblinking as he looks from Kathy to Sam, and they wordlessly climb down to the float and head up the dock ramp to the gate together.

Grief clogs Sam's throat, the tightness of withheld tears crowds his chest when Kathy grabs the Boy, clinging hard, whispering fiercely, "Bye bye, you. Bye."

The Boy blinks rapidly, confused, his eyes dark with fear.

Kathy just nods once at Sam, lets go and hurries back to the boat to pack while she still can, wiping at tears.

Sam feels a surge of optimism as sure as his despair moments ago. No worries; he will find his way back to her, of course—when the Boy is safe, when the world has slept, when they can find their footing and their careful, purposeful balance of joy in the moment again. Everything is temporary.

Sam takes the Boy's hand with a wink. "Good to go, Admiral? See Paula?"

———

Through the damp of last night's deluge, Sam walks his bike and the Boy along the bay front lane, this morning devoid of the usual joggers and cyclists. Approaching the long, rust-stained concrete quay of the island ferry terminus, Sam sees the hulking stern of the dead *Sea Mist 1* still bobbing uselessly and wonders if they've expedited replacement. By the open air shed of the terminal, the first tourists have gathered, or the last, more accurately, of the block-long line already formed to wait for it—families and college kids and their gear, a confusion of color as they mill in murmuring groups. A hundred? Two? More, of course, since their numbers disappear around the far edge of the terminal.

Before they're spotted and mobbed, Sam quickly, gently touches the Boy's shoulder, steering them around the corner of a kitsch emporium and along a narrow access lane to the beachward boardwalk.

The boardwalk is empty too, but littered, trash-strewn, soaked and steaming in the intermittent baking sun, the eerie stillness like a held breath foul with the stink of low-tide mudflats, dead fish, rotting clams.

Up ahead, in the shimmer of damp heat rising from the planks, a pile of dark soaked clothes seems to stir. Foreboding stops him: what's happened here? Everywhere?

Sam smiles grimly at the Boy. "Wait here?"

He rushes forward in jarring steps along the planks, sunlight flaring in the dim periphery.

The body twitches as Sam kneels beside it. A face turns to his, bleary, sagging, foul.

Sam rears back, gasping, but already another sound reaches him from yards away off the side of the boardwalk; in the dunes, another form is stirring, another pile of soaked clothes rises, a pale drawn face, a hand pointing at him: a tourist, laughing woozily: "Pills? A drop in the ocean, man, you have no idea!"

The two stare at each other, red-eyed, haggard.

In his pocket, Sam's cell bursts into a buzz, its ring piercing like a klaxon. He yanks it out but then hesitates, afraid. Whose voice will it bring him this time? He winces as he brings it to his ear.

Paula's voice crackles through, a quick single syllable: "Sam?" And then again as he stands there, his throat raw, words somehow lost to him: "*Sam?*"

3

When did the light in his windows go from gray to orange, the day descend? Bent beneath the side of his head, Chief's arm stings with pins and needles and barely straightens. He flexes his toes to help his heart bring blood to where it doesn't go much these days, and his arch begins to cramp, the tendons there pulled taut, hard as rebar. He stifles a gasp and sits upright, the sheet falling away, his gut trembling, and shuts his eyes to breathe through it.

No way now—to fool himself enough to lie back down and hope his eyes will close, or to even dream that they can, or even that they had at all during the last hours of last night.

Padding carefully into the living room, he sees her last somehow, a detail lost in the décor. She sits almost primly on the sofa, staring at nothing, sponges still taped to her knees.

The face she finally turns to his seems grayish with waxy translucence, and for a moment she regards him with the barely disguised disinterest of a stranger, until her gaze finds him anew, focusing, finally recognizing. How far has she wandered?

"You okay?" It's not a question, both know, but tacit acknowledgment that neither are particularly, even approximately, okay.

"Oh." She looks away and manages something like a shrug. "Tired, maybe, I guess."

They've taught each other well, but today the shared habitual practice of stoic grace fails her and she asks, "*Why*? Why can't we sleep?"

His eyes blur. He shakes his head, helpless. He moves to her and brings his arms around her, pulling her in. She sways a little in his grasp. "Don't know, sweetie. We're trying to figure it out. I'll see about some pills, meanwhile."

She moves away, shaking her head. She bends to tear the duct tape from around her knees, asking, "Linda? Shouldn't we check—?"

"It's barely seven. She hates getting woken up."

Quickly, almost gratefully: "Of course. Right."

"I'll call her in a while from the Jeep."

He feels her head nod beneath his chin, the hard bone and thinning hair.

Suddenly, unbidden, too much comes to him: their arsenal of hurts, their signals of forgiveness, the unfailing secret rituals of their nights, rages and vanities, the children they remain to each other, adversaries and allies.

He swallows and loosens his grip, her question and the day pulling at him. Too many days have borne him surely away to the problems of too many others, for too many years. No strength to fight the current now, and there is still trust that the shallows and the shore will be gained again, as always, in a glance, a touch, a familiar rhythm of everyday motion.

Even now she silently moves to the sink to jam on the tap and fill the coffeepot, the pitch of the swirl and gush climbing as it tops. Clatter of silverware, plates, the *click, click woosh* of the stove burner.

The sand is still damp and cool with dew, the Jeep's windshield streaked and smudged with it as Chief steers along the straight, flat beach between Pines Beach and Ocean View. The tires bounce through ruts of harder sand, the suspension squeaking with a trebly complaint that worries a spot just above his left temple. Fog has gathered close offshore, an intermittently dense bank edging in, the sun a white disk struggling through.

The first Sleepless sit each apart in the sand, cross-legged like yoga students, motionless, until their faces turn slowly—odd how slowly—to watch him pass with impassive eyes. High school girl, tear-streaked face. Middle-aged man, sharp knees splayed, rocking. An older lady in a tent-like caftan, glaring.

But what slows him, instead, is the detritus from an odd turn of tide—a woman's floppy hat floating in the wash, a flip-flop with a broken strap sticking straight out of the sand, a bathing suit top, salt-stained, twisted in rotting kelp.

He pulls over, climbs out to pluck each from the wash to study. But for what? They could be anyone's, after all—things forgotten and swept away by the edge of high tide, or torn by the surf from a struggling woman, or worse, from one gone gladly limp and floating downward with closed eyes, filling her lungs with seawater as she descends.

He turns to the middle-aged man now staring mutely, as if trying to comprehend or recall who Chief might possibly be. Chief wonders himself today, with his service pistol buried or washed away, or just as likely tucked under some homicidal schizoid's waistband.

"Can you give us a hand this morning? We need to form a line, water to dunes, and move down this beach, even spaced. We're looking for a woman. Okay?" He looks at the others. "Folks? Everyone?"

"*Another* one?" The man wants to know, all smirking incredulity, as if Chief has personally lost two adult human beings in as many days.

"The ferry line is two blocks long already, Chief, tomorrow's sold out, too, they're saying. You get my wife on it, I'll help you search every damned foot, here to Pine Glade."

"When it gets here, we'll see who gets on it, okay? Meanwhile, we have all kinds of help on the way to deal with this."

"Not soon enough."

"Pills? It takes forever to see the doctor to get a scrip—"

"It'll all get sorted today. Meanwhile, I need some eyes looking for a missing woman."

The woman in the caftan stands, staggering a little, still glaring as she nods at Chief. Another, tall as a basketball pro, shivers and smirks in a sleeveless tee as he steps up beside her. A hollowness in his stomach, lightness in his knees, Chief swallows and turns away from the dumb slowness of these tourists, their blithe hostility, the rising edge of his own fear.

But no, crazy, because how bad can it really get? Each night without means they're all more due. It comes to him, even as one stands, and then another, to dust the sand off their legs and peer at him and one another with their mouths slackly open; he suddenly, unmistakably knows that this day, at least, will be his last without sleep.

4

"We'll be fine. It's okay." At the first soft grip of the Boy's hand in his, a knot tightens in Sam's chest as they stop a block from the clinic to stare at the crude queue of Sleepless already formed.

The Boy nods solemnly up at him, and they start forward again, even as faces turn toward them and sudden silence descends, as though they have happened upon the sharing of a secret. In that pause, faintly, the sound of the surf a quarter mile across the island reaches them and fades.

Tiny burst capillaries vein the eyes that follow them, filled with light that shut lids no longer block; sallow skin shudders loosely as though days have been decades aging these bewildered tourists who have come here seeking respite and found only interminable brightness and sound and motion. No voice rises up to whine or insist or beg for solace; these are like the faces of doomed refugees who finally understand resistance will only hasten their end.

Inside the clinic, better than fifty of them fill the waiting area, standing in small clusters, twisting their hands, peering at each other peevishly, cramping each other. One steps back on another's foot and shrugs at the other's glare. Two women spot each other across the room and mime back and forth: one makes a prayer steeple of her hands and holds them against the side of her tilted head, the other laughs and shakes hers "no," rolling her eyes.

The rest stand back and watch, as if respectfully, as Sam takes in their sheer number and guides the Boy quickly through and around the admittance counter to a seat in the back hallway. Still within earshot, they begin to murmur again among themselves:

"He's really writing scrips?"

"What I heard, why I'm here."

"Yeah, he is. Saw a guy passed out on the beach with a pill bottle in his hand. Before somebody else grabbed it."

Sam pulls out his cell and dials from still too-recent memory. It's been the number called too many nights—when he couldn't turn off the ceaseless redundancy of his own condemnation, the replaying and second guessing, the merciless voices of verdict. The voices are back again today, gleeful whispers of perfidy. He blinks and sees Kathy's face, and the Boy's, wanting only to trust, watching him, waiting.

When he opens his eyes again, out in the waiting area the Sleepless are there—as if they have always been and will always be there, watching and wanting. How far is it to go to escape them all?

The message beep in his ear startles him, and he struggles to regroup for a blank panicky second, searching for the calm, resolute tone he fails, predictably, to find once more: "Professor, hey, Sam here. Said to call first thing. I am. Please get back, soon as you get this. I do definitely have a situation. CDC should be apprised. I've left word again. This is escalating, if anything."

He clicks off and suddenly Paula is there. Has she been there, is she always? He takes in the faint puffiness around her eyes, the pallor of her lips, the weary rasp of her voice: "Howard called, it's what we heard, the D vitamins are working. But he's running out. People are lining up."

"Okay. Tell him to hand out some other tablet, nothing too recognizable, nothing with any side effects or contraindications. Maybe . . . coated aspirin. Whatever off-brand he has most of. Sure, coated aspirin."

The moment seems an echo of an earlier moment, or perhaps the earlier moment presaged this one. Or it's a rewind and replay, stuck in a loop.

Paula gives him her wary look and nods and goes off to dial Howard again.

He blunders away to the counter to take a breath, but now Andrew is too near, hovering by the sample drawer. A flash of pink, Andrew's hand slips into and back out of his lab coat pocket. Was there a glint of plastic?

It comes to Sam slowly; it's no surprise, really, given Andrew's aggrieved, prissy attitude around here; now he's stealing meds.

"Put it back, Andrew. Those samples are all we have."

Andrew backs up a step, all blinky faux-outrage, laughable. His face experiments with expressions—shock, fury, self-pity. "Jesus, Sam, one pill . . ."

"Why didn't you ask?"

"Well, what would you have said?"

Sam shakes his head, puts out his hand, as one might to a child.

"Turns out not everyone agrees with you and what you think." Andrew lifts a smug eyebrow.

Sam just keeps the stare on, his best chance, since words seem to fail lately.

Finally, Andrew sighs theatrically, digs back into his pocket, and tosses down the sample pack. "You got more of these somewhere, too, I know it. You're just holding out. You know what all this is?"

He nods at the Boy, who sits in his hallway chair, watching all, his little game a blinking rectangle in his lap. "It's because of that kid. From the day he showed up, it started. Walking him around, marina and boardwalk and back. I'm not the only one who thinks so. He's a doctor, too."

Andrew points through the plateglass window at a silver-haired man just outside, looking in.

Wearing sterile gloves and a surgical mask.

5

Sometime during the night, Cort's mother's face has become a map, all dead ends and detours, miles of bad road marked in fine red lines, branching off to smaller and smaller roads that lead everywhere and nowhere. Her eyes have yellowed; the light they give back is dull, reluctant, but her voice unnerves Cort most: thick with a wet rattling edge deeper and uglier than her usual smoker's rasp.

"You okay, Mom?" Cort stands in her bedroom doorway staring at her mother, who has suddenly become the one she hates most to imagine a decade or more from now, helpless and cruel, shrunken and squinting. The planes of her face have sharpened even while the skin seems looser, sagging. A crease crosses one cheek like a sheet mark. Her hair has thinned to clumps of strands, limp, unwashed.

What's happened? Mom isn't sleeping either, for sure, but now it's *aging* her, unless it's making Cort see things like she did in the dark last night, lying there for so long the shadows made shapes.

She's torn: stay here with Mom, or go find Madison, who last night frightened her so badly with her weird hysteria?

Her mother steps toward her, glaring for some reason, and Cort backs up; an edgy, thin scent of dried sweat over something heavier—wrong, malevolent—hits her.

She pinches off a breath, eyes darting, and offers, "Mom, I know! Let's take showers and go out for a bacon fix. Want to?"

Mom backs up a step now: "Whoa no. Not for me. This is your world now. I'm in here, I'm in here. *You* go on."

Mom is sick with something, has been sick, it must be, because it explains everything. "Mom, are you—"

A hiss, her face shuddering with unaccountable fury: "Go!"

The room seems to tilt and turn a little as Cort turns back into her bedroom to slam the door and dress, trembling with her own anger. She rubs at a spot on her forehead where a sharp pain has begun to pulse. Her throat feels tight, her stomach sour. Why does Mom have to be such a bitch, always, and even more now? Every mom knows her girl goes out with boys and lives with it as normal, which it is, anyway. But Mom needs her to lie and then is furious at the lying when she finds out; it's twisted.

In the tragically tiny bathroom with the gross gray mildew in the ceiling's corner, she peels off her boxers and tee and steps into the shower, blasting it hot to cry, fingertips hard on her scalp to scrub with shampoo. Peppermint soap from the bottle, quick with a washcloth, rinse and out.

When did she step out, dry herself? She turns from the mirror where she must be the girl looking back at herself, but it hurts to think so, wet hair plastered to a flat cheek, thin pale lips.

The room seems to slowly turn in place as Cort checks her cell—no need, anymore, for the timer and the tweet every fifteen minutes—but when she brings up Messaging to try Madison again, she sees the old cascading green thought-balloonish back and forth texts with Tay, and new incoming from Evi:

cant sleep anymore cant stay awake what's left god god

This, from best frenemy Sioux:

I know you hate me but is evi okay I got weird text have u heard from her

Scary, from Madison, who is never not the cool one, queen of smug disdain:

nowhere to run nowhere to hide

A chill lifts the tiny hairs on Cort's arms, and she quickly yanks on a clean suit, the tankini with straps that don't hurt or need pulling every five minutes. Cutoffs, thin boyfriend work shirt, and out to the front room where she slows to see Mom standing in the middle of the front room flooded with sunlight like a statue that would crumble if touched, tears running down the side of her face.

"Mom—"

"I'm sorry, baby," she whispers, tenderly. "You go on." This last like a hiss, a barely expelled breath. "Babysitting, right?"

6

Just outside the clinic doors, Silver-haired Man turns out to be a Long Island pediatrician. Sam glances again at his card, embossed in prissy serif:

Doctor Stan Fleisher, Pediatrics
Mercy Children's Hospital
Melville, New York, 10068

The day presses in, the hundred watchful faces barely yards away; he hands the card back.

The man gives a tepid, joyless smile, continuing a wandering prelude: "... vacationed years ago but now here on sabbatical, though it's not much of one, I admit ..."

Sam shifts his weight, edgy. "Sorry. I'm a little time-challenged. What's it about?"

Fleisher looks sixty-and-change years old, slim and ruddy-faced, calm and self-assured. Maybe to a fault, given the surgical mask, and what's next: "From what I'm told, you have a boy who may have answers, since cases began when he was brought in. But . . . he refuses to speak?"

So trusty aide Andrew turns out to be worse than a disgruntled employee and would-be thief, but a careless violator of physician/patient privilege, as well.

Sam looks more closely at the man, trying not to squint with the suspicion that every second with him seems to justify.

Fleisher continues blithely, blandly, "My background's in epidemiology, and from what I see, you have a communicable illness spreading on your watch, and this boy's recent and overall history is key to what sort of pathogen we're dealing with."

"Pathogen," Sam repeats flatly. "It's a theory. That's why you're wearing the mask?"

"I've been sleeping fine, Doctor. I'd like to keep it that way. Can't say the same for you, can we? How many nights has it been?"

They're rounding the wrong corner; Sam is attending here, no jurisdictional ambiguity, he'll ask the questions, thanks very much, and damned if he'll call this glad-handing blowhard "doctor." He fixes Fleisher with a flat gaze. "The Boy's been sleeping, no problems. How do you account for that?"

Fleisher seems to be suppressing laughter. "Come on, Harvard, could be a thousand reasons, a thousand times too many variables. Typhoid Mary, for instance, had no symptoms. It's infectious disease boilerplate, pre-med."

Weariness pulls at Sam. Too many variables would be too many to contemplate at present, so he won't. "And . . .?"

"We need to isolate the boy, make sure he's not spreading it further, and strongly encourage him to share everything he knows."

The man smells of Phisohex or some other dermatological soap, old cologne, cigarettes, some vague underlying sourness.

The skin below his eyes looks powdery, pink. Makeup? Sleeplessness exacerbates pre-existing issues, and the language of "isolating" the Boy and "encouraging him to share" suggests there may be some at hand.

Sam hesitates, pretending to think it over. As if learning a new word, he repeats it: "Encourage . . ."

Fleisher presses on. "Hemorrhagic fevers, Marburg, Ebola—anyone close to you ever die of one of these?"

Now it fits: someone close to this man has, of course. Grief, guilt and sleeplessness have conspired to conjure a waking dream of redemption, a last chance to relive some personal drama with a better ending. "Thankfully, no. But—"

"Kaluamba, Congo. One boy, back from clearing traps in the jungle. Finally told his story. The slow, clumsy monkey they caught, butchered and ate. If he had only told us sooner. If only."

Slow, clumsy monkey? Well, why not? Or why not a meme gone viral as a hashtag, or Gabriel's dreamtime coming through a hole in the world? What is there to say any of it's wrong? "Say you're right. What can you hope to achieve when so many already have whatever it is? Probably some have already gone back to the mainland with it too. You're too late there."

"Four people with Ebola virus got on planes out of Kinshasa. If it had been twenty, we probably wouldn't be here to discuss it. And if we don't get to the bottom of what's happening here, and take steps to contain, it may well be hundreds more who return to the mainland."

Doubt nags at Sam; every moment a crossroads, only hindsight to guide us. But no one is bleeding from the eyes here, so no, nobody is "encouraging" the Boy to speak before he's ready, not on his watch.

"O . . . kay. Well, thanks, but I have patients waiting, as you can see. I'll take it under advisement." Sam tries not to back away too quickly.

Fleisher nods, his eyes shining. "You really think he doesn't know anything?"

"Well, like I said, under advisement. Meanwhile, I do have other patients."

"Of course. I'll check back. But I do think a headcount and quarantine are worth considering, at least until we know more. After all, if it turns out you're wrong to do it, what harm really? Compared to not doing it when you should have? Think it over," Fleisher pauses for effect, and gives the appellation a plummy, ironic twang: "Doctor."

Their expressions shift through poor imitations of deadpan defiance, restrained hostility, chilly dismissal.

Sam turns from him and heads back inside with an even, purposeful pace, refusing to look back.

#

As the island's highest point, Regis Dune is named on any U.S. Geologic topographical map of Carratuck and environs. In hurricanes past, Norman and Ida, and of course Sandy, when much of the island became not so much flooded as simply overrun by the ocean, Regis Point remained above sea level.

Today it seems to hover, surrounded by the misty whiteness of fog dissipating in the island's warmer air. A GTE utility truck has pulled up, and cell-infrastructure maintenance engineer Carl Blonner climbs out. His eyes are reddened, dark-circled as he talks into his cell phone, staring up at the tower. It's sixteen years and a few months old, with three eighty-foot high, die-cast, anodized aluminum support struts, and twelve mounted, variable-azimuth full bandwidth receptor dishes sprouting like steel blossoms up top.

Blonner's voice sounds level, utterly calm and certain as he opines, "It's just some kind of signal coming over the bandwidth, disrupting everybody's brain wavelengths, I'm betting."

Over the line, GTE Senior Field Engineer Tony Blaistro adopts a reassuring tone, as if talking to a man with a gun on a hostage: "Hey, sure, Carl, could definitely be. Sounds smart. How you feeling, anyway?"

"Me? Had a mother of a headache, but that's gone. So all good, thanks, but I got a lot on my plate here."

"Why not come in and we can talk about it? Maybe come up with a solution together, you know, before you go and—"

"—gonna take out the landline switchbox, too," Carl decides. "One right here, highest point on the island. Hank, I'm sorry to say, but I gotta seal this sucker up. People need to be protected."

"Carl—"

"It's okay, you don't need to say anything. You'd do the same thing, Hank, for me and mine."

Carl hangs up. He smashes his cell phone carefully against a cyclone fence post, and then underfoot.

He pulls an axe out of the back of his utility Jeep and carries it to the cyclone fence surrounding the tower. He could unlock the gate padlock there, *but why bother? He swings the axe in a single accurate blow and lowers it to examine the cleft hasp with a nod of satisfaction.*

At the base of the tower, he pauses and swings again, splitting the hasp of the next padlock. He yanks it off the control station housing door and tosses it aside. Inside the housing, there's a nest of landline wires and circuits and switches he'll destroy before he goes for the cell signal junction box a few yards away and the tower strut support cables after that.

The first shower of sparks is like a beautiful reward for best intentions and earnest efforts on behalf of all, and Carl imagines the heartfelt thanks of a grateful company and of citizens everywhere whose brains have been saved, to think and dream of a future filled with equal sleep for all Americans, from every walk of life.

7

Along the beach, sun barely cuts the salt mist and the ocean looks oily and slow, gleaming heavily. Cort walks south toward Sea View to try to find Madison; the servers are back online, but still Madison has failed to return anything, texts, tweets, even an email, so not like her, since she lives with her eyes fixed on her cell screen.

Cort pauses to check #sleepless43 yet again, shaking her head at just how massively multiplayer this truly idiotic contest has become. She stabs the timeline and flicks the screen to scroll back, but still can't find the last of the new players and their absurdly gleeful updates and dopey emojis.

She looks up, turning again and again to see only still dunes and the same sliding sea at the far edges of her sight, but the motion she thought she saw feels like the beginning of more—of gathering ghostly forms from the private world behind her eyes, floating there now even when her eyes are open, too open, wide and aching.

Mom should be here, she thinks. Out of that place smelling dusty and sour, away from the TV and the cigarettes with all the nicotine and tar killing her every minute of every fucking day, another less to share with anyone else. It's selfishness on the surface, but really it's fear inside that drives her apart, deeper even than anger—fear like everyone's, of finding no one, and so to cover it up you deny you need anyone or anything, ever. Just vodka, cigarettes, TV.

Ahead, a group is in a circle, motionless, staring down. A game, a new-agey therapy thing, some kind of ceremony?

Cort approaches, tingly with unease, already half-wanting to run, to hide before more blame finds her. No one glances up. A few thumb cell phones, another starts to cry softly. Cort looks down and her lungs tug in a breath all at once as if it might be her last, to see someone who breathed theirs days ago.

The Boy's mom lies half on her side in the wet sand, motionless, naked, the palest gray and blue of nothing that could be alive. A strand of kelp is plastered across her neck in a shape like an "S," a tiny crab crawls in the shell of her ear, another crosses her hairline, picking its way toward milky eyes fixed on nothing.

The world slides, the sky plunges; the beach seems to rear and plummet with every jarring step as she runs by a jetty and a lifeguard stand and the chief roaring by in his Jeep, until she's lost track of how many houses and lanes and bunches of tourists standing around dumbly looking at nothing she's passed, until she's slowing to finally fumble for her cell again in her pocket, to press his name, finally. Her breath is gone, but the words still spill from her lips in gasps when he answers, "Cort?"

"Tay, meet me, it's horrible! I just saw her, she was staying on our lane, the lady I was supposed to babysit for . . ."

"Wait, hello? Who? The—"

His voice doesn't fade or sink below a wave of static; it simply vanishes, into nothing more than the nothing she hears now, all she has to cling to.

"Hello? *Hello?*" She grips the phone, shouting into it. And then pulls it closer to switch to messaging, but the screen locks there, dead.

With a low sob of fear, Cort stabs uselessly at the screen again and again, her link to everything suddenly cut, gasping at this cruel betrayal, stabbing over and over at it only to see now the white Arial letters in the blackness of the upper edge of her screen, spelling out the flat refusal of what she has never needed more: "No Service."

8

Whatever keeps the world in place while we move has weakened, and the foggy beach sways in a haze of light as Chief climbs out of his Jeep and approaches the cluster of stunned vacationers. They step back and watch him, slack-jawed and wary.

One clears his throat nervously. "It was me who called, sir. I said we should. Call."

Chief nods. "You found her like this? Anyone touch anything?"

They trade glances like guilty children. "Yeah. No one, none of us. She the kid's mother? From the picture?"

Chief's already crouching by the drowned woman, turning back the first surge of nausea at the stench, and the small strange ache at the loss of a stranger. He pulls a camphor stick from his pocket, dabs beneath his nostrils, and lets the details of the scene hit him how they will before he works his way down the basic first-responder forensic checklist.

"Is she—"

He doesn't look up. "Folks, nothing else for you to do here. Please step away."

Chief takes in her pallor, gently brushing aside sand to check for dependent lividity where one hip has run aground. He flicks a tiny crab away from her forehead and lets his gaze travel, from her small white breasts laying flattened against her chest to where one thigh leans demurely on the other, to where the toes of one blue foot point at the sky, the other turned wrong, half-buried.

He starts again, establishing ID first, comparing her general size and hair color to the woman he remembers too well from the nanny cam video, and her wrists for the old scars. Check, and check. He wishes he had a name, for whatever else it might reveal about her and her boy—motive, next of kin—but his two calls to the owner of record of their rented bungalow have so far gone unanswered.

He sighs as a new, deeper fatigue weighs on him; he's got two on ice that the mainland coroner's office is late to pick up, now plus one. In the substation's makeshift cold storage, three's definitely a crowd.

He stands slowly, joints swollen and aching, moving to the Jeep to open the back and drag the stiff, heavy utility tarp out and over to the woman. Panting slightly, he pulls the grommeted edge over her drowned face and her eyes open on nothing.

He straightens and points at two young guys gaping and blinking at him. "I need a second to phone this in, and then I'll need you two to give a hand with her. Nice and easy, into the back of the Jeep?"

They nod dumbly.

Chief steps back, turns away again and speed dials his cell, looking off at the windless gray day, the line of smooth breakers, the bank of fog offshore, hovering.

"Sam, listen, they found her." He hadn't meant to blurt it, and lowers his voice: "Yes, the kid's mother. Drowned. Yeah. Sam, what the fuck have we got here? Where is EPA, CDC? Is any—"

A stocky, hirsute little tourist snaps a cell pic of the corpse, stopping Chief mid-word.

"Sam, gotta go." He clicks off and lunges at the man with something between a laugh and a sob of incredulous fury. "Mother*fucker*."

The man cringes, sputtering, as Chief yanks the cell away and tosses it sidearm, spinning and flashing into the day's lazy surf.

Another tourist laughs outright, but all fall silent and a few step back at Chief's glare.

The worst in everyone is emerging, but how much, how far, how bad? How ugly can ugly get?

As if in answer, his earbud chimes softly. He does his own half-turn now, choking back a curse, and then he pulls just enough of his own cell out of his pocket to see the ID: *Howard's Odds 'n Ends.*

What now? Torn, Chief glances back at the crooked square of tarp. Howard is a prissy, lonely old mama's boy who lucked into the family business, but not one to call for idle chat. Chief clicks him through. "Chief here."

Howard's voice sounds a little breathless, pitched low: "Chief, listen, I got some guy here says he's a doctor—"

The man's voice simply disappears.

"Hello?"

Chief pulls his cell away from his ear to frown down at the screen. His service bars are gone, and he curses softly as he flicks the phone off and then back on again. "Searching," it tells him, and he stares down at it, waiting.

9

Flashing, fading, vanished: Sam's hope against hope—that he has heard the chief incorrectly—is just more wishful thinking, more childish urge to deny. We shut our eyes, but the unseen thing still looms.

His gaze darts sideways down the short hall to where the Boy sits with his feet dangling, urgently lost in the quest of his never-ending game. He wants to go to him, to gather him up and turn his face from the world and murmur reassurance until his little body sags again with sleep. But what reassurance is true today? That the falsehood of placebos is true enough for some, that sleep always comes to us in the end?

Cell in hand, he turns toward the waiting area where too many others wait. From an exam room to his left, the cry of another sleepless child rises to hover and fall and climb again.

He wants to loosen the grip of his own hand clutching at his hair, to ease the throb of fear in his temples and the clenched pit of his stomach. He wants to cut and run and find someplace to drink again the sweet air in deep draughts like a balm to spiral him downward and away.

He rubs a hand over his eyes, but now the cell in his hand is buzzing like an angry insect, and he yanks it up and swipes. "Hello?"

A voice crackles through, loud, trebly, welcome. "Sam? It's Donald Hale. I—"

Breath caught in his throat, Sam tilts his head, straining to hear the next word that will finally offer respite, encouragement, solace, drugs, a team of specialists, or a personal psych evaluation.

Unaccountably, the silence on the line shifts into a different deadness, like the nothing from which too many voices have emerged, from which too many truly awful sounds have lately leapt into being, jack-in-the-box-style.

"Can you hear me?" Sam fairly shouts, "Hello?"

Nothing, less than, since nothing more emerges from it.

"Hello?"

#

On the bridge of Sea Mist 2, *(U.S. Navy-ret) Shell Point-to-Carratuck Ferry Captain Doug Ostermeyer is bent over laughing and doesn't know why. The joke Bob Estes has just told him seemed funny, but what was it again? Estes rocks forward and back in front of the radar and Concord displays, making a helpless little hooting noise, his shoulders quaking.*

Fog is condensing on the wheelhouse plexiglass, little rainbow droplets threatening to gather in windblown rivulets; it's thick out here like weather service said, but since yesterday's scrapped run from Carratuck, he's been politely encouraged to deal with it, revised schedule, late start and all. No problem, really; with Loran and full radar up, Ostermeyer judges them good to go at fifteen knots, halfway there, which is funny too, because every day in every way he's somewhere and back in an endless round trip, so even when he's in one place or the other, he's still halfway there, right?

It's all funny anyway; the all-nighter last night had him kind of in that window of urbane, cavalier irony he sometimes finds between vodka tonics two and three, before it all goes vague and hopeless. And then he spotted the VM from the Ferry Service calling him in, smack in the middle of three days off. For time and half, who wouldn't sober up? He sways a little, reaching for the chart table, knocking over a pile of weather or shipping lane advisories or whatever, but what was the joke again? The bird from the pet store, or the night golfers, or the guy waiting online in heaven?

The first thing he sees of the blue water Chris-Craft fishing rig ahead is a foot of flying bridge UHF antenna a fraction of a second before his bows lift screaming as they smash through and over the smaller boat, crushing the fiberglass hull, freeboard and cabin decks in a shredding, shuddering screech of torn metal and terrified human screams.

The moment shatters into pieces too: ferry passengers are thrown off their feet; near the rail, those clinging see a severed limb float by, shockingly pale in a patch of black water. A spark from the impact ignites the smashed rig's fuel, spreading flames along the roiling surface. Mouths open and close, gibbering sounds emerge, stunned eyes rolling wide at others as some run to the stern to see the props fouled with debris, sucking half a corpse below, one arm waving lazily as it rolls and disappears beneath the churn.

In Suffolk County windbreakers, county police search team members Bill Helke and Scott Ledding scramble to their feet, one helping the other up.

Nearby, Anne Datz, M.S.W. is on her knees in a dark summer weight pantsuit, clinging to a briefcase bearing the insignia: Suffolk County Child Services.

In the stern, Bishop-Merigen Pharmaceutical tri-state area sales account executive Sue Menniger staggers in less than sensible shoes, stumbling over her roll-on suitcase full of bulk bottles of Ambesta.

In the starboard bow, dabbing his bleeding forehead with a handkerchief, Harvard Psychology Department Co-Chair Professor Malcolm Hale climbs to his feet, gasping. He sees a few others step from the rail, faces white with shock, and a mother pulling her little girl to her feet and into a quick embrace, murmuring, "You're okay. Are you okay? You're okay."

He pulls his little cell from his pocket to try Sam Carlson again, and curses softly—still no service bars.

10

Entering Howard's Odds 'n Ends, Chief pauses to wipe at his eyes and try to clear his vision; spots have begun to float in the periphery, afterimages seem slow to fade. Down at the far end of a narrow aisle, there's a jumble of color as tourists crowd together against the pharmacy counter—the khaki of shorts, pale blue jeans, multi-colored tank tops and rock tees. The smell of old sweat and musty dirty hair, like a nursing home room with the windows and doors shut too long, makes him wince, and the crowd of Sleepless barely budges to grant him passage.

"Coming through, okay? Excuse me . . ."

A few finally step aside, muttering furiously down at their cell phones, cursing and stabbing vainly at buttons and touch screens. One looks up and around: "Bars? Anyone?"

"Uh uh. You?"

"—signal?"

"Fuck's sake. No one?"

Chief wedges into the frontmost dozen to see Howard's dead land-line dangling from the counter, swinging by its cord. Wide eyes darting, Howard is backing away from the anxious crowd, and from one man in particular—gray-haired, in wire-rims and surgical mask.

"Look," the man pauses to read Howard's nametag, "Howard. We've been over it. These folks need medication whether they have a scrip or not. I'm a doctor, I'll take full responsibility for dispensing it."

Chief edges clumsily around a tall gawky kid into sight: "Hold up! What the hell is going on?" A little attitude can establish much in crowd control situations, or it used to; he puts a hand on his pistol's stock, protruding from his holster. It's an old, spare .38, enough to send a message, usually all that's required.

The gray-haired man turns to him, oddly calm, maybe even smiling behind his weird surgical mask. "Officer, good. I'm Doctor Fleisher, attending at Mercy Pediatric in New York, and I believe we're all—"

"Hold up, please. A doctor, good, okay. Let's take this whole discussion to Doctor Carlson, where it belongs." He lets his gaze sweep the room, taking in the crowd. "And the rest of you folks go on back to wherever you're staying. Let's clear this area now."

Fleisher lifts an eyebrow at the chief. "I'm not so sure this crowd will be easily persuaded, Officer. Nor that they should be. Things have gotten needlessly out of hand, and perhaps another professional's point of view would be helpful."

Chief hesitates. The guy looks and sounds the part, and though it's not great to wonder, maybe Carlson *is* in over his head.

The surfer Chief has known for years steps up and lowers his voice, as if there's a confidential chat to be had in front of these forty or so anxious tourists. "Chief, dude, come on, man. No one has to know you were even here. Don't you want a pill? Half one? Catch a few hours' worth?"

Chief blinks, trying not to imagine it. Holding his shoulders up against so much gravity has been such an effort; his eyes are burning and his brain is filled with a noise like something frying. Why *not* imagine an hour of relief from it all? Or even just a single blessed moment of finally letting go and giving in?

Fleisher steps closer to Howard: "Exactly what meds have you been dispensing?"

Howard's mouth opens and closes, soundlessly.

A sallow-faced middle-aged woman steps up, dressed absurdly teen, her palm out, revealing three little white pills. "They've been giving us these."

Fleisher actually bows, ever so slightly, with exaggerated courtliness. "May I?"

She thinks, or appears to, before she shrugs and he plucks a pill from her palm, lifting it close, squinting.

He laughs. "You've been duped. These are aspirin." He bites into it. "Over-the-counter, coated, small dose."

A cry goes up, barely intelligible, of incredulity. A weathered local shouts the general sentiment, "No fucking way!"

A young mom in garish makeup brays, "I got a kid who needs to sleep! I'm not going anywhere until I get him something!"

A frat guy tries to push by. "They're just holding out. They have 'em, in back, somewhere, they—"

Chief pushes him back, pulling his gun. A surge from behind pushes another Sleepless into him, and as he stumbles, his arm is jerked backward by recoil from the deafening sudden whip-like crack he only now realizes is a gunshot.

Off to one side, a barbecue propane tank seems to levitate and expand, making a large complicated noise, a kind of shriek with a low concussion, as lawn chairs and chaises burst into flame and go flying, igniting a display, a tourist, and a medicine cabinet behind the counter.

The crowd surges again in a din of shouts and screams of unrecognizable bits of words, as unrecognizable bits of objects appear at their panicked feet and on their heads and shoulders like burning, flung confetti. The crowd breaks apart, fleeing in confusion, pushing one another aside.

Singed, Howard swipes at the burning medication shelf, but his own sleeve goes up.

Chief spots him and hops the counter to roll him on the floor, dousing the flames, while almost everything else seems to have ignited at once, fire climbing the walls in flickering, blinding sheets—roaring, it turns out flames do roar—and crackling with sharp reports like more gunshots.

Chief yanks Howard to his feet, pushing him stumbling out the door between the plateglass windows and burning displays, after the last fleeing Sleepless. Behind them the plate glass breaks into sharp, shining slivers as a flash of blackish flame reaches through for them and they stagger forward to their knees.

Chief looks back at the pharmacy. Flames pour upward from the windows into roiling blackness; the tinkling of glass continues from somewhere inside; another, smaller explosion pushes the burning air outward, hot on his face. Still on his knees, he looks the other way at the Sleepless backing away across the lane, manic, shrieking, laughing. They shout like drunks, stumbling, hooting:

"Lyin' motherfucker!"

"I'm getting on that ferry, steal a boat if I gotta."

"I'm coming with!"

"The marina, let's do it!"

Chief watches them as he climbs to his feet, and he understands everything in a prickly rush, all at once.

He backs away, turning finally, running for his Jeep.

11

Rushing along the Lighthouse Lane boardwalk toward the beach, Cort tries to slow herself down, to stop and breathe, but things are spiraling the way disasters do on TV, when every moment is more likely to bring something scarier than the one before. If there's one bomb, have they ruled out two? If there's one shooter, is he acting alone?

This is some completely new thing: just weirdness spreading, overwhelming people. Mom, and the little boy's mother (though if Cort had shown up that may have been different), and others, too: the couple shouting at each other on their share house porch, the families sitting on the sand staring out to sea, the old guy laughing so loud at nothing. Nobody has slept, it seems like, and everybody's going crazy.

Two kids, maybe twelve years old, look like they've just awakened in their clothes, bed heads and wrinkled shorts and Ts, standing dumbly with upturned faces. Beside them, three ladies in bathing suit tops and shorts who could be wearing more turn in place, looking up behind Cort and then back at each other with their hands floating up.

What is everybody gawking at? Cort turns and sees it: a smear of oily smoke staining the sky over Pines Beach, turning the daylight dim and orangey. Ashes float down like gray leaves onto the rooftops and porches, dunes and bramble. The smell of burning reaches her, some shocked low voices, some curses as a few continue to stab pointlessly at their cells.

Her ears feel hot. A hissing sound like static closes in and then fades. The surf a half a block away? A few tourists take off toward town, jogging and shouting at each other. One almost trips, laughing. A family steps slowly out onto their porch, shielding their eyes, pointing, mouths slack.

Tay, Mom, where are they?

Mom would still be in the unit two miles up the beach, where else, so okay. But Tay, who knows? With some new girl from Five Towns or Westchester, in their same little boat shack, getting her high and making her laugh until she lets him feel her up, for starters, anyway.

Two older guys march by, their heads twitching with anger or panic, clutching dead cell phones. Behind them, past the worn boardwalk steps that climb the last dune to the beach, Cort recognizes Sioux's gray cedar and glass beachfront house where they all took X last year and ended up huddled in Sioux's bedroom laughing and crying until finally they crashed, thank God, sprawled across each other with sweaty hair and blotchy skin and sour breath from the awful speed rush of it.

Cort crosses the lane and heads up the wooden steps to the landing by the glass front door. She peers through the sidelight at the skylit foyer, past the broad stretch of light wood floor to the kitchen where she remembers everything possible was made of stainless steel, like a chem lab or a slaughterhouse.

Halfway down the gallery, it looks like a painting has fallen from the wall, one of those big rectangles of solid color that cost more than Cort's whole house. Cort drops her gaze to the door in front of her and sees now it's actually open a few inches.

"Helllloo?" she calls out, nudging it open a few more inches.

A whisper, a giggle, like children hiding.

Cort steps carefully inside, wary.

Sioux Klein and Madison Schone are standing on the granite kitchen island counter in their underwear, toes painted alike with dumb glitter polish, giggling hysterically, dirty hair hanging in their faces. Their bodies look loose and blotchy beneath orangey tans. On the floor, a bottle of vodka lies spilt sideways, a puddle shining.

Cort slows, finally seeing the single clothesline they have draped over an overhead beam, the ends tied into rough nooses around their necks.

"Hey, what are—let me—" Cort rushes forward, but Madison stops giggling long enough to slur:

"No, we're doing this. Get away!"

Sioux fights a blurt of giddy laughter, loses. She sways, her shoulders shaking, straightens, sways again, the rope tightening with a faint creak, the flesh on the side of her neck bulging around it, reddening.

"Owwww," Madison whines, clawing at the rope around her neck, the slack gone as Sioux staggers. "Wait . . ."

Cort's already clambering up the counter, grabbing Sioux by the waist: "Wait, stop. Let me, okay? And then, you know what? We just leave."

Sioux tries to pull away, tightening the rope around Madison's neck again. "There's no ferry!" Her voice is a shrill, wet sob.

Cort shakes her head, tightening her grip. "There will be."

"It'll be too late! It's already too late! We stopped the game, but we can't sleep. We *can't*!" Her mouth twists into an ugly smile as tears begin to stream.

Cort counters, "What about the boats, the marina? Somebody will give us a ride."

"To where, somewhere we aren't? Where is that place? To someplace, but why, when we would be there, just the same, with this light. This noise. With my stupid fucking brain frying!"

Madison shouts, "Shut up! Jump! Now! Or I will!"

Sioux twists out of Cort's grip and simply steps off the countertop. How can she be so heavy that she falls so impossibly quickly, like some huge, invisible thing has smashed her downward from above?

On the countertop beside Cort, Madison gasps and sputters, arching up on her tiptoes as Sioux's counterweight pulls the rope taut. Her hands scrabble at the noose that has become too tight around her neck for her clumsy fingers to grab. Her nails claw at her skin, streaks of blood appearing as she sputters, eyes bulging.

Where is—something—anything—to cut the line? Cort's eyes dart over the cabinet faces, drawer fronts, countertops. There! A wooden knife block offers up black handles. Cort leaps down and pulls one, which turns out to be a bread knife, but there's no time to turn back for another. She rounds the island and grits her teeth and stands on her tiptoes to reach above Sioux and saw at the rope—some kind of boat rope, thick and braided, it turns out, not clothesline—and slick and waxy enough for the blade at first to skid rather than bite.

Seconds are all. How many does anyone have without breathing?

But even with the rope laid out like a loaf on a cutting board it would take a good minute to saw through with a bread knife, and meanwhile Sioux's feet have begun to kick against Cort's shins, heels hard, searching for purchase. One of her hands claws Cort's hair and face, the other stabs at the air like a terrified blind girl's. Cort dares to look upward, and Sioux's swollen face is a light purplish color, her lips white.

Cort drops the knife with a sob to grab Sioux around her waist again, trying to lift her to create some slack, but there is none, by a missing foot or so of clothesline, there is none.

The sound that comes from Cort is lower than a scream, a long senseless shout that begs and denies and climbs as she struggles to lift Sioux higher into the impossible air.

They embrace, slow dancing. Sioux's feet never touch the ground, kicking at nothing, and her hands find a will of their own to grasp trembling at the clothesline choking the life from them.

Hold her, Cort thinks. *Just hold her up. Just long enough for her to get her fingers under the noose.*

Behind them, above, Madison has grabbed the line just above her noose and has pulled herself upward, like climbing rope hand over hand in gym class, but without the wrap and belay around the leg. Her toes dangle just above the counter; slack sags the line between her grip and the noose, and she lets out a startled grunt, as if at her own good idea.

But then her arms begin to quiver and twitch against failure, failure surely killing her a fraction of an inch at a time as gravity wins and she drops slowly back, the rope tightening again.

Cort has Sioux in an upward bearhug, like a clumsy skater's lift, but Cort's arms, too, begin to shudder until the taut desperate urging of Sioux's body against hers stops, and a new unmovable heaviness prevails.

Behind her, toes skimming the countertop, Madison makes a last sound like a thick, wet sigh, and dangles limply to one side, turning ever so slightly, one eye still seeming to gaze at some distant point, the other simply empty.

Cort's arms give way now, too, and Sioux's feet ghost the floor, one foot sideways, the other straight and so lightly barely touching down just ahead of her, a marionette's.

Cort stays bent, squeezing her eyes shut.

Now, this is the time to finally wake. With a start, gasping to catch your breath while everything returns to the way it was before.

She opens her eyes.

Sunlight makes a shadow of a leaning girl across the floor.

A faint sound like creaking begins and stops. Begins again.

A thin smell like ammonia floats in the air.

12

Under the desk in his tiny back office, Sam has reached and pressed the sides of the phone jack to unplug it and slip it back in, but the cordless in his hand is still as dead as his cell.

He has no earthly reason to doubt it, but like everyone, he can't resist pulling the traitorous, disconnected little rectangle from his pocket to blink dumbly down at it yet again.

He steps into the hall to check; the Boy's still in his plastic chair, gripping his little game in both hands, hunched as if to make himself small, perhaps enough to crawl into that square of light and another, kinder world.

In this one, people have crossed the threshold, finally, of reality into delusion, of sanity into myriad variations of degenerative, dissociative states. Denied the outlet of dreams, the contents of the unconscious always find another way to surface. Driven by some old psychodrama of fear or vengeance, or fantasy of rescue, some deluded insomniac has cut them all off.

What's left, meanwhile, but to backtrack, retrace the origins of the unconscious idea, the involuntary symptomatic behavior spreading? But to what end, since each Sleepless now causes another, sure as the first awakened a second? The Boy or not, no matter. Fleisher is not getting anywhere near him.

Slow down, breathe, focus.

A clutter of noise bursts from the waiting area, curses and half-shouts as the newly injured crowd in. One moans, gripping one arm with the other, scorched sleeve flapping in shreds. Another smiles as if at some epiphany or mildly-amusing *bon mot*, an eyebrow and half of his hair gone. A woman picks at singed threads with a blistered hand, almost idly, in a fugue state.

Paula and Sam are already moving, gathering gauze and salve for burns and blankets to treat shock, as a man with a bleeding ear addresses the room, almost smugly, first to know, "The pharmacy. On *fire*. Some kind of argument, the cop's gun went off, something blew up. Boom."

Sam slows. "Anyone shot? Where's the cop? The chief?"

The man shrugs. Another chimes in, "Shot? Dunno. Cop took off, to maybe get help, who knows. Or just took off." He giggles.

When the next half dozen or so injuries arrive from the pharmacy explosion—more burn cases, a broken ankle, a wrist sprain, a concussion—Sam gives them each a quick look and judges them stable enough. But how many were left behind, or are wandering in shock, unaccounted for? He grabs an EMT kit from the storeroom to head over, evaluate and triage on site, but next in the door is Pete, an auxiliary fire guy with his own kit and scene assessment: a heart attack and skull fracture are down for good, and the rest of the injured have found their way here, either ambulatory or fireman-carried the two and half blocks.

Those already gathered make way grudgingly for the new arrivals, unhappy to think they may lose their place in line.

"Hey, I've been waiting—"

"You and everybody, right—"

Paula silences these with a stern look as she and Sam hand out a few last blankets and the usual Dixie cups of water, and set about cleaning, salving, and dressing the worst burns. Two turn out to be third degree and should go to the mainland for follow-up by a dermatologist.

Sam notices wary glances from a few, even as he treats them. A few looks accuse outright, and a woman in a huge sweatshirt and smeared makeup finally confirms his suspicions: "Fake pills? That's what you were giving us? Why?"

Eyes turn to Sam, the disbelieving look of the betrayed.

Sam nearly backs up a step, but finds his footing, true as any placebo: "What are you talking about? Why would you believe that?"

"A doctor showed up at the pharmacy, said so."

"And you believed he was a doctor? And that he somehow identified the pills just by looking?"

The woman looks around for support, the effort already failing as others murmur and shrug, barely able to track the substance. "Yeah, no. But—some do."

A weathered dockhand turns to the others, "What the fuck are you lookin' at, Doris? You, Chuck? You're back for more of what they gave you because it *worked*, whatever it was. Wouldn't be here otherwise. So shut the fuck up, all of you. Doc, you got ointment for this one? Looks like a bad burn."

———

Bleary, lost in the back hall, Sam turns now to find more gauze or topical antibiotic, or both. He's already unsure, but now he slows; at the end of the hall the storeroom doorway is partly ajar, the light there flickery, somehow, odd.

He moves closer, entranced. An image flashes: a smaller, darker door, a narrower hall. A fragment of a memory of a place to shut back away. A cloying rotten odor is unrecognizable, but then it all disappears into what's there anyway—the thin flat smell of floor cleaner and disinfectant, and the bright hallway to his clinic supply room.

———

Suitcase and duffel beside her, Kathy sits on a cracked leather stool at the Pier View Bar, sipping a Hurricane, rubbing her thumb along the bar's smooth worn edge of polished mahogany, the grain a rich reddish gold, curving around a darker, solid knot she knows by heart. This has been her seat so many summers, fielding the smirky innuendo of Manhattan junior bond traders, or the lame come-ons of Jersey tourists and the desperately single overflow from the Hamptons. Sam had been her storybook rescuer from all that—right up until he turned out not to be.

Bartender Seth has known Kathy her entire adult life, and knows the vague, broad facts of her serial monogamy: the surfer housepainter, the oceanography grad student, the charter fleet owner, and Doctor Sam Carlson. He eyes the duffel and suitcase and shoots her a sympathetic glance. "Hard day, Kath?"

She tries to laugh. "You have no idea."

"Sleep on it, my dad always said. As if."

They share a faint, knowing smirk, and Seth muses, "You know what's funny? We were full up at first, no one could get enough booze, a bunch even broke in and stole half my inventory, but now? It barely works. You have to down enough to kill yourself, they're saying."

Weariness feels different now, like a kind of pressure on the sides of her head, like regret, like tears behind her eyes, aching to spill. She laughs instead, but on a day when she threw back the big one, walked away from a helpless child, and all the phones went dead, like every last connection to anyone, what's funny? She's wanted to call Sam just to be sure the Boy and he are okay, and so she continues to check her little cell's bright screen every minute or so, as if the next time she'll see full signal bars and hear Sam's drowsy, wry voice on the other end, as always.

"You talk to anyone mainland? Before it all went out?"

Seth shrugs. "My sister, last night. Sounded fine. Baby crying, husband pissed off, the usual."

Suddenly, a bunch of gawking college kids crowds the entrance to the patio, shouting to anybody, "—the clinic, demanding meds! We're going in!"

At a far table, a few tourists fall silent, and then trade looks and leap up to follow. One giggles on the way out, another pumps a fist. "About fucking time!"

There have been low points over the years: repulsiveness in long supply, alcohol-fueled desperation to forget or to wallow; friends and couples, strangers and families shouting incoherently, stumbling with faces streaked by tears of bewilderment at real or imagined betrayals, fueled by alcohol and the addictive reality-show ethos of indulgence, all freak-outs and melt-downs. After a while, the view from behind the Coffee Spot counter or a Pier View barstool seemed the same, the faces and voices of the aggrieved interchangeable.

But this is a new, jubilant ugliness: young, determined, and energetic, just getting started. Kathy watches them rush out and turns back to Seth, who's seen it all twice, to gauge his reaction.

But he has stepped slowly from around the bar, staring out the side wall's bank of windows. "What the fuck—?"

Through the glass she sees the white of the fog that's hovered offshore all day—and an ugly, menacing stain spreading across it, inky smoke bil-lowing up from just across town.

She imagines enough for the moment—buildings burning, a mob of these uncontrollable, irrational idiots surrounding the clinic and threaten-ing Sam, the Boy, Paula and whoever else—and she bends to her suitcase, unzipping it, digging through, one hand finally emerging with what Sam had left behind, and that neither had been willing to try—Ambesta, the two perfect oblong pills in their pastel sample pack.

13

The faces of the drowned seem to rise, pale and bloated, behind Chief's shut lids every time he blinks, so he won't. He keeps eyes front as he floors the Jeep through a rut, rear tires spitting sand, but now the names come back too, that could be anybody's, but were theirs: Andy, Doug. Dan, expert whiner, no one lazier. Steve, all of eighteen, baby-fat and red-faced, from out by San Diego, with his Walkman headphones. Pete from Georgia, with his tyro's porn stash.

Chief gives his head a shake against the ringing shouts of these men, but the voices come back, of his guilt and his redemption in the single lucid moment of decision, one that sacrificed some and saved most, they said, and all because he *knew*. In the *Cat 3* off Guam, when the shell rolled off the rack and blew, hull breached and ship taking water fast, he *knew*: the locked bulkhead door would drown a few but keep his ship afloat. Navy let him go, sure, just as glad as he was to part ways—a quick discharge, honorable, uncontested, full benefits. Which said it all, as much as anyone could, without saying too much.

And he *knows* now, just as well, the same hard, incontrovertible truth as he hard-lefts the Jeep, fishtailing a little, roaring down an access lane behind low-end share houses halfway to the marina, where he may just have a chance to seal a breach again.

These are the shabbier, weekender two and three bedroom saltboxes, and the unshaven middle-ager in boxer shorts seems at first like the usual renter, swaying as he goes, gut sagging and smeared with white sunblock, but as the chief steers the Jeep nearly past he glimpses dull dark metal: the barrel of a shotgun almost hidden behind a pink ham hock thigh.

A prickly jolt climbs his scalp as Chief stomps the brakes, craning his neck to watch this man step to a doorway with his shotgun and the doorway open to reveal a skinny, sideburned kid in a rapper tracksuit. Some kind of thrash metal hits Chief's ears, a screech of guitar feedback lost in a sudden, thick blast of louder sound as the kid's torso bursts inward and apart into redness and he flies backward.

Chief is trapped in air that will not part for him, that slows him like water as he spins from the Jeep pulling his spare service pistol from his holster, shouting, "Police! Hold it!"

The shotgunner doesn't turn, but he hesitates, as if actually debating it.

Chief brings the pistol up two handed, but beyond the shotgunner, through the open doorway, there's a flurry of dim movement, another shriek of feedback or a girl's scream. Shotgunner steps in fast, sideways and out of view and fires again, muzzle flash lighting the room.

Chief rushes to the right of the door, crouching close, and there's another blast from inside, a sharp, snapped-off metal screech. The music is gone, and now Chief hears the weeping, worse than the scream. And the whispering, softly confiding, "Why wouldn't you just turn it down? Didn't I ask nice? Wouldn't that have been easy? Now look, look what you made me do."

Chief pulls in a breath and leans to crouch into the doorway low and fast, minimum silhouette, but he's already too late. Why does each shot sound so different? This one has a ragged, scattery sound, and when Chief has dropped and aimed through the doorway to fire, way wide, the man flips his shotgun, barrel to his own forehead.

Chief sees the man smile, or thinks he does: the queasy, mad grin that maybe is just a grimace after all, before the top of his face disappears in a red and white blur and another sharp stinging explosion shudders the air. The man remains standing for another impossible moment, his mouth a gash leaking a last vowel as he half-turns, falling, landing with a leg breaking backward beneath him. Clots of flung, dull pulp and bloody hair litter the room, a hot coppery reek rising thickly.

But for the slow ooze of pooling blood on the floor and a spark from a shattered bulb still swinging, nothing moves now, Chief as still as the rest as he stands there. How long before time begins again? How many minutes go by?

Bark of a dog somewhere, far away gush of the surf. This limp twisted broken thing that was a girl. This man-child of a boy so torn.

Chief feels a knot in his chest go loose. He pulls in a gulp of air with a gasp.

He blinks at the dead shotgunner, steps inside, and without turning feels behind him for the door and shoves it softly closed.

———

On his way to the marina, Chief skids the Jeep to a stop outside Al's Bait 'n Tackle and climbs out with the dead murderer's shotgun—a pricey little

Benelli recoilless, it turns out—and one that can blast the front door padlock hasp to a splintered twig with a single 12-gauge shell.

Plenty more inside, in boxes on shelves stocked for the shark-boaters, maybe even enough.

Some are still down from the blast at Howard's Odds 'n Ends, though others have helped out and carried a few injured away. The rest just kind of dust themselves off and even laugh as they watch the place go up. A gyp joint anyway, let's face it, selling bogus sleeping meds, and that fat ass Howard another gatekeeper prick in a world of more of the same.

But this gray-haired guy, Dale Kelso thinks, is speaking my language. He looks like some snob elite in his preppie Docker shorts and polo, the slicked-back salt and pepper hair and sleek-looking metal eyeglasses, but he's talking some sense about jokers like Carlson, who breeze in from Boston or wherever and snag the hot home girl and good job while they slum and smirk at the locals. The surgical mask is weird, but turns out the guy's a doctor, so he must know.

"Listen to me!" Dr. L.L. Bean shouts. "None of you are getting better! How many nights can you go on? Are you going to believe nothing is wrong with you and let that con man at the clinic treat you with fake pills? It's fraud, nothing less! We need to call him out, and we need to quarantine and question that boy! And find and dispense whatever real meds that so-called doctor is hoarding! You all deserve them as much as anyone!"

The skin on Dale's neck and arms gets a chill and tingle like electricity as he lifts a fist to pump, and he hoots. See, this is key, right there. Fucking-A, yes!

A cheer goes up around him—frat guys who look all right, some share house partiers, the guy from the clinic, the aide, though not anymore is a safe guess.

Mouson Hasmini knows these young people in America can be frightening, this is true, and so many these last days have been without all politeness or consideration, vulgar and wild hooligans who disrespect their elders and their women most of all in the pictures and the tight clothing and less, God forbid.

If there is a prayer to say between the morning and evening prayer times, this is the time to say it; to kneel and be washed in the sea and cleansed of *those thoughts that once were only dreams and so disappeared on waking, in sweetest light of day.*

Uncle from Nariya, nephew from Sanii, these and brother Nasir would call for punishment rightly, these who first feared for the soul of their beloved kin who left to come here and start this beach taxi Jeep business which praise God has flourished. And cousin in Sirt.

Oh, the struggle in a land of infidels to never become one but still everywhere on computers and televisions, on every screen the poison pictures you see them, as if not enough in this place in the bikini bathing suits, lying like whores writhing on their towels on the hot sand to be driven up and down and back and forth into numbness for money to send to Afifa.

So it is time now to climb from this seat out the door and kneel in this same sand and let the white shallows rush up and push and pull, clothes heavy and tugging with it, water salty like tears from our eyes, which close as they must when any man truly begs forgiveness.

But—how has his "Pine Glade Taxi Now!" beach taxi Jeep suddenly started behind his back? How have these men-children in their shirts that show their thickly muscled arms and with their hair that points up like wet bristles, and their cruel laughter and pumped fists, climbed inside his own beach taxicab?

Why shout, what does it mean? Nothing. Why lift hands to plead—not to curse, for that is for God only to visit upon us—because what does pleading mean? Nothing. Running behind, feet slowed by the loose sand, until there is not enough air in the world to stop the chest pains like a knife to bend you double? It means only the same nothing.

14

With intent, determined expressions, breathlessly, people are running. Along the beach they come, across the dunes stumbling, thumbing and shouting into disconnected cell phones, appearing and disappearing in the pall of fog already dimming into shadowless gray as the light fades with the day.

At the edge of a lane, in a last summer home, an old couple holds their drinks, staring out their bay window at a group rushing by.

Yards away, a little girl sits in the sand, crying, her mother whispering curses to no one, rubbing at her shut eyes as if the world will be otherwise when she opens them.

Useless cell in hand, Cort strides quickly along the hard sand by the tide line, eyes front, unwilling to see more than a few yards or a few moments ahead. Why look, why think, when all it brings is more of the same clutched emptiness in her stomach?

Movement teases the edges of her vision, someone running, another leaping. Shouts, the quick blare of a radio, snapped off as suddenly.

She hesitates at a voice behind her, thick with saliva and irony: "Come on with, we'll protect you!"

She turns to see a posse of guys approaching, loudmouths in jams and sleeveless tees, kids from Islip or Ocean Beach, probably, pimp-rolling and sneering: "Have some, only way to sleep—dream big, baby!" They wave a tequila bottle, and Cort tries to put it out of her mind: the sick group scene they imagine behind some dune, taking turns, or worse. How do they get this way, drawn to the grossness where nobody ever matters to anybody? Are they just so afraid?

Running seems dumb since one or more will catch her, and she'll have made herself prey, perhaps before they meant to. But can she just stand here and hope?

They square off, moving in.

One's eyes are sunken deep in purplish sockets, bulging and rolling. He reaches a hand to touch her hair.

She flicks her head away, but his other hand is there already, lightly touching her cheek, his thumb gliding over her lips. She glares, stepping back.

His smile goes crooked; his eyes widen, as if in momentary wonder. Behind him, there's a shadowy movement, and Tay is there, somehow, out of the wet gloom with a ragged piece of lumber stolen from the ocean, tarry and smeared with blood from this creep's head. She didn't even see him hit, but he drops to his knees with a trail of quick drops of blood on the sand, as his posse stands open-mouthed, motionless.

"Cap the fuckers—" he spits.

But Tay has already grabbed her hand, and they're already running. Panic has stolen her breath, her heart beats too loudly to hear a sound over, but she does somehow, hearing herself shouting nonsense: "What—Why is this—?"

"Keep moving!"

Other Sleepless loom, trying to stop them; a woman shrieks, "You're not my daughter! Never been!"

A man in a raincoat approaches. "I gotta get on the ferry. Get outta here. You guys have anything?" He reaches for them, his hands crackling in Saran wrap.

Tay yanks her sideways, away.

A "Pine Glade Taxi Now!" Jeep roars by, rear tires throwing sand, filled with whooping guys, laughing and shouting.

"Hells yeah, sand monkey!"

"Left!"

"No, that way!"

She and Tay watch the Jeep zigzag twenty or thirty yards down the beach, accelerate, and right-turn up over a dune and plow straight into the base of a powerline pole. The end of motion is too sudden, a shock, but in nearly the same instant, the dark shape of a head bursts like a jack-in-the-box from the windshield with a thick, crunching sound, and a scream from inside dies as if strangled.

A heavy black wire sags downward, swaying, and then one end of it twists down onto the roof of the taxi in a shower of smoking sparks. Inside, vague dark shapes seem to jerk in ugly lurching movements—until they don't.

Words come only in a choked whispered rush, because what words are there but these, when being awake is the real nightmare, after all: "What the fuck is . . . *happening*?"

Only the wire is alive now, sputtering and twisting, sparks now setting the seagrass on fire, hissing and crackling.

From behind them again, shouts echo in the pall, furious unintelligible curses, more laughter.

Across the sand, the ocean makes a sound like a low rumble, and then a wide distant sound like applause.

Tay's face goes crooked, eyes glittering with fear: "Come on, quick. I know where."

Behind them as she turns to look, the lights in the houses along Starfish blink out all at once, and the ocean makes its sound again.

15

In the back hallway, Sam has gone still, a roll of bandages in one hand, a bottle of clear fluid in the other.

The ceiling fluorescents make dull rectangles of light on the linoleum. The smell of burnt coffee lingers. The quick, shallow breaths he hears are his own.

Why is he back here, again? Gauze? Antiseptic? Done.

He hesitates, half-turns one way, then the other, and moves back down the short hall to the exam room area where the Boy sits in a plastic chair, eyes wide and darting everywhere.

"Holding up okay, partner?" Sam gives him a small, chancy smile.

The Boy's gaze flickers past his, and he nods slowly as he looks away.

Sam fights another instant's jittery panic; there's just no other responsibility, no other authority, no voice on the end of a line coordinating arrivals of teams of experts who will take the situation firmly and calmly in hand so he can go back to his boat and his girl and their days of wine and summer.

He moves out into the waiting area. Beyond the glass storefront-style windows, evening has somehow begun. Against the walls, Sleepless sprawl in the row of plastic chairs or sit cross-legged on the floor, still sullenly thumbing their cell phones, quietly cursing in disbelief. What have we all become? Attached to the momentary and the elsewhere, lost, unmoored.

But is he any different? Kathy's voice would be so welcome, just to hear it: the mellifluous, wry music of her complaining about mildew, wondering what to cook, whether to make Margs or Mojos for their ritual cocktail hour.

Other voices bring him back—the hum of worried murmuring, a barked laugh from a tourist with eyes fathomless black amid etched lines like dead blood-eggs in a nest of twigs.

He spins away from the sight and the thought and flips on the TV to check the news and see if there's word on the outage. A commercial for Red Bull comes on, of course: handsome hipsters with choppy hair in industrial-chic offices with lots of exposed ducts and glass, high-fiving over computer screens.

Suddenly, the urgent theme music of news blares, all horns and tim-
pani, and now a plummy, tenor voice-over demands to know: "Is heroin in
our suburbs, is your data safe from the next big virus, is your child being
stalked?" In the netherworld between news desk and backdrop of gaudy
graphics, the anchor turns theatrically to face the camera, intoning, as
always, "Breaking news this evening as—"

Gone: sound and image disappear at once as the ceiling lights click
and flicker out.

Sam's first thought is that old TVs used to go off with a fading little white
dot at the center of the screen. These days there's no final, briefly lingering
trace of what you saw—now it all it just disappears into instant blackness,
the same way voices now simply disappear into silence on a digital phone
line. The telltale traces of our world are no longer; we and all we perceive
are—and then simply aren't. Maybe there's a message there about the loss
of the afterimage or the echo that has something to do with memory and
why it matters, but right now Paula is inches away, peering intently through
this larger darkness into which every blessed thing has disappeared.

"Sam?" Why is it always her voice, out of the silence of his cell phone,
or now, out of the blackness, like a mother trying to wake a child? "Sam?"

Other voices join hers, the Sleepless indistinguishably cursing, murmuring, and in the darkness their cumulative breaths and bulk and shifting
nervousness vaguely threaten.

A small bright light snaps on, and it takes a second to realize Paula has
grabbed one of the emergency flashlights from a baseboard outlet. She
aims it away from them and the red retinas of the Sleepless gleam back
at them, like a shot taken in the dark with a cheap flash camera, so eerily
like the eyes of animals.

Nerves ease, laughter erupts here and there, and Sam hears fragments
of comments: "—fuck is going on now?"

"Phone, net, power, everybody weird, it's gotta be—"

"—even *know*?"

"—generator?" Paula is saying now, or asking, or has just said or asked.
Sam shakes his head, trying to keep up. In the waiting room, a Sleepless
finds and flicks on another flashlight. A circle of faces appears there,
peering at one another.

Useless thoughts scatter others: jerry can, powerline connectors like
jumper cables, electrocution. But the Boy worries him most: "Paula, grab
me a light too. I'll get to it. Where's the Boy?"

Paula swings the beam behind them to find the Boy there in his seat
against the hallway wall, oddly calm, even woeful, like a child forced from
the classroom into a hallway timeout. He regards them with even, silent

curiosity, unafraid somehow, as if emboldened by the fear around him. His game blinks in his idle, upturned hand.

"Okay," Sam decides, hopefully. "We're okay. I'll see if I can get the generator up."

A thought stops him, becoming a question: "Which is . . . where exactly? I think I . . . knew."

Paula tilts her head, lifts her light between them, for a closer look at him.

16

By Chief's watch, he's got twenty minutes to stop today's replacement ferry from leaving. If it's on schedule, it arrived an hour or so ago from the mainland, has already sold out from yesterday's backlog and is just gassing up for the return leg just after dark.

The day has disappeared somehow in a stop-motion jitter of moments, too many to run from, but running is all, staying ahead of this night that may never end, bearing down, engulfing, spreading.

Who knows how far? From here to Greenport, along the gridlocked LIE to New York, to Greenwich Village, to *Linda*?

The first all-nighter, she may not think much about it. But the second night? Maybe her friends won't understand her, maybe she won't understand them, and things will get confusing. Maybe she'll take a walk and a truck or bus driver shouldn't be behind the wheel, or a crane operator, or an airline pilot.

He guns the Jeep down the hardpan access road behind Sea Haven's kitschy shops but slows in a double take: from both lamp posts between here and the main square ahead, the light dies, dim yellow circles on the ground just disappearing.

Ahead, between the low buildings, Chief can make out the crowd already gathered around the shuttered, locked ticket kiosk. He slows and parks on the edge of the square, looking out to see a gift, if anything can count as such anymore. Half his problem is solved: there's no second ferry yet—just yesterday's dead, useless hulk, going nowhere.

He yanks the keys and grabs the shotgun and shoulders open the door, climbing out and striding quickly toward the group, a mob, really, a hundred or more, backpacks and roll-on suitcases and litter strewn.

Faces turn, shouting and chatter and laughter die, the stray squawk of a word fading last: "Wha—"

"Folks? No ferry today either, sorry! Let's go on back to where we all were, right now."

"Hey Chief, no fucking way. That's two days!"

"We have a right to be here and get on that boat."

"When it gets here."

Chief is too blurry to track who says what, and why does it matter? The crowd has become one unruly, aggrieved, threatening thing.

"Look, everybody. Let's keep it easy, okay?" His hand floats up, a vague supplication, as if he holds nothing in the other.

"*Easy*? We got cells out, no ferry, now we got no power, no landlines!"

"We're cut off!" another shouts.

Chief blinks away blurriness, trying to focus, to shake off the stutter of afterimages crowding in, the shrieks and explosions and the whispering still ringing in his ears. "The ferry's late, it's not the first and not the last time. But no one's getting on it today, understood?"

"*Why*?"

"Fuck that."

"We'll take the boats, man!"

On cue, boaters climb out onto their decks along the marina float, gawking. Good. They're next.

Chief lifts the shotgun, slowly enough to say it's not about to just discharge, but quickly enough to show some deliberation and purpose. There's nuance to threatening someone with a weapon, something TV gets all wrong these days.

"Try again tomorrow, okay? If I'm making a mistake, no harm, and truly sorry for the inconvenience. If I'm not, you'll thank me, on behalf of your families on the mainland."

It's an unpopular sentiment:

"—What the fuck is he talkin'—"

"You gonna shoot us?"

"*Not* serious—"

BLAMMM! He fires off toward the harbor, the shot skittering the water with little splashes. This little Benelli is smooth as silk, with barely a cushiony backward shove.

The front row of the crowd cringes, a few crouching, hands up, comically wide-eyed.

"Take your luggage, leave it, I don't care. But you all need to clear the dock area."

A tall, rumpled tourist—the dad from yesterday?—glares. "I'm an attorney, Officer. And there *will* be questions. There will be depositions, there will be damages. You willing to risk your job here?"

Chief wants to laugh. "Least of it. Get moving."

The man smiles, an ugly threatening grin over his shoulder as he pulls his roll-on away, clattering down the quay. Where's his family—what's happened to them?

A few at a time, others shrug or smirk or murmur and shake their heads. The crowd thins as better ideas occur:

"Claude's, let's get a brew. If the taps even work."

"Fuck this. Let's go back to the house."

"Check later, whatever."

Going, gone. Finally, he breathes and allows himself a brief appraisal. Not bad: no backup, full crowd control, no one down.

Chief turns to face the rest, the boaters in for a weekend, mutely staring families with kids, fishing buddies, a few retiree couples, but even now as he heads for the main dock ramp, he counts one empty slip.

Could be, with the fog that closed in around Carratuck, that only one boat left for home since this thing really hit, so maybe it's still containable. Or more so than it would be otherwise.

Chief starts with two men on a little O'Day cabin job, middle-agers escaping the wives to fish and beer it up for a few last glory days before they survey and dry-dock her.

Their faces look lopsided and swollen, eyes bleary. He can sympathize with their bewilderment at his shotgun and tries to soften it with politeness. "Hey guys, can you go up on shore, please? I'm clearing the boats."

With bell-like clarity, another thought occurs: they can radio the mainland with their own sitrep, and mainland might send somebody to check it out, and blow to hell all hope of containment. "And grab your ship-to-shore for me, please?"

The two trade dumb looks. "What's it about? We're not gonna just yank out the gear, it's expensive, it's—"

The shotgun muzzle comes up again. "Well, I've asked, and I'm hoping we can leave it at that."

"Why? Where are we supposed to go?"

"Anywhere but off this island. Head up to the Pier View, have some steamers. Take a walk on the beach. Everybody likes that."

In other slips along the float, on other decks, more sailors have gathered to watch.

Money, of course, quickly becomes issue one. "What about the dock fees we prepaid? Some of the others chartered too. Not cheap."

"You are all welcome to file claims when this is all over. And I wouldn't blame you for it."

One says, "Hey, you need a warrant, you can't just—"

Up goes the shotgun muzzle again, gleaming darkly. "Can. Am." Sometimes less is more. Why not hope so?

But the other adds, "Maybe *you* need to sleep. *You're* losing it. Ever think of that?"

Hope disappears. Mutiny begins with one unanswered challenge to authority, and then it spreads.

BLLLAMMM! Chief has aimed off to one side, well clear but point made twice now, with a splintery chunk of piling flying off for punctuation. The man flings his hands up, wide-eyed, quivering.

When the last sailor has disappeared ashore, to Claude's or the Pelican, to the beach, anywhere else into the dark, Chief turns and takes in the lay of the land. He pulls a dock container open, yanking out lifejackets, deck chairs, dock lines, jerry cans, rags.

He slows, his gaze moving down the gangway to the float, finally falling on a diesel fuel pump.

17

In the alley beside the clinic, Sam tugs and tugs again on the pull cord, but salt air and disuse have gotten the better of the generator's plugs; it sputters without result until the fourth try, finally catching with a throaty gurgle.

A square of light appears in the lane out front, throwing long shadows on the ground, and he hears the loopy laughter and "oohs" and "ahhs" of the Sleepless inside.

He stands, wiping his hands on his jeans, looking down with unwarranted satisfaction at the working generator. But it *is* satisfying; he has provided light and comfort, and what more essential can a man provide?

He closes the wooden lid to the generator housing and looks up, hearing the footsteps first—no voices—only the sound of feet moving purposefully and almost stealthily, like a squad moving into position. New light reaches him now, and he looks up to see a group of ragtag tourists and locals carrying hurricane lanterns and flashlights, bunched up jittery and gawking behind a truly unwelcome sight: Doctor Fleisher in his surgical mask, with Sam's erstwhile aide Andrew beside him.

Fleisher lifts a hand, stilling the crowd behind him. "Hold up! We're civilized human beings here! We give them a chance to do what's right. We take the high road, because it's who we are!"

The crowd goes still, blinking and gawking.

Fleisher turns to Sam. "No more fakes, Carlson. Real meds, the boy. Give us them. Or we'll get them. Choose."

Is he smiling behind the surgical mask? His eyes gleam wetly with an unwholesome light, like an adolescent fighting laughter at an obscene joke.

Sam pretends to think, eyeing the crowd, seeing more makeshift gloves and masks. No help for the fear spreading, far and fast as any disease. "I have your word you'll be responsible for the boy?"

"Of course."

Back inside the clinic, all eyes turn to him. A few nod gratefully, almost smiling. A strangely reverent mood has settled over this group, with the sense they are joined by something truly greater than them all, by some unearthly, historic phenomenon with unimaginable consequences.

Sam tries to smile back, but it's shaky. "Folks? I think we can all agree things are getting a little strange out there. Anyone who wants to stay in here and ride this out, welcome. Everyone else, now's the time to leave, and best luck. But I need a hand with these hurricane shutters."

Everyone trades looks, uncertain.

Paula moves beside him, pitches her voice low. "Fleisher? Come back for the boy?"

He nods. "With fifty or so friends."

"So . . . we hole up in here?"

He thinks, or tries to; too many scenarios present themselves, with too many possible consequences that don't bear study. But what choice? Hand the Boy over and trust Fleisher, with his borderline-compulsive chuckling and rheumy eyes and sociopathic self-assurance?

"Sam, you sure?"

"Maybe. Almost." He turns quickly from her, back to the crowd in the waiting room. "Everyone? I'm going to ask a few of you to help me. We need to step outside and as quickly as possible lower the hurricane shutters, step back inside, and close off this entrance."

A guffaw sounds from the back of the room, cut short by an embarrassed silence.

In his chair, the Boy bends closer to his little handheld game again, his lips moving soundlessly, as if davening over a sacred relic.

As if every outcome were his to determine, in the shining light of this little box.

18

With the dock lights out too, it won't help matters, since darkness favors attackers in any engagement. Even worse, if it's some kind of island-wide blackout, fear will spread quickly and dependably, and more might become desperate enough to toss dollars at an impromptu charter, or maybe just outright commandeer a vessel.

"Chief! Come on, man! You can't stop all of us!" A boater's shout rings out across the shut storefronts along the quay, and Chief holds his breath to listen for footsteps.

Redoubts should provide cover and field of fire, and this makeshift version barely offers either, but it does block the bottleneck of the dock gate and ramp down to the floats of the marina. Piled two and three deep, commandeered life preservers might slow buckshot. Coiled line, stacked ship-to-shore radios, empty jerry cans—all of it at least helps provide something to duck behind, if and when it comes to it.

It's all temporary, anyway, just until word arrives and provides clear, straightforward guidance for another course of action, with more manageable consequences—standing down, for instance, with apologies and handshakes all around, maybe a money claim or two and some complicated paperwork, and a dressing down from the aldermen. It's a fond hope.

As if in argument, Linda's face comes to him. She taught him to FaceTime and it's funny now, because when he sees her in his mind, she's leaning into that little window on his desktop computer screen.

He thinks of her easy, melodic laughter, and her expensive, perfect teeth—her orthodontist's office wall shrine to his European vacations. Well, doctors deserve it, even if their parents likelier than not put them through college and med school, silver spoon-style. Money begets money, even if Sam Carlson wants to play working-class hero and salt of the earth, slumming at the Pier View with his local girl.

Whispering? Some faint, stuttery hissing floats in from nowhere, tightening his grip on the Benelli.

Maybe the suicide gunman overspent on this fancy black shotgun, but for home defense or loaded with grape for riot control, the inertia recoil operating system makes it the quickest semi-auto on the market—not that it really bears on the situation now, when it looks as all-business as any other model, all it should need to do—or used to need to do, back when common sense was common.

Which it will be again, of course, since the marina's floodlights will snap again on in a moment, service bars will blip into being on his cell phone screen, and people will step sheepishly from shadows and share houses and motels. Embarrassed, they'll be neighbors all over again, at least for another day or two before the ferry back to Greenport or Hyannis and the silent rueful drive back to their own homes and jobs.

Shadows, now. The darkness almost visible between faintest gleaming, from where? Spots appear like fireflies, dim at the edges of everything.

Forgiveness: it was a sermon once, in a movie or a dream, a stern Lutheran minister booming from his ship's prow pulpit. Jan will forgive him. Linda too. Every neighbor who has family on the mainland will, and who doesn't? The island's children have all gone, for the schools and the smart wild boys in the city.

Somehow he has become gatekeeper again, between the dying and the living. His again to close the door on the last voices, to suffer so much thanklessness, though the doorway he guards here is as real as any between air and water.

But this time will be different. This time the dying will run from the storefront porches, from the boatyard and the dry dock, fleeting footsteps in the gravel to meet him.

19

"That's three. Can we get a fourth?" Sam tries to smile; it's just doubles at the club, round robin, sudden death. The room tilts a little, rights itself.

Like a student unsure of his answer, a guy in a crewcut and sleeveless tee raises a shy hand.

"Okay, good." Sam nods toward a corner of the waiting area, and they gather there to huddle and agree: they'll move fast, opening the front floor-to-ceiling sliding doors, stepping through to reach up, quickly lower the hurricane shutters and duck back inside, hopefully before Fleisher and his group can stop them.

These shutters are just one-by-four-inch painted fir planks, crossmembers nailed back and front at the bottom and top, but to Sam they might provide enough of a barrier to make someone second-guess a poor impulse. The locks are marine hardware-style, tarnished brass rotary latches—something the chief had apparently insisted on when the pharmacy was robbed a few years ago.

Paula, as always, is slow to believe: "Sam, but what if—"

He cuts her off. "Just be ready to lock up as soon as we pull them down?"

Paula hesitates but gives him a somber nod. His volunteers trade looks and follow suit.

Should he count down, to be sure they're ready to move? He can't imagine it. Instead, they simply shove open the two big sliders and step out, already reaching up to free the hurricane shutters.

The first and second pair have unhooked theirs and are already swinging them down behind them as they step back inside.

Sam's partner unhooks his, quickly freeing the galvanized hook from the eyelet, waiting on Sam.

Sam's eyelet fights him; a stubborn burr of corrosion won't give as he wraps his fingers around the hook and yanks, again and again.

In the waiting area, they're already locking the other dropped shutters from inside. *Click click, snap,* a military sound somehow, of readiness, of securing a redoubt. *Shhht-clunk,* the sliders shutting now.

Anxious faces crowd Sam's open slider doorway, peering out. He tries not to glance at them as he pulls.

"Uhhh . . . Doctor Carlson?" Sam's partner is little more than a kid, really, and uncertain how edgy to be.

Sam dares a glimpse over his shoulder across the lane, at Fleisher and his group staring in flatfooted disbelief. Snatches of argument cross the lane:

"You wanna stop them? *You* go."

"What if they got—"

A few of these start across, glaring, and Sam flexes his fingers, tightens his grip and yanks again on the corroded hook. Nothing.

"Hold it, Carlson!" Fleisher shouts. He turns to point the others forward. "Move it, now, don't let them—"

"Doctor?" Sam's partner shifts his weight from leg to leg, a hand hovering.

"Go in. Right with you." He yanks again, two fingers curled aching around the rusty hook's shaft as a flurry of footsteps begins behind him.

Free! The hook slips from the eyelet, the shutter slams down, and Sam almost trips on his volunteer's heels as he dodges a blur of movement and flings himself through the doorway, dropping the shutter banging against the sills. Some are already reaching, turning the last rotary latch. *Shhht-click.*

From outside, shouts:

"Hand out the fucking pills!"

"Not fair, man!"

Shhht-clunk. The slider is shoved shut, barely muffling the manic voices of the deluded, the regressed, bitter as aggrieved children.

With three tourists pitching in, Sam wordlessly enacts active shooter protocol. They shove a bookcase and cabinet in front of the locked sliders and drag a heavy melamine cabinet across the linoleum to stand against the last unblocked slider, just left of the entrance they've already blocked with a tangle of piled chairs.

The front waiting area seems to shrink without the darkness visible outside, without the shadowy lane and vague rectangles of other storefronts.

Sam turns to seek out the Boy and, between milling panicky Sleepless, glimpses him, perched on a chair by the back wall, clutching his game like a rosary. He should go to him, should join him resolutely as they head together into their own trackless night. He should grab him and flee, find Kathy and return them to his boat, cast off and convey them to safety.

Instead, he steps to an exposed few inches of locked glass slider and spots a tiny gap between two planks of shutter, dim light gleaming through, flickering.

He leans and peers out into the dark.

The motion of figures seems jittery, like an old film reel. Thrown by the light of flashlights and hurricane lanterns, shadows cross where the mob has gathered, eyes shining like mad parishioners, staring enthralled at Fleisher in his surgical mask.

Fleisher has raised both hands above his head, a gesture of surrender, or triumph. His eyes gleam as he lowers a hand to point at the clinic, at Sam himself, it seems, for a frightening moment. Sam nearly steps back.

"We have our answer! Inside? They have light, and sleep, and maybe even a way to reach their families and know how they are." Fleisher lifts his voice, searching for the pitch and rhythm of crowd-pleasing rhetoric. "Out here? What do we have? Darkness, uncertainty, unending, unbearable exhaustion. They get theirs, and they pull up the ladder! It's the same, the same old story."

The Sleepless seem to waver. One does a half-turn in both directions, squinting. Another shrugs theatrically. Vagueness ripples through the crowd, murmurs.

Fleisher pauses, his head shifting slowly side to side, reading the restlessness. He shifts his tone, searching for a theme. "You paid for that clinic, your taxes, your hard work, and now they close the doors on you? Our government in action, of the people, by the people, for the people?"

Already bored, a tourist stabs his dead cell phone's screen with an index finger and another closes in to watch. A woman near the back of the group sighs and shakes her head, too tired to track it. A random giggle erupts.

But Fleisher clears his throat and tries again: "And for this they tell you that you can't believe in what you believe in? We remember when a few determined the fate of so many, when our tallest towers fell . . ."

The muttering dies. Stillness spreads now through the crowd, faces slacken with a kind of worshipful longing.

"Can we let it be forgotten?"

Sam can feel the treacly thrill surging, the prickly electricity of the mob's struck nerve. Behind him, his own Sleepless moan and mutter. Can they hear Fleisher?

Tears seem to fill Fleisher's eyes, a gleam as light flashes from his smudged designer glasses; his white, germaphobe freak mask creases as his voice lifts into a cry of peroration: "We remember so that our children will never forget! Our voices will be heard! At a time and place of our choosing, freedom shall prevail!"

It's all a bad joke, of course. Some sensible person will step from the mob and challenge Fleisher and his nonsense demagoguery.

A man does step forward, and flashlight beams converge on him, his bald-spot a floating paleness. "I got a shotgun in my garage. That'll prevail!" he offers.

A grizzled local shouts, "There's a crowbar in the bait shop!"

Inches from Sam's, another eye suddenly appears, rheumy, wide, rolling. Sam rears back. From beyond the locked slider and shutter comes laughter, more shouting: "Peek-a-boo! Shut-eye! Get some!"

Manic nonsense: a harbinger of worse, dependably.

Pale, Sam reassures everyone, "No worries. They're bluffing."

They stare back at him, eyes round with fear.

"But I'll look for a hammer, some nails, or . . . something." Dizziness grips him, the room moving sideways, slowing, stopping again. Absurd, he hears himself asking no one, anyone, "The . . . ferry?"

Paula is peering at him, her hair awry, her face lined. Sam smiles and turns away down the hall to the storeroom. "I'll look for a hammer, some nails." Why, again? "Nails."

Halfway down the hallway, the hallway seems to flicker once, return to itself, then dim again, narrowing. Tilting.

It's another hall now, one his eyes burn at seeing. His heart twitches like a torn muscle in his chest, desperate to stop and never know the place again.

The door ahead ajar, revealing a small part of a bright room.

The bright room.

20

Between the heavy tarp draped above and the hard damp of the boat's floor on their knees, Cort and Tay kneel, bent. Her voice breaks, dry and halting, as the story's unimaginable end spills from her in a rush: "Sioux first, then Madison, I couldn't stop them, I couldn't help them. I couldn't cut through in time. It happened so fast. And then after, I got them down, they were so heavy, how could they be so *heavy*? I only wanted them to look peaceful, like . . . like . . ." she chokes on the word, " . . .asleep."

His whisper is warm breath in her ear. "Don't now. They would've found another way. People are too far gone, too fast. I saw some things too." With the soft roughness of his boy's first stubble, the side of his face touches hers.

Her throat constricts, she nods, starting to reach to wipe at her tears, but his other hand comes down suddenly, hard, trapping hers. Tense.

"Shhh."

He pulls an inch away, revealing a sliver of gap between tarp and rail, a tilted view of the boat-shed door.

A shadowy form hesitantly creaks it open. Another mouth-breathing, conformist jock troll, of course, high on the cheapest thrill of all—making someone feel helpless and afraid.

The same sadist moron, from always.

Why doubt what he might do? What anyone might now? Her shoulders hunch, neck contracting as she tries to make herself small. Not breathing is an ache that grows, a burning from chest to throat; but the real urge is to spit out the poison a trapped breath becomes, before we ever take another.

But *when*? When will this jock lowlife back up through the door and find his jock lowlife crew and move on? Or will he lift the tarp an inch at a time to find them, and bring the others with a shout?

Blood to the brain, hammering inside. Weight on one arm, burning.

Lowlife turns. Head tilted, listening. Turning.

Tay's hand gripping hers, hard and dry. Until Lowlife weirdly, as if thoughtfully, closes the door behind him as he sways out.

From outside, further on, more muffled footfalls approach, villainous B-movie laughter, an evil witch voice cackling, "And your little dog too!"

More jock razzing: "Blow me, Hespeth."

"Your dreams."

A girl whines and giggles, "Jim-*meeee*!" Echoes of shouts, fading.

Only the surf now, always, endlessly, as if asking for silence: *Shhh. Shhh.*

Tay sighs, a held breath they both let go, softly.

A surge of dizziness spins the darkness, which seems to breathe and shift with floating smudges of disappearing color. Moments pass, unmeasured, and then more, until the fear of these last few feels more imagined than remembered.

Which world is this? A girl's, on vacation? In a boat shed with a boy?

It is, it must be, because she desperately makes it so, pulling him closer as he pushes her gently back, moving against her, and her fingers are fumbling at the zipper of her cutoffs. Suddenly, none of it can happen soon enough: her hand, finding and gently touching, guiding; his, urging her knee sideways, trailing upwards.

They take sharp sips of air, heat blooming where they meet and slip onward, carefully pushing, carefully yielding, until their bodies are barely their own.

But here is a thought to forget, to push back into frantic glimpses of others: the sad little room in their same rental, Mom in the slant light of the doorway with her same bitter smirk at everything, her voice coming up out of a sound like static:

"He won't love you, really. Just like your dad wouldn't love me. They say they do, but don't, they never do."

Cort shuts her eyes again because rising now out of shapeless blotches of color, out of nothing and nowhere, comes curled, black edges at the edges of paleness which is flesh charred by flame, and the perfect ashes of a boy's hair, his body slumped beside others in the burned-out beach taxi.

Now in sunlight, there's the milky, unseeing eyes of the drowned woman, her blue-white skin torn, open in narrow gashes to darker, stringy insides.

The doctor guy, the chief, with their bland faces both trying to act like they don't blame her for it all, an orphaned child and the pitiless waste of a life. Grief rises like a thick sob in her throat, swollen. How did she fail everyone so soon and so completely?

Even the stupid contest: she's lost that too, taunted, quit, cut off. Madison and Sioux's faces: she can see them both standing motionless side by side like sick twins, staring unblinking with their filthy hair and greenish shadows beneath their eyes, nooses jutting sideways from their necks.

She pushes away the thought, back into her old somewhere else of other thoughts, the bad ones where her hated self lives to hate herself, the selfish, lazy slut liar. Pushing away, away, the pureness of their need frees her.

The press of Tay's fingers on her shoulder, the whisper of her name like something cherished, her own upward thrust against him: each sensation surges to shake her. His mouth lifts and disappears, his breath shuddering against her neck before stealing hers again.

There is no way back from this exquisite burning, no way forward but deeper into this rich darkness.

His lips are a doorway she passes through to float beyond into their waking dream of each other and the secret world only they can inhabit now, the roof gone and the night theirs as they rise, even as the ocean surges far below, moonlit windblown waves and spindrift, beautiful, to the edges of the turning sky.

The sound of the static rises and falls, and with Tay's deepening touch, she understands the sound is the sea and the dark is now filled with stars, parting to let them pass even as Tay's eyes fill with those same stars. In the spectral night his hair floats slowly now in tendrils around his head as her lips part as if to whisper, and she wonders: how do you wake up when you're already awake?

21

Where is there air to fill his stopped lungs, a sane thought to start his stalled heart beating again? Sam's head pounds as if some pressure within has built to bursting.

At the end of the clinic hallway, which is another hallway now, narrower, in that bright momentary room at the end of it, there are spots on the dirty wooden floor which are drops of blood around and on legs splayed in spattered cargo pants, boney bluish-white feet flopped outward: Gabriel Thomas, second year Australian student, half of his upturned face still recognizable.

Closer, closer to see now the cell phone in one dead hand, the gun in the other, the fingers given up their grip. Like the thin, bloodless line first left by a razor, so pure, so exact: the truth of this failure, deep and cold to the bone.

The sound of static comes like something burning, and from within it the noise of words rises up from the dark bulk always suddenly there somehow, huge, the same cop in dark blue the dark of a fly's wing, white round face split by crooked, laughing lips as he smirks at another cop:

"—thinks he can save—"

Sam spins as it all flickers back into where he is, into Paula beside him in their bright clinic hallway, finishing her panicked shout: "—everyone!" She clutches at his arm, her eyes bulging and bloodshot raw with fear.

He looks past her to the waiting area, past where the Boy cringes in his chair, past Sleepless flapping their hands in furious autistic panic, surging back from a blow against a shutter making the inside glass quiver.

This is where it begins and ends, so perfect somehow, his every evasion leading him more inexorably to a final accounting. Again, the slam of some blunt heaviness shakes his house of poor stone, his beautiful lost sinecure.

From outside he hears his name again, the name of the accused, shouted in a rhythm, as if by an audience impatient for the headliner to appear: "Carl-son! Carl-son!"

Images split and scatter: a floor-to-ceiling glass pane spider-webs and sags into opacity; Sam's hand closes on the Boy's thin bicep to yank him upward and into his arms; Paula's shout bursts free above everything deaf-ening—the chattering cries of Sleepless within and without, the pounding of crowbar on splitting shutter, pulse of blood through knotted heart—"Go!"

Sam feels his feet moving, but so heavily as if through a tide of water surging against him, time moving so much faster than he can, as his Sleepless cover their ears and cower back.

Torn wood and voices shrieking.

Like a blue-black comma, the head of a crowbar appears between two planks of a shutter and staves in the rest of the glass, hesitating before twisting and screeching back out.

Through the split shutter and broken glass of a window, the barrel end of a shotgun pokes through now, blindly, inquisitively, and a Sleepless in flip-flops and basketball shorts cries out unintelligibly and grabs it, pulling.

BLAAAM! In this room of hard surfaces, the explosion is a blade piercing every other sound, ripping into ears already crackling with distorted noise.

Things fly through air, unidentifiable, as the man falls into his own flung blood and more screaming begins. Across a row of salmon-col-ored plastic seats, bits land, patches of dark, short curled hair attached to yellowness.

The Boy writhes in Sam's arms, fighting with his eyes closed and his mouth wide and soundless.

Back, out, down the linoleum into the wide lighted hall that was dark and narrow moments ago, to a doorway once again to hesitate a panicked heartbeat's worth. Now with the Boy clutching his hair, Sam plunges across the threshold, and with one hand flings aside spare medical supplies, scrabbling wildly to topple a wobbly shelf-unit to clear the unused rear emergency exit. He claws at the latch and bolt and twists the lock, yanking hard to budge the heavy door where the damp has swollen it shut, to open it finally on the dark little fenced patio of trash bin and recycling and the big dead HEPA filter he meant to have hauled, to run, the Boy clinging for life, a frightened animal, eyes shut tight and face half-buried in his neck.

Quick steps carry them banging through the little latched gate and into the side lane, seemingly unseen, but how to know? How to hear a footfall or a shout above his own gasping and his own pounding blood as he runs?

"You're okay," he whispers into the Boy's ear. From behind, the night pales toward the lane's corner and rushes them into the shadow of a row of other low buildings, onward, to anywhere else.

Back to the boat and Kathy and off this island.

The Boy answers him with a brief squeeze on his shoulder and a pull on his hair, a reply that stings his eyes with sudden tears.

———

Paula has led her room full of tourists back away from the broken windows where the Sleepless from outside clamber through, wielding pieces of lumber and golf clubs, feet crunching on broken glass as they surge forward. Fleisher is nowhere to be seen, and Paula shouts above the din of fury and panic, "What are you *doing*? How—"

A shoulder catches hers, pressing her hard against the admittance desk in the crush, as Sleepless yank open drawers, rifling through.

"Pills, lady. Now."

"You—" A shove from another Sleepless pins her back, and her footing fails on something slippery.

She clings to the desk edge as she falls to a knee hard on the scuffed linoleum. "Just—" An elbow connects with her cheek, stunning her as another Sleepless squeezes by toward the hall and the stock cabinets there. A foot crushes her hand and she cries out, unheard, as the throng bunches and swirls, the room packed, deafening with unintelligible shouts and another thick blast of the shotgun, farther away now, but the high edge of it ringing.

On her hands and knees, another knee to her temple stuns her, a blinding glare of white spots swimming. The legs around her sway and press in, stifling, rank against her face, feet shuffling, heavy, implacable as cattle's. Syllables—broken bits of them without meaning, "hawl," or "vawl," "gat"— rise from the din like the hands of the drowning from the ocean. Her own too, finally slipping beneath.

22

The first footsteps are faint, like the scrabbling of rabid vermin. The first shadows are fast and long and flung by some trackless wedge of dim light from between the outbuildings of the boatyard.

Chief wants to run, just give in and bolt and leave the pieces of the world to land where they may for anybody else to sort out, but if these weekenders make it to the mainland, his Linda's eyes may not close and she won't know why. She might think it's the heat or more noise again from the street outside her dorm, and maybe it would be, from others awakened by others awakened—not so different than here, this night, with everyone blinking dim and dull as drunks, which many seem to be anyway, maybe trying to put out their own lights any way they can.

Why not, after the days that go on and on and the dread that they may never stop? The whispering of those approaching is nonsense now:

"You know it's sick."

"Hello."

"Get gone, is what. I'm out."

Chief edges up, checking his sight line out between stacks of ship-to-shores and old yellow life vests. "Far enough," he shouts. Let's just—"

"Fuck you, Chief," one of them offers.

The stock of the Benelli presses into his shoulder, barrel grip smooth and warm in one hand, etched trigger guard light and cool beneath thumb and middle finger of the other. His index finger nudges the nickel trigger lightly, a questioning touch. Making sure is making sure, but the stock kicks and his finger has already jerked to pull and shoot a round into the stunned air, exploding.

The blast is a longer sound than he remembers, echoing with a fizzy, spitting finish off the far dark buildings across the yard, and a clamor of shocked cries and tossed shadows from the Sleepless, dodging and cursing in disbelief.

"Motherfucker!"

"Yow-ow!" one actually laughs, worst news of all, suggesting Chief has somehow still failed to convey the gravity of the situation.

"Bluff hand, poker face!" another yells, demented, past reason.

The Zippo feels warm and smooth. The metal click of it brings a small flame, leaping blue to the soaked rag flapping from the beer bottle half-full of diesel, one of his six impromptu Molotovs. He waits, counting, as the flame climbs.

"Now," another whispers, as if to Chief's hand clutching the crackling, burning bottle.

Chief pulls his arm back and flings it forward, hard, fingers letting go to spin the smooth hot glass from their tips as the bottle spirals, fluttering light, *woosh* out over the gravel lot between gate and boatyard.

"It's—" The next syllable drowns as the bottle breaks and bursts ripely into burning fuel, lit spatters flying. Small blotches of flame litter the ground, shadows again flung twisting as the Sleepless stumble and run, footsteps and frantic whispers fading.

Silence descends again across the broad quay until there is only the sound of his own pulse beating in his ears and his breath slowing as he wills himself to calm.

He counts, he sings to himself, he rehearses his reasons. Sleep is the land of every childhood, his ground to hold, so that all may return there. He drifts back to his own, to all the hours of sweet oblivious floating, back to the early evening hours of summer, to the distant sounds of a lawnmower, a dog barking or a plane droning; or back to the forward berth under the dank bow on his and Dad's first sails to the island, up at dawn to cross the great Sound. The loops of rope swaying from hooks, first sun flickering through the hatch on the brightwork, low unending throb of the engines. All the innocent safe pleasure of it. Sinking into a world as warm as the palm of God's hand, to dream of the faces of loved ones and the soft music of their speech.

More shouts echo from the dark now: "Get Carlos!"

Who?

"Chief, you crazy, man!"

"You're gonna die, okay?"

23

Over the last dunes of Ocean Beach, Sam runs, staying low. The Boy clutches his hair and a twist of his shirt, and Sam realizes the Boy has dropped his little handheld game somewhere, his fantasy quest of rescue lost, his escape and refuge gone.

Bonfires have sprung up along the beach. In and out of the dark, everywhere voices call out as tourists and islanders alike emerge from houses and motels to gather, desperate for sense or purpose. Some seem merely dazed, wandering from group to group. Others, drunk, shout their fear and wonder:

"It's terrorists! I heard a guy had a radio!"

"I heard they're quarantining!"

"—whole eastern seaboard!"

A studious-looking young man cups his hands to his mouth, megaphone-style, exhorting anyone, "Everyone? Let's gather our batteries, and please fill your tubs, in case there's some interruption in water service. Hello? Excuse me!"

Others laugh, aping him. "Excuse *me!*"

The young man frowns peevishly, but continues, undaunted, "Does anyone have a transistor radio of any sort? So that we can figure out if—"

A kid holds a boombox aloft, an eighties power ballad blaring suddenly with surging electric guitars and flanged tom-toms, but he's quickly tackled by another and the sound stutters and snaps off.

Confused shouts echo, more laughter, unreal.

A skinny old couple glides by on a golf cart. No clubs in back, but a big wooden instrument—a cello?—and what looks like a picnic basket, as if on a pleasant Sunday's outing.

A woman tears off her clothes and stamps on them, loose paper-white flesh juddering. "Get them off. Off!" she shouts. She tears at her face, and even in the darkness there's darker spots of blood from her fingernails.

Sam slows and stares in disbelief, the Boy clinging, wide-eyed.

Nearby, two more men take turns striking each other in the face with their fists. They laugh and then cry, and finally both, as one falls to his knees, shakes his head and then climbs back to his feet, blinking and swaying to swing at the other again, feebly.

Wearing dishwashing gloves, a tourist runs by, shouting in Russian or German, sidestepping a flabby naked kid who crawls on hands and knees in the loose sand, lighted by the flames. "My contact! They knocked it out!" he bawls, turning his wet gleaming face to them.

But there is light again, stagey and lurid as two middle-aged men in surgical masks carefully touch a homemade torch to the eaves of a one-story beachfront. Brightness leaps, snapping, sibilant, climbing the dark slanted roof. Blackness blots out the stars. Is there a scream from inside?

Someone in the next lane, or somewhere else, running to somewhere else?

Past a shuttered Sunglass Hut and the Marine Supply and Ben's Bait 'n Tackle, over a triangle of municipal gravel, Sam carries the Boy onward, feet and heart pounding. From beyond these low buildings, a generator-powered security lamp sends a wedge of dim light, enough for Sam to guess that the edge of the boatyard lies somewhere ahead.

He pauses, gasping, slowed by muffled footfalls ahead, motion in the darkness. Has he been flanked? Have some faster pursuers passed them in the dark to cut them off? Right, left, he peers into the night, the shapes of storefronts shifting and fading as he turns his head.

From behind him comes the sound of breathless running and more quick footfalls, and he glances back to see the first shadows gather and then more collect and crowd in, a group shoving each other into the faint slant of light, their faces gibbering, jittery with fury and panic again—one or the other, it always seems.

From between Andrew and a grizzled local, Fleisher steps forward in his surgical mask and rubber gloves, cool, unhurried.

"You're making a tragic mistake." His voice floats out, melodic, calm: "Be reasonable. We need answers, the Boy has them. Let us have him. You can do it, Sam, you can, you can save everybody."

It's an idea from a bad dream, counterfeit coinage of the values of wise and kind men, of devoted servants of the common good. A joke only the joker gets.

The Boy presses in against Sam's hip, hands gripping like claws at prey.

Sam squeezes back, their private dialogue.

Suddenly, a new sound reaches him: the flutter of something thrown, a small skittering across the square's gravel.

His eyes fix on tiny, pale movement in the shadowy gravel, and the idea comes to him, chary as doubt, but then with a kind of awe as he remembers the bubble pack of Ambesta samples he left behind with Kathy, now flung to land bouncing among the small sharp stones.

Across Pine Beach's little public space with its brass anchor and kiosk, she steps from the shadowy colonnade of shops: "That's what you really want!" she calls out. "Take them!"

A second's confused hesitation, and Fleisher lifts a hand to stop the others, who bunch up gawking behind him. He strides forward with prissy dignity at first, but then abandons it all, dropping hard to his knees with a faint sob to shove aside his mask and another Sleepless to claw at the ground, to grab up and rip apart the bubble pack, and shove both doses blindly into his mouth, face to the ground.

He rises slowly, chewing furiously, his eyes feral, all animal fury, searching the darkness for Sam and the Boy and Kathy.

He makes a show of spitting. "More fakes! Get them!"

But Kathy has already stepped from the colonnade to grasp Sam's shirt—everyone is pulling his shirt, it seems—to yank him and the Boy stumbling into the dark of the colonnade, behind its wide posts and around a corner into a narrow, hardscrabble alley.

Again the gasping and pounding of his own body drowns the sounds of pursuit, but they must be there, who knows how many or few steps behind them, vengeful and terrified, crazed as Furies.

"This way," she hisses, between her own gasping breaths. She points them forward, toward a low fence she climbs, quick as a girl, turning to reach for the Boy Sam half-hands and helps over, murmuring uselessly, "Quick, now, easy. Good."

The Boy moves with them, crouched low and silent as they rush on through the boatyard between the dark hulls on sawhorses, the yardarms, cable spools, winch hooks.

Somewhere along the way, Sam realizes, he has become lost, the thought itself so emblematic he wants to laugh—but each breath is too sharp and dear in his lungs, danger too close, his charge too helpless, time too short.

So why does she slow, shaking her head, stopping? He stops too, and puts a hand out to halt the Boy.

"We can make it. The marina. Come on . . ." He lifts the silently yielding Boy and looks at Kathy.

Behind them, having gained the boatyard, the Sleepless are searching, shouting.

"Sam, we can go right, other side of the yard, into town. Hide until help gets here. They are, right? Getting here?"

"They'll find us. We need to keep going." The moments left to them dwindling, wasted, too soon irrecoverable.

Confused, she steps closer. "To . . . where?"

"Off Carratuck. He can't be here, he can't . . ." Sam tightens his grip on the Boy, who stares from one to the other. "I can't let anything happen."

Kathy tilts her head at this new pitch of insistence. His look is wild, stubborn past desperation. "Sam? Through the inlet, tonight? You haven't run the engine in weeks, you don't even know if—"

"Come on. We're going."

She reaches a hand to him, slowly, as if not to frighten. "Sam . . ."

Footsteps sound, too close, behind a row of boats on blocks, ever nearer. Indecipherable whispers, a choked sputtering laugh, hushed too late. Dim forms appear at the end of their row of boats, shouting: "Here! The kid and the quack!"

Who is more deluded, Sam or their pursuers? Kathy chooses, hissing at Sam: "Go, I can lead them off."

He hesitates, paralyzed.

The men, spreading and moving closer, breathing heavily from the chase.

Her harsh whisper again: "Go!" She steps back into the shadows, as if from shallows into deeper darkness, submerging, gone.

"Fuckers! Go back to Bayshore!" her voice rings out, brazen, echoing from aluminum hulls and the high corrugated roof above the dry-docks.

Another flurry of footsteps turns Sam one way, then the other. No choice, he lunges with the Boy in his arms between two boats, clambering over a trailer as quickly and silently as he can toward where he imagines the marina must be.

———

Kathy knows the yard's cyclone fences from her high school days, when kids passed Everclear and sensi and made out behind the clip joints by the fishing pier. Beneath one, she finds a remembered gap where the concrete had to be graded for drainage after Hurricane Francis. She goes to her knees, lays flat and rolls through, ducking behind a dumpster while a group of Fleisher's vigilantes approaches. Their scuffling steps hesitate, uncertain, before continuing past.

"Bitch!"

"Fuck her."

"Did, twice, on Calvin's rig, Junior year."

Laughter, fainter.

She breathes again, peering under the dumpster into the night, black as a blind man's day.

24

By the last hulks of dry-docked boats, over another low fence and into the big gravel wharf before the dock gate, they run stealthily, Sam with a hand on the Boy's arm to guide him.

Sam slows them at a body on the ground ahead, a man, groaning. Stuttering from time past, a memory rises up from nowhere, disappears with the echo of someone laughing unkindly. This morning? Days ago?

And then he sees him: Chief, peeking over a pile of stuff gathered from dock boxes and boats, blocking the gate in a crude fortification. The low oily gleam of the shotgun barrel.

How have they led each other here? Over these days of moments imagined or remembered, created or relived, vivid as if crossed into the corporeal, all reason has fled.

"Sam?" Chief calls out, voice ringing off the shut storefronts around the wharf.

"Yeah, Chief. What's—"

Behind him again, the crunch of gravel, rasp of labored breaths, as Sleepless crowd into the square, slowing.

"Chief," Sam turns back, "we're leaving. Don't let them through, they're trying to stop us. They want—"

"Can't let you. Nobody."

Sam looks back again to see Fleisher has appeared—his absurd surgical mask, the unnatural gleam of his watching eyes. Beside him, a grizzled shark-boater Sam recognizes carries a shotgun casually under an arm, like a parvenu at a skeet shoot. Beside him, Andrew glares triumphantly.

Sam calls back to the chief, "What are you saying? We need to—"

"Told you, Sam. My last Navy tour? Typhoon, a shell rolled and blew, engine room flooded. I shut that bulkhead door, Sam. Some drowned inside, but we made it back."

Sam blinks at him as it dawns: the Navy episode Chief had once obliquely mentioned, a tragedy that presumably averted a larger one. Chief is back in it now, confronting the hard choices of sacrifice, finding the courage to make them, deep in some rewound drama of heroism.

"I understand, but this is different." Sam's eyes find a haphazard pile of sharp angles—the square metal radios piled up. Commandeered from all the boats?

Chief tracks his gaze. "Sure, I took 'em. Boats, harbormaster's. If mainland hears and sends anybody, they'll get sick too, bring it back to wherever. It's not drugs or chemicals—DWP said so, your blood tests said so. So it's a virus."

"Chief," Sam explains, "it isn't. I can't find anything—"

"—can't let it spread, Sam, I got my girl ashore in college."

Fleisher jumps in, louder: "Then let us have the Boy, Chief. Before it's all too late. You're tired. Before you lose the ability to reason at all."

Chief looks from one to other. Reason? The memory of it is a kind of nostalgia now, as if for love and laughter, for any human kindness.

Sam lifts an empty hand, as if proof. "Chief, man, there's no disease here. Blood panels, nothing." Sam ticks off a finger. "Environmental samples, all in range—"

Fleisher pretends astonishment. "In *range*? Of testing by your friendly neighborhood clinic?"

Sam keeps eyes on Chief, imploring. "Chief, this is just us, giving it to each other—like yawning, laughing, like being afraid. There have been other cases, it's hysteria. It'll all go away, always does, it'll go away if we can just—"

"—just *what*? It's all in our heads, right? So you gave out fake pills? Fuck you, Sam."

Astonished gasps spread through the crowd, murmurs of shocked dismay.

Sam points a finger, glaring. "And they *worked*."

"Not anymore!" a college kid, one of the frat boys, hoots from the back of the crowd.

"But they *did*." Sam nods sideways at Fleisher. "Before he came along."

Fleisher calls out, "Chief, you know what to do. You seal the breach, and if the seal leaks, you fix it. You know that."

Chief nods. "Yes, yes I do."

Fleisher warms to his subject like a method actor to a monologue, finding a chummy, humble timbre, an ingratiating cadence. "But if you let these two go now, how will you ever be sure it wasn't them? Maybe these are the two that tip it all over, that make it too many to track down and isolate. Low probability? Maybe, maybe not, but a high-impact scenario, way too high, on your watch. Worth the risk?"

Fleisher's eyes glisten with cornball ersatz empathy, but he sways ever so slightly, a hand drifting up as if for purchase.

Sam points a trembling finger at Fleisher: "He hasn't slept either. He's not making any more sense than anyone else. There's no disease! It feels like one, but it's just hysteria, mass hysteria, and he's fueling it with his fear-mongering paranoid nonsense."

Fleisher looks around, inviting assent. "A sleep-deprived psychologist's fantasy, of course."—the *s*'s slurring now. He nearly staggers. "What else would he think? My god, has no one looked up this man? No one knows why he's here, treating hangovers? Maybe he needs to save a boy." Fleisher nods toward the Boy. "And look, here's one! Whom we hope will tell us what he knows, where he's been, what birds or animals he or his family have been in contact with, and where and when. We need to track this thing. Can we really take a chance on so many lives?" Fleisher actually smiles at the Boy, one side of his mouth drooping, ghastly. "You want to help us, don't you, son?"

The Boy cringes behind Sam, and suddenly everything happens too fast, sped up like a jerky home movie reel, grainy and veering: Fleisher nods to the local. The local lifts his shotgun and aims at Sam. *Shh-click*: he cocks his trigger, but there's no evil leer, no sadist's grin; this one is frightened and in over his head, but in for a dollar too, in front of his cronies.

Sam's hands flutter upward. "Chief—"

Fleisher shouts, "Shoot!"

The local shark-boater sharpens his aim, and starts to squeeze the trigger, but Chief shoots him first, the Bellini barely kicking, quick and accurate. The man falls in a spray of blood and the chunky, sharp report seems to register an infinitesimal beat later, with another louder blast from the shotgun wildly fired by the local on his dying way down. A choked cry fades as another boater falls, spinning.

Shouts ring out, hoarse and shrill as boaters now gather in the shadows opposite the square:

"Fuck! Let's get the boats! He's out! Now—"

"He can't—"

A group of a dozen or so surge forward, then hesitate, losing their nerve, running into each other, shoving.

Sam grabs the Boy and moves them sideways, crouching. Where is there to run? Who's on what side? Agendas seem to have crossed, shifted, died in the blur of fatigue.

Fleisher shouts again, pointing, "The Boy!"

Chief yells at Sam, "Quick, now, back here! We'll hold them!" and lights a Molotov to hold off the others.

Sam lifts the Boy and swings him up in an awkward clutch as he rushes forward, but the Molotov sloshes and spills, igniting Chief's sleeve. Chief hesitates, slapping at it, and the bottle explodes with a thick grunting sound, turning him into a bleeding, spinning torch. A gout of flame goes flying, a lit blot of fuel, and splatters the dock behind him, igniting the last-resort gasoline trail he spilled along the ramp, down to the float, to one boat after another—charter fishing rig, luxury sloop, weekender.

Sam goes to his knees and bends himself over the Boy against the blast of murderous heat. He turns his head sideways, wincing. Between the blurs of running Sleepless, he sees the chief kneeling in a shroud of flame, swaying to finally topple, consumed.

In berth after berth along the float, furled sails burst into fire with a spitting, flapping noise, and then a series of explosions as tanks go up screeching, the air itself deafening, concussed, burning. The marina has become an inferno, consumed by fire crackling in antic, joyous fury as Sleepless run screaming in the chaos.

Through the smoke, Sam glimpses the burning spars and the hull of his erstwhile home, lost, and he lifts the Boy and plunges back through the square, backhanding a Sleepless in their way, shoving another away. A thought of Kathy, quick, flashing. Gone to a girlfriend's couch, one of the local waitresses, or a B & B hostess, he's met them. She knows her way. The chief, he—

From behind them, Fleisher cries out, "The Boy! Stop them!"

Sam veers left along the side of the boatyard, tracking the low silhouette of the boardwalk toward the beach. Dark squares of unlit homes, motels. Grip of the Boy's hands, his breath hot and rushed as they run without destination through the night reeking of cinders and ash.

25

In Cort's waking dream, Tay has led her miles away and back again to this damp shed on a stretch of night beach, as if for the first time. Hers are the eyes of someone dazed into clarity by a life divided into before and after.

"Shhh," he says softly, as if she has stirred or begun to say something herself, but why when the sweat of their bodies and their hot, wet breaths have said everything so completely, again and again?

But again his lips part around a sound like the one after a cherished secret is told: "Shhh."

"What—" His hand slips again over her mouth, and now she hears it, half-hidden in the rhythm of the surf, the Sleepless returning, shouting to one another, voices vibrant with youth and alcohol and menace:

"Must be around here, check it—"

"Already looked, okay?"

"Look again, dipstick."

Cort and Tay struggle, yanking zippers, fumbling blindly with buttons and twisting to straighten clothes. His hand, hard now, grips her wrist as he shrugs the tarp off and sliding stiffly away, and pulls her upward. Her shin bangs on the rail and she stumbles over and down, pushed.

They hesitate, breathlessly listening for a pause in the spill and gush of the ocean to reveal a laugh, a footstep, a taunt.

Quickly, they move through the door swinging silently open onto the beach, out into darkness nearer the hollow, booming ocean. The night weighs like a pall, windless and heavy, barely lighted by iridescence in the wash of the breakers.

There was a street once she lived on of houses with fenceless front yards and stunted shrubs beneath metal-framed windows set in blotchy stucco. There was a town and a school with a playing field and trees beyond the cyclone fence they climbed to smoke and dare to pretend to touch each other. There was carpool and homeroom. There was a life once lived by her, but barely.

Feet heavy in loose sand to the damp, harder stretch along the tide line, they run, dodging kelp and driftwood, through salt mist and spindrift, into the next.

26

Beneath the flickering sky, by firelit dunes, Sam and the Boy stay low, running, always. In the blackness, at the corners of Sam's eyes, afterimages of ephemera float, blotches and streaks of paleness, gone at a glance.

Behind them, distantly, small lights drift and gleam. Ahead, there's another bonfire a group of tourists feeds with furniture, books, clothing—like something hungry to consume the last of what we were. Howl of an animal from nowhere, everywhere, rising into a peal of laughter, even less human.

Sam turns the Boy's face into his chest, hiding his eyes from vague pallid figures kneeling in a circle, surrounding a naked woman on all fours. In the quivering beams of flashlights, she laughs, gasping, spitting and crying as they use her, whispering curses, chuckling.

Turn away from it, away, leaving the group in the dark to cross under the boardwalk to a narrow lane.

They stop between the hunkering shapes of bungalows, crouching low to avoid another flashlight beam leaping out long and snapping back to its origin, yet another group of tourists. The beam tilts and rears and finds a fortyish man in boxer shorts and a ball cap at the group's center. He laughs, exposing bloody teeth, holding a pill bottle high.

"Ate 'em all, fuckers!" he shouts, triumphant.

Again Sam pulls the Boy in, hand hard on the back of his head, his hot breath on his neck, small body shuddering.

The beam jerks, exposing flashes of gritted-teeth grimaces and limbs yanked back and flung out in clumsy blows that stagger the man to his knees, gasping, until one lands him prone sideways, and his eyes lose their focus and his lips form a dreamy smile. The shadow of an axe or a shovel lifts and falls. The man's shoulder seems to part, tee shirt gaping to show bright bone white against stringy red as he sighs and rolls onto his back.

Again, up and stumbling to carry this helpless creature, half-weightless now, to anywhere away from so much horror, if there is such a place anymore.

———

Between a dark motel and a row of share houses, Sam flinches back at two figures approaching, but a voice calling, "Doctor Carlson?" slows him—it's the teenaged girl, her name gone again, who led him to the Boy and his mother's little rental where he watched the depth of the woman's despair and her undoing.

"It's me, Cort. From . . . yesterday? Was it yesterday?"

Sam stops and Cort steps closer, her face etched with tear-streaks and too much seen, years older. Closer still, her voice worn: "This is Tay."

Sam nods to the teenager with Cort, a handsome, fit kid, white teeth and surfer-tan, a likely enough choice. His eyes dart quickly back to her again. "You okay?"

She stares at the Boy. And then she slowly steps forward. "It's you. Hi . . . I met you. In the market? Remember me? Hi . . ."

Her voice fades into his silence. The Boy gives a nearly imperceptible nod, staring with wide eyes, and Cort's eyes fill with tears.

Sam has no words to console her, to keep her from wondering what she always will: what would have happened if she had babysat the Boy and given the mother a break? Would the woman have walked the sandy lanes and the boardwalk to the beach the next day, waded in like anybody else, let the ocean and sky calm her, found some kind of hope again? He shuts the thought away, useless now.

Tay watches Cort, a quiet waiting in careful attendance, his eyes red-rimmed but calm.

Cort's gaze shifts to Sam and her voice cracks with the desperation of her question: "What's *wrong* with us? With everyone?"

"It's . . ." He hesitates, but belief is all he has, all anybody has. "It's almost over. We'll all be asleep soon. Out like lights, like none of it happened. Believe it."

For a still moment, each seems to dream of it, until Sam reaches quick and hard to pull her close as if for solace, for some last fleeting purchase when all is slipping.

From behind them, beyond their row of low dunes, sounds near: more Sleepless, shouting, always, approaching.

Sam lets go as the teenaged kid, Tay, glances back. "We need to go. I kinda hit some guy in the head with a board, they were hassling Cort. They're pretty pissed off."

Sam indicates the Boy. "We need to go, too. They think he started it all. I need to get him off this island."

Tay glances at Cort, as if to have her vouch for this man bearing another's child away. But Cort asks Sam, "Tonight? But, how? Are you sure you—"

"Come with us."

Cort thinks, demurs: "No. My mom's crazy, but she's still my mom."

Tay takes her hand. Sam gives him a brief appraising look, seeing the watchful stillness of him, beyond his years. "Okay, then, you two had better go on."

Cort and Tay nod, hesitate. And then he tugs gently on her hand and they start off, into the trackless future like sweet, hopeful newlyweds.

Sam calls out to them, softly, "Hey, know where I can find a boat?"

They stop and look at each other.

———

Sam and the Boy skirt the lurid last bonfires surrounded by sweating red-faced men and hollow-eyed women, running beyond the dunes and the island's big, oldest summer homes, passing the great distances of ocean rolling and sliding in the dark, the whisper and thunder and breath of it, vast, living.

One home looms hugely from a dune's crest, beach steps littered with confetti and party hats, plastic cups strewn. In the circle of light from a candle, a couple in soaked formal wear sits on separate benches, sagging slumped and gazing with dull eyes out at nothing.

A small, dark rectangle obscures the gleam of the ocean ahead, like a sentinel's desolate outpost, guarding the last approaches to nowhere. As they near, the boat shed door yawns open, creaking softly in a fetid breeze from the ocean, a parody of welcome.

The Boy looking on, Sam shoves the creaking wooden doors wider to see the little sailboat there on the trailer, half-hidden by tarp, mast stepped and lashed.

He looks from the boat to the surf, a hundred sandy yards away.

Suddenly, a voice turns him and brings the Boy's hand drifting upward, as if to ward off this Sleepless in a tattered bathrobe, spongy ear plugs, sleep mask pushed up on his forehead. The cheesy stink of dried saliva drifts from his mouth, sweat stiffens his matted hair. He points a flashlight in one hand and a pistol in the other. "Pills. Now. Before they find me. I know you're that doctor."

The pistol he holds looks like the chief's—the Navy-issue heavy Walther he carried on the beat in his belt and holster, so absurd with his khaki Bermuda shorts. The pistol trembles, the Boy trembles, the world itself with the possibility that seems now a certainty: death, pointless, just when there finally seemed to be one.

Sam lifts his hands, palms out, stepping ever so slightly sideways away from the Boy.

"I haven't got any, I swear but . . ." His voice trails off as he sees it: the safety is still on. "Even so . . ."

He flashes out a hand and grabs the gun away in one quick smooth motion, surprising everyone. They stand there, blinking at each other.

"The safety's still on." He thumbs it off, with a heavy metallic click. "Now it's not."

Aiming now, the gun a black improbable thing in the foreground, a blurred shape that makes people afraid. His now, their deliverance.

The man shoots his hands up, cringing, nodding enthusiastically.

"Drop the flashlight. Find another place to be."

The man smiles and does both, fleeing into the dark.

27

Sam moves quickly, finding some gas in the boat's little outboard, but no jerry can anywhere to top it off. Lines are coiled in the fo'c'sle, the mast is lashed across the cockpit from bow to stern, and the stepping hardware looks simple enough.

His little body tensing in fear, a sound like a whimper escapes the Boy as Sam lifts him into the bow.

He bends again to lift the trailer hitch, and the weight staggers him like a living thing pulling downward. He drops it again, bends at the knees, lifts again, just enough to roll the sailing skiff almost through the doors before his shoulders and back give. He lets it drop again, still a hundred yards to the water's edge.

In the bow, the Boy trembles and cringes, eyes downcast, unable to lift his gaze forward to the sliding vastness.

Sam winces, a stab in his side, thin and blade-like.

Too heavy to lift, too hard to believe that a single human effort can change all that has sped so quickly and relentlessly into such chaos. But another foot of wheeling this trailer will bring him and the Boy and the boat a foot closer to escaping. If only the feat can be repeated, again and again. It doesn't bear thinking about; looking up to gauge progress can only disappoint.

Keep your head down, pull. Drop the hitch.

Breathe. Lift. Pull.

A breeze has begun, warm and dank and gathering strength out of the darkness. The Boy lifts his head at it but turns away trembling again from the rush and roar ahead.

Lift, pull, into this last struggle against the strength of the earth pulling him and the boat downward forever.

Why look back? It can't be at the sound of footsteps, because what sound is there to make by even a hundred cresting the loose, dry sand of the dunes behind them?

But he does, to see the hundred or more Sleepless gathered at the ridgeline around Fleisher and Andrew, watching, silent. More gathering.

"We can make it, we're good," he tells himself and the Boy. We cling, against everything.

Head down, just pull again, over the long beat of believing the mob will turn and shrug and go their separate ways to lie waiting, each for their own sweet, private darkness to return. If only it could be.

He tugs the pistol from his cinched waist and turns in a single motion to fire at the first wave of Sleepless, winging one who goes down shrieking, his tee shirt blown into a hole in his shoulder, a confusion of cloth and blood. The others pull up short, some cringing, others eyeing him and one another, muttering senselessly:

"Whoa. I'm out."

"What up, doc?"

"Just do right, man. You go, everyone gets it."

The Boy quivers there, between the sea that took his mother and these Sleepless who believe he's to blame.

Sam tightens his grip on the gun, takes a quick step and aims point blank at the throat of one, a beefy middle-aged tourist with slicked hair and smudged skin nearly black below his hollow eyes.

"You. Pick up this hitch, pull it. Now."

Fleisher steps from the crowd now, lids heavy, blinking. "He's not going to kill anyone. Or he would have." He staggers sideways, rights himself with a chuckle, stumbles again with something between a sigh and a laugh.

Emboldened, a few from the crowd venture closer.

Sam backs up a step, gripping the Boy. Will Fleisher pass out before he exhorts the mob to murder? It's all guesswork: the near-asleep and the Sleepless, as blinded by shadows as by light, lost.

Fleisher goes down on a knee, head bobbing, but lifts a hand to point at Sam. "Him—don't let—"

Now. When choices narrow from a maze to a single narrow hall to a door he opens by lifting the gun he holds in his own hand and firing. Here, now. The blast somehow flat and echoless, factual.

Fleisher's eyelids flutter as blood erupts in a flung, twisting rope from the side of his head. He collapses sideways into the sand.

No thinking now, just point this amazing, heavy black object at someone else. They all cringe away, terrified—those who aren't flat-out running.

Quickly, Sam steps to another cowering back stunned, pressing it against this one's ear. "You. The trailer."

Eyes wide enough to burst, the man nods convulsively, eagerly. He rushes to hoist the hitch end of the trailer, strengthened by adrenaline.

Shouting spins Sam to point the gun at still another, a younger, aggrieved

Sleepless jumping in impotent fury: "Do you know what you're doing? Do you have any idea?"

Who wouldn't wonder? It's not an unreasonable question, after all.

Too late, no thinking now. Sam points the gun again at his conscripted helpmate. "Move it."

The trailer tilts back, the wheels turn slowly over the sand. In the bow, the Boy kneels, eyes wide at the surge and hiss, the slap and gush of the darkness leaping and collapsing ahead, a darkness to engulf them all, and the light of days.

Behind them now, the mob has backed up halfway to the dunes, shouting accusations of cowardice and betrayal at one another.

The cold uprush shocks Sam's calves, a gust of spray stings his eyes. Before the bow, the Sleepless man gasps beneath the burden of such weight. Sam grabs his shoulder and pushes him away.

The man flees, sobbing or laughing, splashing through the knee-high wash.

Another wave collapses, and the seething shallows deepen enough for Sam to yank the gunwale sideways and float the boat free. Pushing now, harder, out and deeper as the Boy tries to hide himself in the bow.

Sam hoists himself on, rushing to tilt the outboard motor back, blades in the water. Gasping, a stitch like fire in his side, he yanks the starter cord.

Nothing.

A new wave catches them and pushes them back, almost grounding them. Sam loops the cord around his fist and yanks again.

The motor coughs, sputters, catches, roaring to life. The little boat leaps forward, and they smash bow first through a breaking wave. Soaked, bent, the Boy opens his mouth twisting wide and soundless, so dark in the pale roundness of his face as they head out into open sea, past the surf.

Sam secures the tiller and rushes to hold him hidden from the plunging tumult of the waves as they pull away.

Behind them, the Sleepless stand silently, eyes gleaming in the dark.

The Boy shivers and Sam pulls him closer as they push on, free.

———

Kathy knows her way along the edge of town from childhood, cutting through the narrow yard between a utility shed and a fenced easement, continuing on to a girlfriend's bungalow. Gail, who worked breakfast shift with her before she quit, was never Kathy's friend exactly, but on this night a door locked behind her and a couch and blanket are nearly all that's required.

Her tears have begun, finally, quietly, almost contemplatively. Why did she waste these months with a man whom tragedy made so indecisive, equivocating? Gail had been jealous and derisive: "Good luck, too big a fish to throw back. If you even have him on the line."

She wipes the wetness from her eyes with a soft laugh at herself. Treacly self-pity: no place for it now.

To her left a few yards away, the shadows seem to gather into a sideways oval, hovering. Kathy steps closer, slowing, drawn, and sees it's a deer, one of the island's hundreds, at once quivering and still. Its round liquid eyes glint with a distant light, a stray reflection of a star, or some human trace, a far torch or beach fire. It lifts a hoof, sets it down, looks away and back, chary and breathless, suspended. So silent a creature bearing its shape into the world with barely the stirring of a blade of seagrass, or a mark on the sandy hardpan.

She remembers the rough press of her father's cheek against hers, his breath faintly rank from gin and cigarettes, his hair from sweat, as he held her up to see a deer like this one. The air hung heavy and dank, flown by fireflies as the creature regarded them, bobtail twitching. Out of the dusk, others seemed to materialize, a shy bevy stepping forward slowly to stop and step again, hopeful and wary.

"You can't feed them." Her father's voice returns to her. "Or they become dependent and die."

When she arrives at Gail's little guesthouse bungalow, Gail is gone, or refuses to answer her door, but the passing night no longer seems to threaten, a climax of fury abated, exhaustion beginning.

She walks on, habit leading her to an accustomed spot, affording a vantage of the longest stretch of boardwalk, anyone coming or going, fleeing or returning. She sits in a shut doorway and leans back, imagining them safely out to sea, making straight for Greenport, safe but lost to her now: the man she might have loved had he loved her better, and the Boy who in a dream might have been their own.

28

In the last dimness, Cort and Tay linger outside to whisper, the boards of the porch soft and damp beneath their feet. Slowly, her mom's windows give back pink light, blurred with dew.

What is there to know, to believe about ourselves, after so many became more vicious and heartless than animals, who after all at least are innocent?

To have ever worried about who said what, who looked how at who, or texted what, to have ever lived by the fickle judgments and murmurs and glances in the cinderblock hallways at school, what girl was that? To have ever for a second hated her own mother, to have laughed at her sadness, to have rolled her eyes in disdain, who was she?

If there is a way forward to choose, to turn from the twisted faces and fires still flickering in the blink of an eye, the shouts still echoing and the stink of char, his touch and his voice begins it.

She lets a small, careful hope begin to bloom inside, unfolding, urged by the lightest brushing of his fingertips across her cheek, his leanness just inches away from the whole length of her as they stand wordlessly watching each other, his gold-flecked eyes giving her back to her new self.

Words seem like a new language too, and his sound like music at first, his voice rough and soft at the same time, almost a melody. "Don't go in. Stay out here with me awhile. I'll watch over you."

How can she not? She nods, speechless. They lower themselves to the damp porch, to lean in one another's arms against the cedar siding of the wall. He brings his lips dry and sweetly to hers and they kiss shyly, as if for the first time at the end of a first date, in another life, before the end of sleep.

The island has grown quiet with the long fading of the dark, as the numbness of exhaustion has driven so many off by themselves to sit in doorsteps or on benches, or in the soft sand stupefied by the slow, sure failure of thought and speech. Angers forgotten, the will to threaten and harm has fled, replaced by the weight of a greater terror: that each will suffer the vertiginous daylight again and again, the interminable sea, the thrum and beating of their blood in their own dying hearts without respite.

———

Dale Coop partied hardy, his posse giving a surfer queer and his slut a scare until Hespeth started whining and Nicky Z bitch-slapped him, joke, but Hespeth round-housed him, bamm, *side of the head and Mindy and Dave got into a fight, over who knows what, but so what anyway because whatever. This* fucking day now.

———

Elise Herkimer from Shirley, Long Island, has wandered back to her room in the share house where these two SUNY sorority pledges, one engaged and the other at least supposedly serious have hooked up like total round heels with guys who look like muscle-head Jersey Shore *clones—orange from tanning lotion, trimmed little beards, cheap gold chains and steroid pecs. No one notices when she walks in; they could be all dead, so motionless and blankly staring at nothing, barely breathing. The chlorine stink of cum, the dead ashes of cigarettes. The loose flattened breasts and lipstick-smeared mouths half-open as if about to remark. The stillness of it all like a painting no one should've ever painted, that no one would ever want to see.*

———

Carl Beineke remembers pajamas with feet, blankie, teddy bear. The blue sheets with white clouds. The carousel lamp that threw the shadows of animals. The little yellow nightlight.

———

Denise Obermeyer has had a second thought but can't remember what it is.

———

For a while, motionlessness has been a good way to nearly tolerate the pain of the light. Pete Keegan keeps his eyes on his hand there at the other end of his arm, so far away, resting on the sand becoming warm beneath it. Grains sticky on his cheek. He needs to get up now, though, and find some shade and cover his eyes with something, and his ears, to stop his mind, mostly, from thinking thoughts that go nowhere and his nowhere thoughts about them, wife daughter job house, his life like an image in a mirror image of an image in a mirror, but how will it stop unless he stops it?

Just telling the arms to flex and hands to hold onto the ground so the legs can get underneath. Standing, wobbly fun. One foot, two foot. Funny. Walking.

In the sand, a shard of broken amber bottle.

By the house on the dune, a child's swing made of rope.

The ocean, opening.

#day_eight

1

The sea is glass out here, rose and gray, the sky's mirror.

Sam and the Boy sit parched and slumped in the bobbing stern, in the blooming of so much light, the skin around their eyes like the bruises of the beaten. Dew shines slick on the rails, too mixed with last night's salt spray to sip.

In his too-big mildewed life vest, the Boy listlessly watches the still water, and Sam dares to flick his cell phone on yet again, as if this time it will bring their last connection back to life.

No bars, only the battery indicator at four percent. But does powering it up and down use more than low battery mode? Or leave it on, but turn cellular off and on with airplane mode?

———

Hours in the white dazzle of endless water. Joints throbbing, tongue swollen across cracked lips.

Against the stabbing of that light, he would move his hand to shield his eyes, but there is strength enough only to test the mainsheet for a breeze and find nothing as the sail sags in so much heat and stillness. And then to lie back again against the stern gunwale, where the outboard has died, out of gas, from where their last sight of land faded so long ago.

The Boy barely blinks, hunched against the cockpit bench in the patch of shade Sam has made with his shirt hung from the barely swaying boom.

Without measure, time is lived too long and hard, only guessed at by the blaze of day and the trail of spume passing on a ghost current to nowhere.

———

Fever dream of agony, the unthinkable choice: turn the cell on and risk the last of the battery but find no network, when later they might find one? But how else to know if they've already crossed some invisible line, a threshold

232 | ROY FREIRICH

of data on a wavelength? Even here, in sight of nothing, it must be possible, because when Sam succumbs and flicks it on, suddenly a service bar flickers darkly, hesitantly upward, and then a second. Sam lifts the little phone to arm's length, peering through the blur of salt-crusted lashes, a sound between a sob and a laugh as the tiny black arcs appear.

Full bars, connected!

He yanks the little phone back to thumb at it, "0" and "send." He murmurs prayerfully, "please, please," a croaking not his own, but some dying, desperate foolish man's.

"Operator." A voice crackles through, brusque, officious.

"Operator? Thank God, this is a ship-to-shore mayday." His throat is clogged, swollen raw. He coughs, a loose rattle. "Sam Carlson, calling from a daysailer, drifting, probably ten or twelve miles south-southeast from Carratuck Island. Hello?" He stands and limps toward the bow, into clearer air, perhaps.

"Sir? I have that. Ten to twelve miles south-southeast of Carratuck—"

"We're becalmed, out of gas. Got a boy here needs medical attention." Say anything, anything can be legitimately said.

"Is he conscious? What's—"

"Barely. We need help."

"I have that and will relay that. Do you want to hold while I contact Coast Guard?"

A laugh rises in him, an unstoppable, manic blurting of noise. "Sure. Okay, yes."

A burst of static intrudes, a loud gush of it, but the operator's voice surges through again: "Say again? Did not copy."

Sam shouts it now: "Okay, yes!"

"Got it. Sorry, static on this end." Another burst of it. The word again, "static."

He glances back behind him, and again. Why is the Boy somehow suddenly standing at the stern? Why is he staring into the water, the glassy flickering there? Where is his life vest?

Sam's hand floats up as his other drifts away from his mouth, and he looks to see the life vest lying there in the cockpit. Carefully now, he sets the cell gently down to approach the Boy with both hands spread as if their emptiness is an argument to persuade.

"Hey, Admiral. What's up?"

The Boy glances at Sam, but then turns back to the water.

How, to have come so far, to lose him now? "We've had some days, huh? You and me?" The honest desperation of it, the helpless truth: *please, let this Boy hear it.*

Breathe. Go on, step closer.

"You're not afraid of much, are you?"

The Boy looks at him now, pleading, shaking his head *no*.

Here, always, searching out a way toward, a way in, to some solid purchase with which to pull the deathward, helpless children back again. "Your mom was brave too. But she got tired. It wasn't your fault. You're not in any trouble here. She—"

Turned away to face the water again, the side of the Boy's face quivers.

"Hey, wait . . . just—"

The Boy steps from the gunwale, plunging straight downward like a dropped stone, vanishing with a small thick splash into water so sluggish it seems oily.

Where, what? Something to throw first, before himself, for them both— there! A stained cockpit cushion, looped loose handles he grabs to fling hard and fast, an arcless path to splash down a dozen yards out, drops like rainbows spattering.

The sky and the boat's bright hull sideways as he dives.

Sounds gone in a sudden violent coolness, returning in a rush: his own pulse hammering, basso echoing thrum, faster with panic as he turns, eyes wide against the sting and in the dimness searching through shafts of sunlight from above. His hand hovers, nearly reaching out, but for what? The moment held like a drowning man's last breath.

He kicks away and sweeps an arm sideways to spin himself to find the Boy there, floating as if in space, hair like slow living tendrils, eyes closed, skin blue-white.

With a frantic push, Sam grabs the Boy and yanks him upward.

They burst into air, gasping, the Boy coughing and sobbing, "I couldn't . . . she . . ."

Sam holds him, reaching out for the dirty floating cushion. "Shhh, it's okay . . ."

" . . .she got pulled out in the griptide! She shouted! I ran in but then she yelled no! She yelled no . . . so I didn't . . . I didn't!"

The cushion his now, Sam brings it quickly beneath the Boy as pain expands in his helpless heart.

"You couldn't. It's okay. It's okay."

"She said, no, to wait! But—" The Boy's eyes find Sam's, his voice a thin rasp, pleading, ashamed. "So I did, I waited, but then she yelled, she yelled help, she did, please help but I couldn't because—"

Sam lunges to reach out roughly for the Boy, to put a shoulder between him and so much pitiless sky, blurred by his last choked whisper: "I was afraid."

The Boy breaks down, finally, in his arms, shoulders hitching, his face crumpled around a wail that rises into the sodden air, harsh and echoless.

Sam pulls him in as if to shield him, if only he could, murmuring mindlessly, "Okay, okay." We cling, against everything.

Finally, his eyes scan the yards of flat, unending horizon to find the boat, not far, the mainsail loose and lines hanging limp.

Tiny cat's paws ripple the surface around it, and the mainsail fills just enough for the boom to creak like a haunted house's door opening.

Well, but maybe the mainsheet has caught a little on something, a kink in a block, or a block fouled with salt or a burr of corrosion. The mainsail fills a little more now and ghosts the boat just another slow yard or two away.

From the cockpit Sam can hear the voice of the operator leaking from the dropped cell: "Sir? Hello?"

The first fear is little more than a glimmer, all he allows himself before he shakes it off with a bemused chuckle as he turns to the Boy. "Can you hold on real tight? Can you? I'm coming right back."

The Boy nods, too weak for words, too stunned and numbed by grief.

Sam kicks away, hard, cupped hands flinging water, drops scattered with glimpses of glaring sky, water in his eyes and mouth. Swimming, he smooths his stroke to cut through more cleanly until his lungs burst with burning and he slows to lift his head to see how far, how very far.

The boat no nearer. Farther. The yellowed sail a loose belly of air.

He stops, just treading water now, gasping at so much precious effort for nothing.

The little boat moves so slowly but unstoppably away as he suddenly understands everything. He shakes his head with a faint, sick smile of disbelief.

But no, of course, he needs only to understand instead that they will trace the cell signal and then the current and wind direction right back to them. Coast Guard helicopters with infrared heat signature technology, search and rescue vessels. Not long.

He swims back to the Boy, peels his soaked shorts, shreds them once and again with his teeth, and ties the boy onto the cushion with it, knotting it with half-hitches.

He looks again back to the boat: farther now, smaller.

2

Vastness, sparkling. Faces seem to float in the glare, edged in light, spectral. Gabriel, gone. Kathy, alive, laughing.

Treading water for too many years in each spinning moment.

The Boy who barely shook his head when Sam asked his name, beyond exhaustion now. Bleeding from a lip cracked by dryness. Sun dappling from water into motionless eyes.

The light shifts, brightening. Heat deepening. Failing of limbs that continue anyway, pushing at the water to keep his nose and mouth above. All there is to measure these hours in the endless tormenting day.

Once he reached to keep from sinking, clinging to the Boy's cushion for just the blessed sweet second of it, and then he let go to tread again.

A new sting of salt in one eye. Wiping it away, making it worse. Blinking blindly, the edges of light blurring. The fire in his lungs from gasping as fear grips his chest. The fear that fear will exhaust him, muscle failure from the tensing, heart racing beyond its rhythm.

Easy, calm now. Nothing but waiting. Smallest motions to float. Easy, so very calm.

The bonds are still fast and tight on the buoyant cushion and around the Boy's thin back and chest, hollow and bony through his soaked tee.

A lapping of warm saltwater fills Sam's nose and he coughs, the pain in his arms of ceaseless use a shearing beneath the skin. He reaches to cling to the cushion again, to rest for only a briefest moment, but it bobs lower and the water sloshes up into the Boy's face, and Sam pulls his hand back and coughs again with a weak gasping shudder.

No thinking, no choices, just shutting the mind to all else but the moment arrived with its simple undeniable truth. "Well, it seems like . . . two's a crowd. But they'll find you. They'll . . . find the boat and track the current and the wind back to you. Just hang on tight. I promise, they're coming."

The Boy only stares dimly, lost in the hours of dehydration, the insensate daze of dying.

"You can't save everyone." Sam touches his shoulder, gives his weary smile. "See you in my dreams, Admiral."

Sam treads water and lets the Boy drift on.

———

Is it hours? The steadfast glare of the sun, the sound of it like static now. The small darkness of the Boy's head lost in the fire of the horizon.

He thinks of Gabriel, backing away out his door, turning, fleeing. His unappeasable fear of the dreamtime coming through a hole in the world, of the malignant blooming of the seed of a notion.

Click your heels together. Wish upon a star. The innocent adage of empowerment: believe and it will happen. Was there ever a more truly horrifying idea?

The longing comes now like a hollowness for something to blame instead of each other: bird flu, Lyme's disease. Subsonics from shifting ocean currents. The blue color temperature of the new lights along the lanes. Hashtags, destroyers of truth and lies, of despots and democracies. Or the very screens we live by, the billions of synapses of our brains finally become like the binary bits of all we listened to and looked at, on/off, awake or dead, no in between.

The small, choked sounds he hears are only his own weak, weary laughter, because what was that, any of that? Every thought the thought of someone sleepless, every Sleepless made so by another, spreading each to each as sure and simply as belief, as laughter or fear.

He blinks again from the sting of salt, and in that brief unseeing conjures the ferry's stern growing smaller across the bay, fading into sunlit haze. How many brought sleeplessness home, a souvenir from their summer idyll? Would it spread in the larger world or dissipate with time and distance? Will it end, only to happen again, somewhere else, and be misnamed or forgotten?

Only children believe in answers to everything, and here is childhood's end.

But not the Boy's, *please, please,* if only a prayer can rise high enough, whispered as it is, weak, ragged, the single word again and again, faint from bleeding lips.

———

Some echo of Sam's voice, or the memory or a dream of it, nearly turns

Kathy's head as if to look behind her, but there is only the Coffee Spot's warm hard door she leans against, sitting in that doorway waiting for her life to begin again.

She remembers another door, ajar, from her childhood bedroom to the hallway, that welcoming rectangle of soft light, and she imagines for a moment that nothing can harm her as long as that light shines, and that no fear and no regret can ever reach her.

She knows it to be true: Sam and the Boy are safely away from the howling vengeful creatures so desperate to blame, well on their way off the island to some other shore. And in her waking dream, she dreams she, too, will find her way home again.

———

The salt stinging Sam's burned skin and blinding his swollen eyes makes him wince and flinch in smaller motions as he tries to lie floating with his face to the empty sky.

Where there has been only the rasp of his breathing and the slosh and splash of his fingers just breaking the surface, like tiny fish as his hands waver and float, another sound reaches Sam now—like the truest reason to submit, finally, to all that has been weighing so long, the unendurable sun, the inescapable water.

The distant *thwok thwok thwok* of a helicopter.

Hovering at the edge of everything, lower, lower, the black angelic machine bringing mercy.

The ocean rises around him, even as it pulls him downward.

A cough, and his arms push helplessly for purchase where there is none. His mouth, filled as if drinking, as if breathing in air, but there is none. A stab and spasm of pain in his chest. The shuddering clutch of terror but then the pain is further, fainter. Fainter, until it's gone.

Why struggle? The world is right without him now. We let go, as we must, in these last living seconds of volition. Smiling with tears of awe and gratitude up at the sky, through the blur and coolness of the water closing over it.

The last faces returning behind his eyes, a lovely woman's, a rescued boy's.

Falling slowly in his cathedral of light and silence.

———

Up, up in the rescue basket, from the circle of blown spray, the Boy ascends.

Eyes unblinking, focused so very far away, far from the roar of the massive blades of the search helicopter beating at the air.

Thwok thwok thwok.

The soundless shouting of his rescuers.

The water below, shining away beyond him, finally.

#day_nine

1

Shuffling in circles to the foggy beach and back again and again for hours that wouldn't stop, so no one did: Mom and Tay and his parents, the waitress, the fisherman and the beach taxi driver and the police chief's wife, the slumped staggering tourists with unclosing eyes turning milky like the eyes of the blind.

The man who saw his old dog alive again enough to lick his hand and whimper and disappear into the dunes. The woman whose husband woke up from a coma, and they laughed together for a little while. Another man driven mad by music. Another woman who saw the boys who chased her when she was little, exactly the same. The other men whose fear made them blame and murder. Everyone living what they used to dream of.

These are the stories.

And these: Roscoe's supermarket trashed and looted of candles and cans, shopping carts half-buried in the dunes like skeletons in the desert. Beach house doors creaking in the warm wind smelling like low tide, seagulls' cries that go up at the end like questions. Sand windblown smooth around the base of the boardwalk posts and the empty high lifeguard chairs, a page of newspaper flapping along like a dying bird.

But then, there was a shout from down the beach and another woman stood and lifted a shaking hand to point out to sea and it was okay, a light glimmered in the shifting whiteness of the fog, red and then green, the outline of a boat, and another, with flashing blue lights, bobbing. People were onboard, in uniforms!

Another shout, and down the beach more shapes of people came, in uniforms too, in a group they came together, but their voices were kind as they turned this way and that to look around at everything and even stop to speak quietly and hand a blanket and bottle of water to someone else just speechlessly staring. We were all silently staring, hoping that maybe somehow they bring the end of all the bright noise.

2

They kept the islanders separate while they searched for a virus or poison, but found none, and quarantined us on the mainland in an empty middle school they turned into a dorm, with lumpy cots and cafeteria food.

They never told us what was wrong with us and kept us carefully from anything that could give us information: no cell phones, or computers, or TV. They walked among us calmly and smiled reassuringly, and the sleep they gave us was hard, deep and dreamless—until the evening they took the wrapped bandages from our wrists—mine, Tay's, everyone's. They slipped the needles out of our veins and wheeled away the metal poles and tubes and hanging medicine bags, telling us that they would be near, they would leave a small light on and the door open just so, that we had to learn to do it on our own.

But I kept seeing his face, his wide blue eyes wondering as if in amazement, though I know now it was more likely fear. If the Boy had been rescued, wouldn't he be here, too?

I slipped quietly from my cot. In the glow of the nightlight I padded to the end of our auditorium and out in the hall where the polished floor felt chilly, and I climbed short wide stairs to a landing, and another, and stopped to catch my breath.

Slowly then I went down halls of rooms of piled desk chairs and boxes, to others with more rows of cots where more strangers lay. Some I remembered from the island: another tourist family, a short, dark guy always fighting with his exhausted wife or girlfriend, a boat guy. No one turned their head to watch me cross by their row of cots, their curiosity gone.

On a far bed, though, he lay on his back, a hand cupped by his side, the other limp on his little chest, his face shining, smeared with ointment. He moved his head slowly, as if a little at a time, to look up at me as I moved closer, his eyes wide and unblinking, curious, maybe wondering: am I the girl who never showed up to take care of him, here after all?

"Hi lo," I said.

"Hi lo," the little boy answered, and then lifted his arms to be picked up, which I did, holding his warm, living weight against me. I lifted him and he held on, the room blurring for a moment around me.

———

Back downstairs, we lay together in the dimness, the boy curled like a question mark against me, Tay's arm flung across us both from behind me. Across the aisle between rows of cots, Mom rested on her side, almost childlike, with her elbow crooked and a hand flat beneath her pillow, her eyes blinking slowly, her weariness becoming like a kind of peace.

For a little while more, the old fear gnawed and twisted inside like a living thing, that being awake would never end, but after the hours and hours of just lying there staring, some quietly telling sweet reassuring stories and tucking their thin blankets up higher under their chins, I think maybe I just got too tired to care. If we were still awake later, even forever, why worry about it now? "About that which you can do nothing," Mom always said.

Waiting, I remember I heard the gentle sounds of a voice murmuring, a fly buzzing against a windowsill, the longest day finally seeming somehow to end now, and all of it folding into a sound Tay made like a kind of soft laugh. "Now I lay me down," he whispered, or I thought he did, and the last small light seemed farther and farther away, to slowly dim into sweet darkness.

#epilogue

Sleep returned to us all, of course, and our week of "civil unrest" became a story that faded, like those of so many unexplained events. The hysteria in LeRoy, New York, for instance, gets mentioned in the same obscure books and articles and websites about "phenomena," with the same questions always lingering: what caused, and then what stopped, the spread of it, and will it reoccur? Yet in the end, dependably, it seems, newer mysteries—the crater in Siberia, the Marfa Lights, the Taos Hum—capture the public's fickle imagination before those stories, too, largely disappear.

There were deaths on the island, to be sure, but in each individual case, medical experts, police, and reporters fixed on personal animus—depression, delusions fueled by alcohol or drugs, excessive heat, insects, or yes, even extended insomnia—as causes, and in the end shrugged off the confluence of these factors as coincidence, or yet another exacerbating factor.

Later, since the story continued to be of personal interest to me, I read that psychologists had finally agreed to call the Carratuck Island Incident, as it came to be known, a case of Mass Psychogenic Illness, which by all accounts was the initial diagnosis by Dr. Samuel Carlson, attending physician at Pines Beach Urgent Care. Further study revealed that a phone company lineman, my classmate Cynthia ("Cinder," who created the #sleepless43 hashtag), an unnamed fisherman, and others all visited Dr. Carlson (whom I met too) for various individual, unrelated complaints before the onset of their insomnia. Consequently, interviewers asked others, as well, and discovered the same common link to Dr. Carlson, perhaps causal, some theorized—in the sense of a "patient zero," as every sociogenic illness begins somewhere.

I recall his face as a kind man's, evincing weary good humor. By all accounts, his self-sacrifice and heroism remain beyond dispute. And so my eyes, my throat, my heart aches at the sad, innocent guilt of his true role as origin of all that occurred on Carratuck.

Nevertheless, the Boy chose to rename himself after Doctor Carlson, "Sam," long before I finished my studies and Tay and I married and applied for and were granted custody.

These years later, in this modest mainland home we share with him, late when the drone of a far-off plane, or a dog faintly barking, or the creak of the house settling into itself lulls me into drowsiness, I still sometimes startle from remembering too much, or from the quick thought: somewhere, in some exotic tropic or snowy latitude, or perhaps just some bland, temperate suburb, is someone opening their eyes, woman, man, or child, waking from the very last of their sleep?

I hold this against it, the same vision that closed my eyes, finally, lying in that makeshift dorm with the Boy in Tay's loose arms: running along the beach with Tay, the sun flashing rainbows in our eyelashes, feet slapping the warm backwash until we bent, out of breath, laughing, over the Boy playing with his toy pail and shovel in the damp sand. His hair is stiff with dried salt and funny, his jams are wet and the skin on his hip is pink where the waistband sags, and his eyes are bluer than the ocean. And then we all look up to see his mother coming down a dune toward us in a bright cover-up with a beach towel over her shoulder, pausing to shield her eyes with a glad thoughtless smile as she lifts her hand in the air to wave.

acknowledgments

Thanks always to my first inspiration—my lovely wife and tireless, perspicacious editor, Debrah; to Deborah Dill for her encouragement; to Jeff Dorchen for his astute thoughts; to Fran Lebowitz for her steadfast advocacy, and to Tricia Reeks of Meerkat Press, of course, for seeing something worthy in these pages, and for knowing when to pry the manuscript from my sweaty, white-knuckled grasp. Thanks to L.Mai Designs for the beautiful, disturbing cover design.

If this book reads as a cautionary tale, I'm content with that. Empathy requires effort, and it's among the first faculties to fail in weariness. Sleep deprivation is an invitation to the supremacy of our own stories and points of view, to the tunnel-vision of solipsism, gateway to delusion. The ability to read the room deserts us. We feel misunderstood—the beginning of righteous anger, the prelude and pretext to every form of violence.

Sleep enables us to dream, and dreams enable us to relive unresolved moments in disguised form, and so diffuse their power; little by little, dreams free us from our pasts and allow us to live more fully in the present. Without sleep, denied the outlet of dreams for too many nights, the unconscious finds other ways to surface. The past stalks our waking lives, old wounds bleed anew, urges can become obsessions, worries become terrors, and our worst selves win. Emotional stability is lost, confusion and chaos rule.

Sleep matters.

Good night.

about the author

Roy Freirich leads multiple lives as a writer. He adapted his novel *Winged Creatures* for the film *Fragments*, featuring Forest Whitaker, Dakota Fanning, Guy Pearce, Josh Hutcherson, and Kate Beckinsale, and has written screenplays for Fox Searchlight, Dreamworks, Warner Brothers, and Sony. His lyrics have been sung by legends Aretha Franklin, Smokey Robinson, and Patti Labelle, among many others. He lives with his wife, ever-patient editor and frequent cowriter, Debrah, in Malibu, California. Together, they've written the libretto for a musical adaptation of Anne Rice's *Cry to Heaven*, for Seattle's 5th Avenue Theatre. Visit him online at www. royfreirich.com.

Did you enjoy this book?

If so, word-of-mouth recommendations and online reviews are critical to the success of any book, so we hope you'll tell your friends about it and consider leaving a review at your favorite bookseller's or library's website.

Visit us at www.meerkatpress.com for our full catalog.

Meerkat Press
Atlanta